An UNFAMILIAR SEA

A San Juan Islands Murder Mystery

by

BETHANY MAINES

 Blue Zephyr Press
2661 N. Pearl, #360
Tacoma WA 98407

This book is a work of fiction. Names, characters, and incidents are products of the author's imagination or are used fictitiously.

Any resemblance to actual events or persons living or dead is entirely coincidental.

Cover art by **LILT**.

ISBN-13: 978-1-7332813-9-3

DEDICATION

To the woman at the tourist center who looked shocked
when I said Orcas Island was a good place to murder people.
Sorry.

TABLE OF CONTENTS

CHAPTER 1

FRIDAY - TISH YEARLY THE LIFE COACH

Twenty-eight-year-old Tish Yearly carried folding chairs across the lawn toward the gazebo in the glorious June sunshine and rehearsed the words she was going to say to her boyfriend.

"I'm pregnant."

Tish's thoughts and her feet came to a stumbling halt. "What?" Tish stared at twenty-two-year-old Penelope Drue, who was clasping and unclasping her hands in front of her chest. Penelope looked like she needed more than a one-word question, but Tish needed more than a two-word announcement. "Congratulations?" Tish tried.

When Tish had set about opening her own wedding venue on Orcas Island, she had been prepared for inclement weather, she had been prepared for irate brides, she had even been prepared for the inconvenience of bribing the local Sheriff's deputies with food to keep them from ticketing her guests, but she had not been prepared to play den mother to employees that were barely younger than she was.

"I'm not trying to ditch out." Petite, purple-haired Penelope looked tearful. "I'll carry the chairs, but I don't think I should lift the dancefloor sections."

Tish had not been planning on asking Penelope to lift dancefloor sections. "OK," said Tish. "Uh… that's fine?"

"They say that, right? That pregnant women shouldn't lift heavy things?"

"I think so," said Tish. Penelope had big hazel eyes and a tawny complexion that always looked slightly sun-kissed and strangely natural with her purple hair. Currently, those eyes were set to maximum hugeness and Tish wondered if she could mimic that puppy effect with any sort of effectivity or if someone had to be twenty-two to pull it off.

"Bowen asked me to carry dancefloor sections," clarified Penelope. "But I can't! But I really need this job!"

"OK," said Tish. She had loaded three chairs onto each of her arms, and her left was starting to go numb below the elbow. "Just tell Bowen I put you on chair detail."

"I'll only be like four or five months along by the time wedding season is over, so it won't be a big deal. No one even has to know."

"OK," agreed Tish. She didn't know what else to say. Her experience with pregnant people was limited. *OK* seemed to be working so far—Tish decided to stick with it.

"I haven't actually told anyone else yet, so can maybe you not…?"

"OK," said Tish.

"But I just thought I should tell you because I didn't want you to freak out that I'm not a hard worker or that I'm being difficult and fire me."

"I won't fire you," said Tish. She didn't add that she was pretty sure that firing pregnant girls was not only illegal, but probably also a sure-fire way of going to hell.

"Oh, thank the goddess!" Penelope had been raised in a commune on Shaw Island and therefore had some unique views on spirituality.

"You just found out then?" asked Tish, trying to do the math.

"Yeah. It's kind of an accident."

How is it only kind of an accident?

"Some of the coolest people are oops babies," said Tish reassuringly, since Penelope looked like she needed reassuring. "You don't have to plan everything."

Penelope laughed. "I plan almost nothing. That's usually what I have Azalea for."

Azalea was Penelope's best friend and the OCD yin to Penelope's wild child yang. Tish had hired the pair of them and so far they were both operating above her expectations. Although, the pregnancy thing was a bit of hiccup that she hadn't included even on her top secret list of potential Orcas-wackiness.

"I guess I won't be able to have Azalea help me with this," continued Penelope, looking sad. "I also guess I won't be doing anymore drinking for a while. That's fine. Like I need beer calories anyway. I am nervous," she said with a nakedly honest expression that hit Tish right in the hug button, not that she could do anything about it with her arms full of chairs. "But the weird thing is, I think I've got this. I know what I'm supposed to do. And it's not going to be easy, but at least I'm not confused."

"Well," said Tish, "that makes one of us."

"Thanks for being understanding," said Penelope.

"No problem," said Tish. "Uh, but maybe you can carry one of these chairs though?" she asked, holding out her left arm.

"Oh! Sure!" Penelope took two of the chairs and Tish sighed in relief.

"It's really cool?"

"That's good," said Tish. "I'm glad you're happy. Babies seem nice."

Theoretically. For other people.

"No, that was a question. Is it really cool with you?"

"Oh. Uh…" Among the other things that Tish didn't think she had prepared for properly in her business plan was the idea that she would have any say or sway over the life of another human being. She wasn't the boss. As a former actress, she was ready to be a star. Maybe. But never the boss. She was at one with the proletariat. She loved the idea of contributing jobs to the Orcas Island economy, but she didn't think she was supposed to be able to devastate the hopes and dreams of another person. "Yes," said Tish. "It's fine. We can make it work."

Penelope's shoulders dropped as if a weight had slid off. "Thanks," she said, tears sparkling in her eyes. "This wasn't supposed to happen. I'm excited about it. But it's complicated and—"

"Tish!" yelled someone from driveway. "Tish, we've got a five-alarm emergency!"

"Is that Terry the florist?" asked Penelope.

"Yes," said Tish, looking down at her arms full of chairs. "Uh..."

"Just leave them there," said Penelope. "I'll take care of them."

"Thanks," said Tish, setting the chairs down on the grass with a clack as the wooden seats banged together. "I'll be back in a minute."

These last two days leading up to her very first wedding ever had been full of Tish telling people she'd be back. Unlike the Terminator, that wasn't remotely true.

Terminator, 1984, starring Arnold Schwarzenegger in a role that was originally slated for O.J. Simpson.

She felt like she was being pulled in a million different directions at once. She was trying not to place too much importance on this one event. She had six more weddings booked over the next two months. But this was the first one and she couldn't help feeling that if it didn't go right, then *none* of them would go right. She'd been having constant naked-on-stage dreams for the last week. It was the worst case of opening night jitters she'd ever had. Only this wasn't a play and she couldn't slink home and drown her sorrows in red wine if the reviews came back poor. Orcas Island was now her home and if she screwed this up everyone on the entire island was going to know.

Tish walked up the rise to the driveway and gravel parking area in front of the house. Terry's bulbous, dark-blue Subaru was parked awkwardly in the middle of the drive as if she had seen Tish and promptly stopped the car where it was. Terry was standing at the edge of the drive watching her approach.

"Hey Terry," said Tish, swiping a chunk of her blonde bangs behind her ear. She really needed a haircut, but she winced at the idea of going to an on-island stylist. And then she felt pained and uppity for wanting to go off-island and then she didn't do either. "What's the emergency?"

"The flowers didn't make it on the ferry and now my flower guy is threatening to charge double-hourly for the wait time to get on the next ferry. I can't pay that. And if they make me pay that, I'm going to have to pass it on to you."

"So our emergency is that you want to charge me more money?" asked Tish and Terry froze seeming to think over the situation.

"I don't want to Tish, but I can't pay that amount of overage or I'll lose money." Terry was a constantly frazzled, forty-something brunette in her second year of business as the island's florist. Like many of the island's residents she was used to a level of informality that Tish found strange in a business person.

"This is why we have contracts," said Tish. "It's not like your address has changed. It's not your fault if your vendor didn't accurately account for the ferry time. Call them back up and tell them that they will not be charging you anything and that threats to change prices at the last minute are unacceptable and illegal."

"Well, what do I say if they say they're still going to charge me no matter what I say?"

"You say that you'll discuss it later, but you can't talk about it right now. Because the most important thing is that they deliver the damn flowers. You can refuse to pay afterwards and get Sam to send them some sort of strongly worded lawyer note."

"Oh," said Terry. "I don't know… I just I can't… That's so confrontational."

Tish didn't know what to do with that. "Uh… OK, so don't say anything."

"What?"

"Well, how are they threatening you? Did they call or email?"

"They left a voicemail."

"Well, just don't call them back," said Tish.

"Oh," said Terry. "I guess I could do that."

"Right. They can threaten your voicemail all they want. Just don't pick up the phone. As long as they deliver the flowers, they can say whatever they want."

Tish had long ago mastered the art of aggressive non-response. She didn't understand people who thought the phone had to be answered.

"Right," said Terry, perking up. "Right. I can *not* answer the phone."

"The phone is not the boss of you! You are the captain of your own ship. You are the florist of your fate!"

"What?" Terry looked confused.

"Never mind," said Tish. "The point is that you are in charge."

"Thanks Tish!" exclaimed Terry. "You're so good at this stuff."

"Tish!" someone yelled from the house.

"OK, gotta go. Keep me posted on the flower situation."

"Of course," said Terry, "I've actually started on the boutonnieres already. I ran into a situation with the Baby's Breath, but..." Tish backed away as Terry continued to talk. She didn't think she'd ever actually concluded a conversation with Terry. She just slid out from under it and sidled away.

"Hey Tish," said Azalea, when she reached the front porch of the craftsman bungalow that was the home of Yearly Events. Azalea was Penelope's best friend and probably already knew about the pregnancy thing, but Tish had promised not to say anything, so she didn't immediately ask about it like she wanted to.

"Hey Zales, what's up?" asked Tish, looking up the few feet to the auburn-haired waitress on the porch.

"I've done an initial count on the silverware. I think we're solid, but I'm worried about plates. We look short. I don't want to unbox everything, but if we're short tomorrow…" Azalea had a sharp pointed chin and a heart-shaped face defined by her widow's peak and dark wing-like eyebrows. At the moment those eyebrows were starting to V distressingly upward in worry.

Tish nodded. Somehow, despite being raised on the island, Azalea had mastered the mainland sense of urgency. She understood that it mattered when things happened and that *it will all work out* was not a realistic philosophy in the face of an Amazon-employee bride.

"OK, we'll grab a couple of box cutters and we'll just do a quick manual count. You're right we don't want to find this out tomorrow. If we're short, I've already talked to Quest down at the Orcas Hotel and he says we can borrow up to fifty plates."

Azalea nodded, looking relieved. "That would cover us." Her nod bounced one of her curls loose from her ponytail.

"I don't like the idea of not matching though," said Tish, as Azalea quickly undid the rubber band and swept all of her hair back into the proper form. Azalea always looked tidy. "So let's get counting."

An hour later Tish found herself on the porch and couldn't remember what she was supposed to be doing. Her phone burped up an incoming text and she looked at it with a nervous flutter in her stomach.

You coming?

Tish left the porch and walked down the meandering trail that took her to the wooded area of the property and lead to a ramshackle barn. It was her goal to be able to do fall and winter weddings in the barn, but that was a whole level of renovation that she couldn't afford. Maybe if she made it past her first year of business, she might consider it. Once out of view of the workers on the lawn she jogged to the barn and swung open the door. She had barely crossed the threshold when a pair of strong hands grabbed her around the waist and pushed her up against the wall.

"Hi," she said, throwing her arms around Emmett Nash's neck and kissing him. Dating Nash had never been in her plans, but kissing Nash was always on her top ten list. He made her toes curl and today was no exception.

"Hi," he said, pulling back smiling down at her with those blue eyes that made her melt.

Sheriff's Deputy Emmett Nash was tall, gorgeous, stubborn, well-read, and utterly delectable. He was also the divorced father of the absolutely adorable ten-year-old Claire who knew nothing about her father's relationship with Tish—Claire's preferred babysitter.

"I was starting to think you weren't coming," he said.

"And I'm starting to think that I'm the life coach for half of my employees."

"Oh God," he said, looking horrified.

"I am an excellent life coach!"

"Tish, baby, you live with your grandfather, and routinely find dead bodies."

"Twice is not routinely. And I don't think living with Granddad should count against me. It's for Granddad's own good."

"One more and the coroner has threatened to get you a punch card. And then there's the commitment phobia and the fact that you won't introduce your boyfriend to your grandfather."

"You already know Granddad! I don't have to introduce you!" He gave her a look. "I want to tell him about us." She knew it didn't sound authentic.

"Then why haven't you?"

"Because…" This was where the rehearsal would have come in handy. She should have her answer down pat already. She'd known this was coming. And she really did have a plan. She just wasn't sure everyone else would agree to her plan.

"Tish, I like afternoon delight as much the next guy—"

"After… Who *are* you?"

"A child of the oldies station. But I'm kind of over having to sneak around to spend the night with my girlfriend."

Tish's phone rang and she pulled it out to check if it was an emergency.

SAN JUAN COUNTY JUSTICE DEPARTMENT.

"I want to tell him, but every time I think I'm going to, he brings up how happy he is that I'm not dating anyone who's divorced."

"This is starting to feel pointed," he said. "Are you sure Tobias doesn't know already and he's just messing with us?"

"Always a possibility," she said, picking up the call. "Ronny, I swear to God, I have all the permits. The cars are allowed to park there. If you ticket them, I will sue. Not just the department, but you personally."

Nash rolled his eyes and made hurry up motions. Ronny was his least favorite co-worker.

Tish listened to the speaker on the other end of the line and felt an on-coming headache.

"Thanks," she said at last. "I'll be there as soon as I can."

She hung up the phone and looked at Nash.

"I'll talk to Ronny when I get back to work," he said. "But seriously, it's been months. I want to tell Tobias. And I want to tell Claire. And then we can stop sneaking around the damn island. It's ridiculous."

"I want that too," said Tish.

"So you'll go home and tell Tobias right now?" asked Nash, looking suspicious.

"I can't," said Tish. "I have to go bail him out of the Anacortes jail."

CHAPTER 2

TOBIAS YEARLY THE JAIL BIRD

Tish stood at the railing on the upper deck of the MV Tillicum and felt the metal plating under her feet vibrate as the ferry shoved its way across the dark blue water toward Anacortes, Washington. Below her a pale yellow jellyfish drifted away, tossed on the churning wave of the ferry's passage. She still loved this portion of the trip. As a child, the journey from Seattle out to Orcas to visit her grandparents on the ferry had been endlessly fascinating and the joy of traveling by ship made even the boredom of enforced family time fun. She thought the other island residents frequently viewed the journey across the water as a massive inconvenience, but for Tish it had yet to lose its allure.

Tish had left Seattle just after high school with no intention of returning there to live. She'd gone to L.A. to be an actress.

I went to L.A. to be a star and when I realized I wouldn't be, I came home.

Only Seattle hadn't been the same Seattle of her youth. Amazon bros, tech giants and rent prices that jumped every two weeks had changed the landscape beyond recognition. Tish had settled for what she had considered a temporary job in marketing at an architecture firm only to be fired after reading her boss the riot act.

Tish snickered to herself to think of it now. Her boss had dropped the ball on a million-dollar proposal that put the jobs of at least three other employees at the firm in peril and Tish had told him in no uncertain terms just what kind of jerk he was.

Apparently, calling someone a lazy bastard who hasn't bought a new album since New Kids on the Block is an HR violation. Who knew?

But that disaster had sent her back to Orcas Island and the one person willing to give her a free place to stay while she got back on her feet—her father's father, seventy-nine-year-old Tobias Yearly. Only when it came to Tobias, nothing really came without strings. Tobias Yearly was an ex-test pilot and, unknown to Tish before coming to stay on the island, an ex-CIA agent who was still wanted in the former Yugoslavia. He was an unrepentant troublemaker and a self-proclaimed nosy old fart who still kept files on the entire population of the island.

Tobias might have kept his retirement to island gossip and playing bridge with his best friend Reginald Stokley down at the Grange, but shortly after Tish's arrival Reginald had been killed and Tobias took that more than a little bit personally. It had taken Tobias and Tish's combined efforts along with some deadeye shooting from Nash to stop Reginald's killer. It was Reginald's old property that she was currently turning into what she hoped would be the premier wedding venue on the island. And it was Tish's legwork that Tobias was parlaying into a very tiny, very relaxed private investigation firm. It was the kind of business that left room for afternoon naps and Matlock on VHS. Tish mostly ignored Yearly Investigations and threw herself into building Yearly Events.

Yearly Events wasn't supposed to succeed. It was just another dream that was sure to bust up in my face.

But Yearly Events was *this* close to succeeding. Partially thanks to the marketing efforts of Tish's best friend and ex-co-worker Sarah Brook, a bit of manual labor from Nash, a lot of manual labor from Tish, and some cash from Tobias.

Tish gripped the rail and tried not to think about yelling out her frustrations in one long prolonged scream into the wind. There were too many tourists on deck for that today. Screaming only went un-noticed in the dead of winter when rain spit down in angry torrents and the waves sloshed over the bow and onto the cars parked below and everyone with any sense was inside.

Tish was petrified that Yearly Events wouldn't succeed.

I'm scared shitless that it will.

Tish was determined not to let her friends and family down, but she had no idea what to do if she did succeed. She felt like she was on the cusp of some life-altering transition. She had felt this kind of shift before—when she left L.A.—and she had welcomed it. She had happily thrown herself off the cliff of her old life, killing off any chance of returning to it, launching into something new, even though she hadn't known what that new life would be. But here on Orcas Island, hovering on the brink of success had her more frightened than any performance she had ever given.

I know how to fail. I know how to roll with the punches and come up with something new. I have no idea how to deal with winning.

And compounding that fear was something else she'd never had. Nash.

The blue-eyed boy next door. If the boy next door were six foot four and gorgeous. And funny. And secretly trained in the library arts with an in-depth knowledge of Shakespeare that turned her on more than she would ever admit to anyone. He also had a funny, adorable, sweet, darling, wonderful daughter Claire that Tish loved beyond reason.

Tish took out her phone and dialed Sarah.

She needed to tell someone about Nash. She'd been keeping the secret for months. Tobias had a weird aversion to divorced people and Tish had an aversion to breaking Claire's heart. Which would be what would happen when Tish broke up with Nash. Not that she wanted to break up with Nash.

But I break up with everyone sooner or later. Or they come to their senses and break up with me.

Nash had been ridiculously patient, but even Tish knew that it was time to bite the bullet and just tell everyone. What she had wanted to tell Nash was that she wanted to wait until after this first wedding and then have Nash and Claire over to the house for dinner.

She figured Tobias couldn't yell in front of Claire and Claire would probably be OK if she could play with Tobias's dog, the plump black lab, Coats. Only Tobias had managed to surprise her once again.

Sarah's phone went to voice mail.

"Hey," said Tish, trying not to feel hurt at the lack of response. This was the weekend of Yearly Event's first wedding. Sarah had been with her every step of the way. Sarah was practically a partner. But this was the third unanswered phone call. "Um... I really need to talk to you. Um. Also, Granddad is apparently in jail and I'm going over to Anacortes to bail him out. So... yeah. Anyway, just call me."

Nash had given her detailed instructions on how to post a bond, which was a relief. Otherwise, she would have been logging some very awkward Google searches. She parked at the jail and saw with a sinking feeling that Detective Spring was waiting for her.

"Tish," said the balding detective as she exited her white Toyota POS.

"Detective Spring," said Tish. Their relationship had marginally improved since Detective Spring had stopped accusing her grandfather of murdering people, but she thought that he still resented the fact that she was taller than him.

"Here to bail him out?" he asked.

It was exactly this kind of question that annoyed Tish. He knew the answer. Why even ask?

"No," said Tish. "I brought him a cake with a file in it, but other than that, I figure he's on his own. I'm going to spend my evening recording over his Matlock collection." Detective Spring raised an eyebrow and gave her a look. She gave him a look back.

"I had a word with the arresting officer. He says he gave Tobias every opportunity to go someplace and sleep it off. The officer said it was like Tobias wanted to get put up on a drunk and disorderly charge. I tried to go see him last night after I got off my shift, but he told me to piss off!"

"Last night?" repeated Tish. "How long has he been in jail?

When the hell did he get arrested?"

"Yesterday at six-thirty in the morning. Didn't you know he was gone?"

Tish counted back and tried to figure out when the last time she'd seen her grandfather. Wednesday night she'd snuck out to be with Nash. Apparently, she hadn't been the only one sneaking out. Then there was the fact that yesterday at noon, she'd bumped into George Fujiyama who'd passed on the message that Tobias would be eating dinner with his not-a-girlfriend Eleanor. If Tobias had already been arrested at that point, why had George given her that message?

"I've been really busy getting ready for our first wedding at Reginald's. I haven't been home much."

"Well, is he on some sort of medication? What the hell was he thinking?"

"I have no idea."

Like I ever know what Granddad is thinking.

"Look, with a good lawyer, you can probably get the charges dropped. But seriously Tish, this is so weird I think you should probably get him checked out by a doctor."

You think that because he's old.

"Well, I'll definitely talk to him," said Tish. Detective Spring's eyes narrowed.

"Why do I get the feeling you're holding out on me?"

"I really have no idea why Granddad would be drunk and disorderly in Anacortes on a Thursday morning," said Tish. "I'm not even sure how he got over here since his cars are still at home."

Come on. All of that together and you're still not going to ask yourself what secret plan Granddad has up his sleeve?

"That's what I'm saying! It's totally bizarre! You need to have him looked at by a doctor."

"I'll do what I can," promised Tish, which was no promise at all.

"Damn Yearlys," muttered the detective giving her an angry glare, pulling out a pair of aviator sunglasses and shoving them angrily on his face. It made him look like he was trying too hard, but Tish didn't say anything. "You're both crazy. Good luck."

"Thanks Detective," said Tish. He grunted in return and headed for his car. "Seriously," she called after him, "thanks for checking in on him. I really appreciate it."

He waved but didn't respond and slammed the car door of his unmarked police car with extra vehemence.

Tish went inside and waited in three different lines, filled out the six forms, wrote the check and then waited on a bench for her grandfather to be escorted out to meet her. She felt like she was trying to collect lost luggage.

GET HIM YET?

Nash's text popped through and Tish smiled, trying to remember when that little chirrup of sound hadn't made her irrationally happy. She now had a Pavlovian response to texts because of Nash. It was ridiculous.

NO, STILL WAITING.

WHAT'D HE DO?

DRUNK AND DISORDERLY AT SIX THIRTY YESTERDAY MORNING.

Tish waited for the response, knowing that there was going to be one.

I'M NOT THE ONLY ONE WHO FINDS THAT INCREDIBLY SUSPICIOUS, AM I?

Tish grinned at the message.

IT'S YOU AND ME, KID. DETECTIVE SPRING SAID I NEEDED TO GET HIM CHECKED OUT BY A DOCTOR.

I'M REFRAINING FROM COMMENT.

Tish rolled her eyes. The blue brotherhood was a real thing. Detective Spring had tried to arrest Nash for murdering his ex-wife's boyfriend and still Nash wouldn't ever just come out and say that Spring was an idiot. Maybe not a total idiot, but he didn't exactly leap to the right conclusion very often.

The door swung open and Tobias came out, escorted by a police officer who stopped just outside the door and handed Tobias his cane. The officer went back behind the locked door as Tish stood up.

"Oh shoot," said Tobias, grimacing at her. "They were supposed to call George."

"They were supposed…" Tish stared at her grandfather, words utterly failing her. "Go get in the car," she finally said, pointing to the door. "We will *discuss* this when we are *not* in a police station."

Tobias grinned, wide and impudent. "You sound just like your Gran when you're mad."

"Grandma should have married the opera singer!" Which was something Grandma had always said when Tobias had been working her last nerve.

Tobias chuckled. "They get fat when they get old. She wouldn't have liked that." Which is what he had always replied. The familiar call and response of old family arguments soothed Tish more than any amount of faux contrition would have.

"Car!" she said, pointing again.

"Yes, ma'am!" he said with a cheerful salute and headed toward the door.

CHAPTER 3

HOME AGAIN

Tish watched as Tobias eased himself into the passenger seat of her Toyota. It was a long way down for a man with a leg that no longer bent the way it should. One too many plane crashes in his test pilot youth had left him with a leg that set off metal detectors. He settled himself back against the seat and leaned his back on the headrest. Tish thought that despite his gung ho attitude in the jail itself that he looked tired. Tish waited until he got his cane tucked in by his feet and closed the door and then went around to the driver's side, trying to text as she went.

Got him. Heading for home. I'll let you know how it goes.

"Texting Nash?" asked Tobias sourly as she dropped the phone into her pocket and got into the car.

"Yes," said Tish. "I had to have him tell me how to post bond. Funnily enough, I've never actually had to do that before."

"You weren't supposed to have to do it this time," said Tobias grumpily. "I think Detective Spring must have redirected them on who to call."

"Yes, I gathered from the way George was providing you an alibi that I wasn't supposed to know about this," said Tish, steering toward the ferry dock. "Didn't we have an agreement that you weren't supposed to cut me out of the loop? What the hell are you up to?"

"You got the wedding thing coming up," said Tobias. "I didn't want to distract you."

"Granddad, *why* did you get yourself thrown in jail? And don't tell me you were actually drunk and disorderly because I'm not going to buy it."

"Didn't think you would," he said. "It was for a client who had to meet certain timelines."

"A timeline in jail?" demanded Tish.

"Yes," said Tobias.

Tish mulled that over. A fair percentage of islanders had relatives who might be in jail, but if any of them wanted to see said relatives they'd just go—they wouldn't need to send anyone.

"You weren't a drug mule were you?"

"No!" He glared at her and then leaned back in the seat again and closed his eyes.

If it was a client, then it had to be someone he saw relatively often or who he would be able to meet on the island. It had to be someone who had connections to jail but wouldn't want to go into the jail itself.

"If you wanted to see someone in the jail why didn't you just go visit?" asked Tish.

"They record those," said Tobias without opening his eyes.

The client would be someone who didn't want to be recorded and wouldn't want Tobias to be recorded.

"Why didn't the client get someone else to go?" she asked.

"I'm old," he replied. "Odds are good that I can weasel out of the charge and at my age having it on my record won't matter. You did keep the receipt for the bond, didn't you? That'll go in reimbursables."

Tish considered that as well. The year-round population of the island wasn't overly wealthy. But Tobias's scheme was far from cheap. That narrowed her suspect pool to one of the summer home owners or one of the few genuinely wealthy people. Once more, she wished that she had the resources to convert her grandfather's paper files to a database with cross-referencing and search functions. Currently, the database was her grandfather's brain and that didn't exactly help her in this situation.

"Who came up with the idea?" she asked.

"I did, if you must know," he said, shifting in his seat, tugging at the seatbelt as if it were cutting into him uncomfortably. "I've done it before. It's not hard. Except for the Southern Comfort. Terrible stuff, but it gets the job done and it stinks enough that you smell drunk."

"When?"

"What?"

"When have you done this before?"

"Oh. Um. When I was in Panama? Might have been Honduras. Don't remember. In the early eighties. South American jails, for the record, are not as cushy as ours, but the guards are a damn sight easier to bribe."

"Oh dear God," said Tish. "Please tell me you didn't try to bribe a corrections officer. I will never be able to look Nash in the eye again."

"No one looks Nash in the eye," said Tobias. "The man's eight feet tall."

"Foul, no rhetoric," said Tish, quoting *Rosencrantz and Guildenstern are Dead*.

Rosencrantz and Guildenstern are Dead, 1990, starring Tim Roth and Gary Oldman as the permanently befuddled side characters of Hamlet.

"You being actress-y again?" demanded Tobias.

"Probably," said Tish. "Stop evading the question. Did you try and bribe someone?"

"No, not worth the effort."

"Good to know you weren't prevented by moral qualms or anything."

Tobias chuckled and then shifted in the seat again.

"Granddad, at no point in the planning of this did it occur to you that maybe this was a bad idea and that it might be bad for you?"

"Well, it's jail. It's not supposed to be good for you. I'll be fine after I get home and sleep in my own bed for a bit."

"Mm-hmm. Granddad, are you going to tell me who hired you for this cockamamie plan?"

Living with old people gives me the least cool vocabulary.

"Confidentiality agreement," said Tobias smugly.

"Granddad, you know I'm going to figure out who it is," said Tish.

"Five bucks says you can't do it within a week," said Tobias.

"A trip to the dump says I can," said Tish.

"You can't possibly have anything left to clean out!" exclaimed Tobias in outrage.

"Your closet," said Tish. "The attic. The jam cellar. The shed out in the lower acre that you think I don't know about."

"That's my in case of emergency shed! You can't touch that!"

"Granddad! I looked in there. You have half a car and like eight million tubs of junk."

"That I might need in case there's an emergency."

"One of the tubs had nothing but *National Geographics* in it. What kind of emergency are you going to use those for?"

Tobias glared at her. Tish waited, sensing winning was moments away.

"Papier-mâché," said Tobias. "You never know when you'll have a crafting emergency."

Tish tried to hold it in, but a giggle burst out of her. Tobias snorted out a chuckle of his own. Tish spared a thought to wish she wasn't driving so she could get that quote down. Her Twitter account, *Words from Granddad,* had five thousand followers. She hadn't told him about it yet. She wasn't ever planning on it either. He'd probably stop being pithy on purpose just to spite her. But someone ought to appreciate the sheer gold that he came up with and she could only text Nash so many quotes before his co-workers got annoyed.

"But Granddad," said Tish, returning to the subject at hand. "You can't be going around getting arrested!"

"I don't plan on making a habit out of it," said Tobias. "Don't let it worry you."

"Detective Spring said I should get you checked out by a doctor," said Tish. "You know, because you're nuts. He didn't say nuts, but it was heavily implied."

"That man is about as imaginative as a fence post," said Tobias, shaking his head. "But Tishkins, don't go telling him any different. The whole point of this being a secret mission is that it's a *secret* mission."

"Yeah, don't worry about it," said Tish. "Between now and Sunday I'm practically going to be camped out down at Reginald's for the wedding. Who am I going to talk to?"

CHAPTER 4

SATURDAY - WEDDING DAY

Tish bounced on her toes and wished she could take a jog. It was nearly 8:00 A.M. and the bride was already pulling into the driveway. Tish pasted on her most realistic smile and went out to greet Yearly Event's very first client.

"Oh my God," said the bride, climbing out of a Tesla. "The weather is going to cooperate. Please, please, please, tell me it will."

Tish looked up at the lone fluffy cloud in the sky and then back at the petite brunette with the short clipped hair and the cat under one arm. The cat was a snub-nosed, fluffy looking thing that looked like it was permanently auditioning for a Fancy Feast commercial.

"All signs point to yes," said Tish. "All the forecasts have perfect sunshine all day long."

"You are crushing it, Mimi," said the maid of honor, climbing out of the driver's seat. Kara was a mid-sized amiable blonde who seemed to be permanently cruising for alcoholic beverages.

"Good," said Mimi. "Because I waxed every damn thing on my body and it better not be for nothing."

Tish managed to stop herself from suggesting that waxing and weather were in no way corollaries or in fact related on any level. "If you want to head into the house and start getting set up, I've got mini-brunch bites and mimosas waiting."

"God, yes," said the bridesmaid.

"What about Wellington?" asked the bride hoisting the cat.

"I have a tin of sardines in the kitchen," said Tish, thinking quickly. "I'm sure he can have an extra special wedding day too."

"Yay!" exclaimed Mimi.

Tish led the way into the house and tried to keep her expression set to this-is-totally-normal.

Because, sure, everyone brings their cat to their wedding.

"Oh my God, Mimi," said Kara, as they entered the half of the upstairs designated for brides. "Look at these! Tish these are totes to diiiiiiiie for. I'm instagramming everything."

"Hashtag Yearly Events," said Tish with another smile. Tish was aware that living with her grandfather had possibly permanently stunted her vocabulary to the 1950s, but listening to the bride and maid of honor gave her severe whiplash to the twenty-first century. Never mind that the duo were thirty-five and thirty-seven respectively.

Why do they sound like seventeen-year-olds? Are they being ironic? I'm pretty sure even teenagers don't sound like that.

"Eee! How cute is this?" demanded Mimi, picking up the decorative basket containing the emergency kit of tampons, safety pins, bleach pen, clear nail polish, deodorant and band-aids. "What is this called again? There's some sort of uber cute name. I'm going to have to quag it. Fir realz, don't remember."

God, I hope they don't sound like that.

"I think it's just an emergency kit," said Kara.

"No, there's a name. Like a super, super cute name with a rhyme."

Kara was studiously taking pictures of the mimosas and didn't respond.

"I'll go down and see about sardines for Wellington," said Tish.

"Thank you!" trilled Mimi. "God, I can't believe I'm doing this!"

Tish didn't think that statement actually needed a reply so she left the room quickly before anymore non-sequiturs were forthcoming.

Terry arrived while she was dishing up the sardines. She carried a plastic milk crate full of bouquets.

"Hey Tish!"

"Hey Terry. I see the flowers arrived all right," said Tish, eyeing the soft pink roses.

"Yes! And I did what you suggested and just ignored the phone message. And this morning they sent their invoice and it was for the original amount. So we're good to go!"

"Sounds like someone just got frosted about the ferry and then thawed out by morning," said Tish.

Terry laughed. "You've been spending too much time with Tobias. Your slang is hilarious. The only people that make less sense are my kids."

"I like it," said Bowen coming in with another box of flowers. He was a fifty-ish, off-the-grid, pot head type. Tish used him for odd-jobs and heavy lifting. And he seemed pleased to have a job that didn't have a set schedule and only required that he get up early every once in a while. "And I think she makes way more sense than most of the kids these days. I overheard some kid on the ferry say they totally yiked some girl and I couldn't tell if I should file a police report or not."

Tish laughed. "It's a dance move. Police report not required. Although, parents will probably be horrified."

"Good to know. Where am I putting these?" Bowen hoisted the box of flowers.

"In the study. I've got the air conditioning unit going already."

"Is that going to be cool enough?" asked Terry looking worried.

"I ran a test last week. It stayed below sixty the entire day. I think we should be OK."

"Great. I'm so excited for this Tish. I think it's going to go great!"

Terry and Bowen disappeared down the hall and Tish nodded and took a deep breath. She wanted it to go great, but she'd woken up this morning with the same peculiar sense of foreboding that had presaged the worst play she'd ever taken part in. They had made it all the way to intermission when, during a storm scene, the background set had come crashing down and set a portion of the stage on fire. The phrase *it was a stage fire kind of day* had taken root in her vocabulary after that and she was hoping desperately that today was not that kind of day.

Tish was barely down from serving Wellington when the kitchen staff arrived, followed by Azalea hurrying up from parking in the lower pasture and tying on her apron.

"Hi," she said with a breathless smile. For once Azalea's curls were out of a bun or ponytail and looked slightly mussed. "Hey, I talked to Pen this morning and she said she might be running a few minutes late. She and her brother are sharing a car right now and she thought he was spending the night at his girlfriend's, so she has to wait for him to give her a ride. Her Vanagon broke down... again."

"It's fine," said Tish, nodding. "I scheduled everyone a half-hour early to account for Orcas time."

Azalea smiled but didn't look particularly amused to find out that she'd arrived a half-hour earlier than she needed to. "Probably a good idea. I would have given her a ride, but I was already past her house. Maybe I'll call Tate and see if he can pick her up."

Tate Donovan was part of the wedding band and Azalea's boy-friend. He was a good-natured twenty-three-year-old with boy-band looks and the hair to match. Tish thought he was a fairly talented musician who was better at marketing and showmanship than he was at singing, but sometimes that's all it took to succeed.

"I talked to him this morning," said Tish, going back to her clip-board. "He was going to run into town and get a spare cord for the amplifier or something."

"You talked to him?" repeated Azalea and Tish heard an alarm bell along with Azalea's chilly tone.

"Yeah," said Tish not bothering to look up from her list. She refused to be drawn into tweeny-bopper drama. "He called to dou-ble-check his arrival time. He wanted to make sure that he had time to get the part."

"Oh," said Azalea, with an exasperated sigh. "You know, this won't be a problem when we move in together."

"What won't be a problem?" asked Tish looking up, genuinely confused.

"He's always so forgetful," said Azalea with a complacent smile. "When we move in together, I'll be able to look after him better. Anyway, I'll tell him to stop and get Penelope."

"There won't be time," said Tish. "He was taking a different ferry. The timing is going to be tight and I need them to get here in time for the processional."

"I'm sure—" began Azalea.

"There really isn't time," said Tish, cutting her off. "If Penelope needs a ride, she'll have to call someone else." For a moment, Azalea looked ridiculously pissed off.

I'm sorry that I can't be as accommodating as a regular Orcas employer, but I've got a bride paying a ludicrous amount of money for this to go perfectly.

"Sorry," said Tish. "But I'm not telling the bride we're delaying the ceremony because the band stopped to give someone a ride."

"Of course," said Azalea, calming down. "I mean, that makes sense. Leave it to Penelope to make things inconvenient for everyone."

"Great," said Tish. "Can you stay here and keep an eye on the bride? I'm going to go double check all the electrical cables out at the dance floor."

"You got it!" chirped Azalea, seemingly bouncing back from her momentary anger.

"Oh," said Tish, one hand on the door. "And remind everyone to keep the doors closed. Mimi brought her cat and the last thing we need is for Wellington to get out and be eaten by an eagle or something."

"She brought her cat to her wedding?" asked Azalea, looking perplexed.

"Yeah," said Tish. "That's pretty much the face I made. Anyway, keep an eye out and make sure everyone knows to keep it in the house."

"On it!" said Azalea, enthusiastically.

Tish found her photographer laying down in a flower bed on her way out to the gazebo.

"Hey Neil," she said leaning over him. "How's it going?"

He rolled over, looking up at her in surprise. "Hi! Great! It's going great! The place looks great! This shot of the gazebo through the flowers is going to be epic. The lighting is ethereal!"

"Cool," said Tish. "The bride and her bridesmaid got here a little bit ago."

"Awesome! My assistant Quincy will be here in about twenty-minutes. She's going to do some dressing room shots. I mean, that's not her thing. She's really more for the tech stuff, but this way I'm minimizing any sexual harassment risk."

"Um… K," said Tish. "If you go up to the house and ask for Azalea you can get a print-out of the itinerary."

"So organized!"

"You had a lot of coffee this morning, didn't you, Neil?"

"Yes, I did. I'm very excited about this opportunity. I really think that advertising shoot we did at Christmas is what sold my portfolio," he added. "Thanks so much."

"Of course," said Tish. "I'll see you in a bit. Good luck with the bride."

Tish continued on her rounds. The staff arrived. The band arrived. The officiant arrived looking nervous and slightly drunk. He was one of the groom's friends who'd gotten himself ordained online so he could perform the ceremony. Tish confiscated his flask and sent him off to rehearse with two protein bars and some orange juice. Wellington escaped and ate a boutonniere, but Terry came to the rescue with three extras to account for pinning mishaps and assurances that none of the plants were toxic to cats. By the time the ceremony started, Tish was feeling slightly more settled, although the sense of foreboding hadn't quite left her. But when no one stood up to object to the marriage, Tish felt her shoulders relax. It wasn't until meal service started that she realized that Penelope had never shown up for work.

Tish stood on the back porch and watched the reception unfold. The late afternoon sunshine was giving everything a golden glow. The guests all seemed happy, pleasantly buzzed, and generally bent on reenacting a Tommy Hilfiger commercial. Neil was in absolute heaven, snapping through a million bytes of memory card.

Azalea came around the corner of the house with her phone in one hand. "Hey Pen, it's me. Why aren't you at work? Call me back." She stopped when she saw Tish and smiled awkwardly. "Hey."

"No answer from Penelope?" asked Tish.

"No," said Azalea. "I don't understand it. She's usually so responsible. I know she comes off as a little… granola. But she's a really hard worker. I promise."

"We're doing OK without her," said Tish. "I'll talk to her about it later."

"Thanks for being so understanding," said Azalea. Tish shrugged. Tish didn't really want to think about firing Penelope. On the other hand, maybe she wouldn't have to. Penelope was hourly, so it wasn't as though Tish was going to have to pay her. As long as she came up with a good excuse, Tish would probably just give her another a chance.

Azalea scooted by her into the house and Tish scanned the crowd again. She was about to go back into the kitchen and sneak some food for herself, when she caught sight of a familiar lanky form and frowned. Matthew Jones was the island's most eligible drug dealer. Brushing up against six feet tall with dark hair and intense brown eyes, Matt had been raised on Orcas and while no one could prove that he smuggled in weight from Canada before shepherding it south, it was one of the island's least well-kept secrets. Tish liked him, which annoyed Nash. Tish at one point had attempted to point out the irony of Nash being mad at her for liking Matt considering that he and Matt had gone to college together and the two were remarkably cordial for being on opposite sides of the law. That conversation hadn't gone over well.

Matt was currently wearing a pair of slacks and a button-up, and he was doing his best to blend into the Amazon crowd. Out of habit, she checked his watch. He never dressed like he had gobs of cash lying around. He usually looked as Northwesty as everyone else in REI and North Face, but his one splurge point seemed to be watches. She couldn't quite tell at this distance, but she thought today's watch was Cartier.

Matt lived in Anacortes mostly these days but showed up at a lot of island events because his mother still lived on Orcas. Tish couldn't quite figure out how he'd gotten an invite to this wedding though.

On the island a lot. Lots of money. Knows Granddad.

The crowd rotated and Matt turned to head toward the appetizer table when he spotted Tish. He immediately attempted to divert and swing right.

"Hold it right there," said Tish stepping off the porch.

"Patricia," said Matt, pausing and smiling at her.

"Don't Patricia me," hissed Tish. She grabbed him by the elbow and pulled him away from the crowd. "You got him arrested, didn't you?"

"I don't know what you're talking about," said Matt innocently.

"Liar. What the hell are the two of you up to?"

"Which part is worse?" asked Matt taking a sip of his drink. "The fact that we didn't tell you or the fact that you haven't figured it out?"

Tish straightened up and folded her arms across her chest. "You think you're cute, don't you?"

"I think you think I'm cute," he said with a cocky grin.

"You're lucky I do," said Tish. "Otherwise I might accidentally bean you with a champagne bottle and tell everyone your middle name is Cornelius. Look, if you—"

A crowd of guests drifted by and Tish waited until they were out of earshot.

"If you get him in trouble I will be very upset," she finished, feeling annoyed that the timing delay had robbed her threat of impact.

"He's a big boy," said Matt. "I didn't make him do anything. I offered to hire him for his services, and he accepted. He thought it was a worthy cause."

Tish considered that piece of information. Her grandfather hated drugs, but Matt had always flirted with decency, which was why Nash liked him. If Tobias really thought that Matt's case was worth taking then it probably was, but she was having a hard time picturing what the reason would be.

"He is seventy-nine," said Tish. "I realize that a misdemeanor isn't exactly going to impact his life at this point, but jail was *not* good for him physically."

Matt grimaced. "Sorry," he said.

"You should have told me what was going on. I could have scheduled more time with his physical therapist and badgered him into a massage."

Matt took another sip and eyed her amusement dancing in his eyes. "He said he didn't want to distract you from this." He waved at the wedding. "Which turned out great by the way."

"Is it going well?" asked Tish nervously, looking around. "It feels like it's going well, but I can't tell."

"It's going great," he said. "The place looks like a frigging magazine photoshoot."

Tish felt her shoulders relax a fraction of an inch. "I know it's ridiculous, but I keep having this sense of impending doom."

"Everyone is having a really good time," he said reassuringly.

Tish ran a hand through her hair. "Please just promise me that you're not going to send Granddad off on some other crazy top-secret mission."

"I promise," he said reaching out and squeezing her shoulder. "I needed him to deliver a message and he did. It's done. Whatever the impending doom is, it's not mine. Promise."

Tish looked up at him. "And you're not going to tell me what it was?"

"And rob you of the fun of figuring it out yourself?" he asked grinning. "I wouldn't dream of it. And now if you'll excuse me, I have to go try the delicious looking hors d'oeuvres."

"You're going to hit on the bridesmaids," said Tish, scoping the crowd by the food.

"No, I'm going to chat up their wealthy parents," he said. "Wish me luck."

"Good luck," said Tish watching him go with a frown.

What does he need with wealthy parents?

Tish shook her head. She didn't have time to worry about Matt. She needed to focus on getting through this day and the next emergency. So far, all the emergencies had been minor, but she was still expecting the other shoe to drop at any moment.

CHAPTER 5
DISCOVERY

Tish breathed a final sigh of relief as the last guest exited the property. She had checks in her back pocket and three envelopes full of cash for tipping out the band, bartenders, and staff. Doom was not going to descend upon them. Nothing horrible had happened. The sun was setting on a glorious day at Yearly Events.

She grabbed her phone and quickly deposited the checks via her banking app before anyone could change their mind and then went downstairs to distribute the cash. The staff was slamming through clean up. Word was that they were collectively heading for the Olga bar and everyone wanted to get done as fast as possible. Tish flitted through the mad house like a cash depositing fairy and everyone looked delighted. Tish felt the impossible swell of success. She felt like she had just taken three curtain calls and booked a movie with Disney.

"I've got some for Tate too," said Tish as she handed the bass player his cash. "He didn't leave already did he?"

"They went outside. Azalea wanted to *talk*," said the bass player, rolling his eyes. He was your basic bearded hipster in a black vest and tattoos. Tish thought he was possibly named Marty or Morty. Which seemed unlikely enough that she didn't want to say it out loud. Neil had practically squealed like a little girl upon seeing the band. *Trendily photogenic* might as well have been their band name.

"Trouble in paradise?" asked Tish, feeling sympathy for the bass player's low threshold for drama.

"Eh, who knows? Azalea's always tweaked about something. Everything better go exactly to plan or she is not happy."

"I know," said Tish. "I'm attempting to harness that for my own evil wedding planning purposes."

The bass player laughed. "Yeah, I hear that. Except Tate's never met a plan that he wanted to follow. They are the worst couple. He keeps swearing he's going to break up with her, but I don't see a lot of movement in that direction. Probably because Azalea won't let him."

And I am backing away from this situation and giving zero commentary.

"All right, well, I'm going to go see if I can shove cash at him and then run for cover. I want to get everybody out of here and straight to drinking as fast as possible."

"You are exactly the kind of woman I like to be under," he said. Tish was already a half-step toward the door and didn't bother to turn around. Either he was making a definite inappropriate statement slash joke slash pick up line or he'd made an inadvertent double entendre. Either way she wasn't sure she wanted to have to respond. In her model slash actress days, she could have returned with something equally inappropriate but dismissive or flirty depending on how she felt about beards that month. But being the boss made her feel weird. How was she supposed to handle that in a lady boss-like way? In some ways it really would be easier to just be able to let everyone know she was monogamizing the hell out of Nash on a regular basis. Even if the various randos didn't respect monogamy they did respect Nash's height and Sheriff's badge. But that seemed like a literal cop-out. She shouldn't need to hide behind Nash.

Tish made it out to the parking circle just in time to see Tate's Dodge pick-up take off down the gravel drive. Azalea was standing, arms folded, an expression of extreme dissatisfaction on her face.

"Uh," said Tish.

"He is just so immature," said Azalea. "He's going to have to realize that he can't just drive away from every little argument."

"Right," said Tish, trying to backpedal.

"Did you need something?" asked Azalea, smiling forcefully at

Tish.

"I was going to tip Tate out," said Tish.

"Oh, I can take it," said Azalea, holding out her hand.

"Sorry," said Tish. "That's illegal. I've got to give it directly to him."

Not that I'm actually sure about that, but I'm not going to hand out cash to significant others without a wedding ring and even then I'm not sure about it.

"Who's going to know?" asked Azalea, laughing.

"Well, me, for one thing," said Tish. "And it's the kind of thing that gets around. I don't want the other kids knowing I hand out their cash to whoever happens to be standing around. I worked a job like that and it got ugly really fast. Have to keep the *Lord of the Flies* vibe tamped down before I end up needing to be rescued by the Navy."

"What?" Azalea looked confused.

"Never mind," said Tish. "I'll just give it to him next time I see him."

"OK," said Azalea with a shrug. "I think today went really well, by the way. I don't know what the client said, but from the staff side I thought it ran smoothly."

"It seemed like everyone had it under control," agreed Tish, heading back to the house. "Having Lane as the bartender really helped."

"Yeah, stealing him from the Orcas Hotel was a smart move," said Azalea, with a smug smile.

"I did not steal," said Tish firmly. "They cut his shifts. The guy has to make a living. It's just that we're decidedly not mentioning it to anyone."

Azalea chuckled. "You know it's going be all over the island in two minutes. It's probably going to be on that dumb blog by tomorrow."

"What blog?"

"Haven't you seen it?" demanded Azalea, her eyes lighting up. "It's called The Grapevine. Some nosey little bastard is putting all the island gossip online. Last week they ratted out Mrs. McAllister for letting her rooster loose on her neighbor's chickens."

"We all knew it was her," said Tish, with a shrug.

"But we did not have photographic evidence of her doing it on purpose," said Azalea. "Everyone thinks she did it to sink her neighbor's egg business."

"Well, now they've got a chick business," said Tish. "Could be worse."

The staff trickled out in waves and, in the case of the bass player, invitations to join them at the Olga bar. Tish declined and finished her final sweep of the house before locking up. She was headed home for a bath. Which was a bit of a disappointment because what she really wanted was to head over to Nash's for naked hot tub time. The beauty of living on two acres of land with about a hundred pine trees was that hot tubs could be clothing optional. With a sigh she headed out into the glowing orange evening.

In the driveway, Azalea's red two-door was parked with the hood up.

"Car trouble?" asked Tish, sensing her bathtub getting even further away.

"I think the battery's dead. I don't suppose you have jumper cables?"

"Granddad probably has some," said Tish. "Not that I know where."

Azalea sighed. "I don't suppose you could just give me a ride home? I'll have Tate come help tomorrow. Right now I just want to head home."

"Yeah, I hear you," said Tish. "Sure."

As they bumped down the gravel drive, Azalea took out her phone and made a call. "Hey Penelope. It's me. Again. Can you call me?" She hung up and looked at Tish with a worried frown. "Penelope hasn't even texted me today. I don't understand what's up with her."

Tish once again wanted to ask about Penelope's pregnancy, but decided against it. Penelope had said she wasn't telling anyone yet. That might include even Azalea.

"Um…" said Azalea. "I don't suppose you would maybe be able to stop by and see her before you drop me off. Maybe she's sick or something. Then you could just leave me there."

Tish felt the beginnings of a stress headache.

I should have eaten something when I had the chance. Do I still have that protein bar in the glove box?

"Sure. We can do that. Where does she live?"

"Just before Otter's Pond Bed and Breakfast. It's got the ferry boat mailbox."

"Gotcha," said Tish. "No, wait. The regular one or the one that got weird?"

"Weird," said Azalea. "Paxton, Pen's brother did some shrooms and went decorating."

"Ah. That explains the statue of Buddha on the foredeck."

"It explains a lot of things," said Azalea drily.

"I don't know. I thought the unicorn was a nice touch."

Azalea did not look amused by the unicorn.

Tish turned right at the mailbox shaped like a pink ferry boat with the gold statue of Buddha and Unicorn on the roof and bumped down a pothole ridden road to a pre-fab single wide house that was still on cinderblocks. Golden streaks of sunlight streamed through the evergreens. Dancing dust motes clogged the almost palpable rays and attracted early night moths and diving swallows. Penelope's Volkswagen Vanagon was parked off to one side radiating hippiness.

Azalea climbed out of the car and went to the front door. Tish watched her knock and then wait. Tish surveyed the yard again. It was mostly a barren gravel parking area with a trash heap off to one side. Like a lot of Orcas residencies, all the pretty stuff was in the back yard. If you could call acreage a back yard. Tish rubbed her neck and tried to shake the bad feeling she was getting.

The curtains in the house were all wide open. Not a problem exactly except that the sunshine was beaming directly through the window and hitting the edge of a TV. That seemed abnormal if someone were home.

Tish got out of the car and stood listening to Azalea knock again.

"I'm going to try the back door," said Tish.

"They always lock it," said Azalea, dismissively. "Everyone knows Paxton has drugs, so he has to lock it so his low-life friends don't rip him off."

"Yeah," said Tish. "I'm just going to look."

She could see a small pond on the far side of the house and a chicken coop. There was even a cute little water feature and tiny little island in the middle. Someone had loved the place once upon a time. The sunlight was hot on the back of her head as she came around the corner—bouncing off the white house paint and doubling the heat—but then she stepped into the cool shadow of the house as it stretched out onto the pond. It took Tish's eyes a long moment to adjust to the change in lighting and when she did, her heart sank. Azalea came trotting around the corner after her and Tish put out her hand to stop her too late.

"Really, they lock the door all the—" Azalea stood still, her breath coming in short sips.

Penelope Drue's body was lying face down in the water at the edge of the pond. She was dressed in nothing more than underwear and a tank-top and her purple hair drifted like seaweed in the green water.

CHAPTER 6

REPORTING FOR DUTY

Nash stood next to her and Tish tried not to simply throw herself into his arms.

"This is becoming a bad habit," he said.

"Not funny," said Tish. "You need to call Detective Spring."

"We already did. It's standard procedure."

"Right," said Tish nodding. "Right. Good. That's good. I'll talk to Granddad too. We need to do something."

"Tish," said Nash.

After pulling Penelope's body from the water, Tish had sent Azalea back to the front of the house to wait for the police. Nash and Colin had done all the appropriate things: covered the body, called the coroner, and taken statements. Colin was taking photos and talking into his phone, recording notes like he was an actual detective on a TV show instead of a local Sheriff's Deputy. Colin was about forty and a bit pudgy with dark hair starting to go salt and pepper. The coroner and his assistant had been able to make an afternoon ferry and were still looking at Penelope's body using an enormous hand-held flashlight that put out enough wattage to light a movie set. The sun was fading and the coroner's light was starting to leave spots in her vision. Tish was waiting for him to stand up and declare something.

I don't want to even think what I'm waiting for him to declare.

"You know Detective Spring will try hard," said Tish. "But we have to be prepared in case he decides to be an idiot again."

"Tish," said Nash, again. He was tilting his head and trying to catch her eye. She didn't like it when he did this. It meant he was trying to be kind and serious at the same time. "I'm not sure…"

"She drowned in less than a foot of water," said Tish. "It's murder." Her voice sounded flat.

A director would be calling for more emotion.

"Tish…"

"What?"

"She and her brother have a long history of drug use. She might have just slipped and passed out."

"No," said Tish firmly. "She was not doing any drugs. I talked to her yesterday. She was… excited about stuff. But this morning, she didn't show up for work. She didn't answer her phone all day, but her body was still a little warm when I pulled it out of the water. What the hell was she doing all day? And why was she only in her underwear?"

"I don't have the answer to those questions," said Nash. "But what I've learned from this job is that drugs make people do weird things and we may never know the answer."

He was being gentle, and Tish found that infuriating. She found Penelope being dead infuriating. Penelope should not be dead. Penelope should be alive and planning baby showers and wondering whether pregnant women were allowed to eat sushi because she heard one time that they weren't.

"Not good enough!" snapped Tish. He reached out a hand for her arm and Tish yanked it away. "No! No, Penelope was killed. She was not doing drugs. She wasn't drinking. She wasn't lifting heavy dance floor sections. She was pregnant. And someone killed her."

"What?"

Tish spun around to find that Azalea had come around the house again.

"She was what?" Azalea's eyes were huge.

"Shit," said Tish.

"Azalea, Azalea!" Deputy Ronny Fullbright came sputtering around the house after Azalea. "You're not supposed to be back here."

He grabbed Azalea by the arm and took her back around the house.

"Tish is back here," protested Azalea.

"Yeah, well, Tish knows how to deal with dead... Uh... You know what, Azalea, we're just going to go back to the squad car, OK?"

"Shit," said Tish, again.

"Tish," said Nash and once again Tish wanted to wrap her arms around him and feel safe and know that everything would be better. But over Nash's shoulder, Colin was watching them with a thoughtful expression.

"I want to go home," she said. "I've been awake since four because I couldn't sleep, and I didn't eat any lunch or dinner and I'm really tired. Can I go home?"

Nash glanced over at Colin who shrugged.

"It's not like Detective Spring doesn't know where she lives," said Colin.

"You want me to drive you?" asked Nash.

Yes.

"No. It's not very far. I can do it."

Nash looked like he had a hundred things he wanted to say and since she wouldn't let him tell anyone they were dating he wasn't going to say anything.

I know this is my fault. If I weren't so weird about relationships, we could at least be hugging right now.

Tish sighed and made a sad shrug flap motion. She wanted to say more too, but also couldn't come up with anything that could be said in front of anyone else. She turned around and walked back to her car. Azalea and Ronny were out by the trash heap. Tish knew she ought to go talk to Azalea. She ought to do a lot of things, but instead she got in her car and drove toward home.

Chicken.

She made it all the way to her usual parking spot in her grandfather's driveway and then found that she couldn't muster the energy to get out of the car. Her grandfather's house was a long horizontal strip built around a grand central A-frame. It was set back on the property and on a grade so that while it was two-stories it appeared shorter. The driveway was horseshoe shaped so that anyone could simply drive around the loop and back out to the road. To the right of the house was a shed and to the left was the recently fenced area with the arbor and dog run. And in the center of the driveway loop was another shed slash garage that had Tobias's home gym. Tobias tended to park his beat up old white truck off to the left and she pulled hers in under the slanted carport area to the right in front of the storage shed. Tonight, Tish found herself staring at the door of the shed and counting the slats of wood, soothed by the monotony.

Thunk.

Tish jerked upright and looked around, her heart pounding in her chest. Tobias was standing outside her car with a concerned expression on his face. He had tapped his cane on the glass.

"Hey Granddad," she said, opening the door slowly.

"Why is Nash calling me to make sure you got home?"

"Nash called you?"

"Left a message on the machine. Heard it as I was coming in from throwing the ball for Coats."

The black lab wedged himself around her grandfather's knee and he panted up at them looking from face to face as if inquiring what we were all doing, and could it involve more ball.

"What happened?" asked Tobias, looking at her severely as she rubbed Coats' soft ears. "Something bad at the wedding?"

"Wedding went great," said Tish, shaking her head. "But one of my employees didn't show up for work. And I drove her friend home and we stopped in to see if she was OK." Tish stopped, her throat clogging up and her chin wobbling.

"Not OK?" asked Tobias and Tish shook her head.

"And Nash said she had a history of drug use, but she was pregnant, Granddad, and she was happy about it. I just don't think… It was only a little duck pond. It was barely a foot of water."

I'm not making any sense.

"I'm really tired. Nash let me come home."

"Uh-huh," said Tobias, nodding. "OK, well, inside with you. I'll make you a fried egg sandwich."

"Thanks Granddad," said Tish. Her grandfather's cooking skills, or rather lack of cooking skills, were infamous, but since her arrival he'd made real strides in the fried egg sandwich department. They were now almost always edible.

Tish sat at the kitchen bar and watched as Tobias got out the cast iron skillet and made his way around the kitchen. A few minutes later she had a sandwich slathered in butter and egg with a dash of tabasco because Tobias thought everything was more interesting with tabasco.

"Eat your sandwich, Tishkins," he said, when she didn't immediately move.

"Granddad, I don't know what I'm doing."

"You're sitting there not eating your sandwich," said Tobias, scratching his nose.

"With my life," said Tish.

"Well, you ain't gonna figure it out on an empty stomach. Eat your sandwich."

Tish did as she was instructed and after a few bites found that life probably wasn't an empty wasteland devoid of meaning. By the time, she'd finished her sandwich Tobias had procured a cup of decaf and was leaning against the kitchen counter. As she pushed the plate away, he reached into one of the overhead cupboards and pulled out a bag of animal cookies. He dumped them out onto her paper towel napkin and Tish eyed their pink and white shiny icing. Granddad knew her weakness. She just hadn't realized that he stocked her weakness. She picked up a pink lion and shoved the entire thing in her mouth.

"Feeling better?"

"A little bit," she admitted.

"Tell me about this girl."

"Penelope Drue. Sweet kid. Hard worker, but a bit Orcas-y." Tish bit the head off a camel.

"Artsy and never arrives on time?"

"Yeah. Anyway, yesterday, she told me that she couldn't lift anything heavy because she was pregnant."

"How pregnant was she?" asked Tobias, looking confused.

"Barely. She said she'd be four months along at the end of wedding season which is late September."

"I think lifting heavy things is only when you're further along," he said, taking a cautious sip from his mug.

"I don't know," said Tish wearily. "I don't know anything about pregnant people. But I do know that she was excited about it. And she was planning on being at work today. But then she didn't show. And we found her body in the pond."

"Doesn't seem right," said Tobias.

"No! It doesn't. And then Nash said it was probably drugs, and I wanted to punch him."

"Well, Tishkins, in all honesty, it might have been." Tish stopped with a bear half-way in her mouth and glared at him. "But give it a day or two and the coroner will be able to say for sure. In the meantime, we can poke around if you want."

Tish rubbed her eyes and then sighed. "No. I mean, probably we shouldn't. With our luck, Detective Spring will just accuse me of murdering her. He's gotten everyone else. He's bound to get around to me at some point."

Tobias snorted in amusement.

"And I don't know. Maybe I'm wrong. Nash has been here a lot longer than I have. He knows about a lot of the island stuff that I don't."

"Suppose so," said Tobias. "But he hasn't been here longer than me. And while the Drue family is as kooky as they come—I think the parents are currently in Hawaii learning about aquaponics or some such—the kids have always struck me as a bit more together than the parents. Did Penelope say who the father was?"

"No," said Tish shaking her head. "I didn't even know she had a boyfriend. Although, I guess there might not be a boyfriend. She just said she wasn't telling anyone yet."

Tobias nodded thoughtfully. "Well, I tell you what. I think you ought to go get some sleep and we can see how things look tomorrow. Ten to one Detective Spring will fetch up here in the morning and then we can see what he thinks and find out what he knows."

"He's going to make comments about you having dementia," said Tish, trying to pick between a white hippo and what was possibly a pink elephant.

"Well, sure," agreed Tobias. "I wouldn't expect anything less from him."

"In his defense, he was really worried about you," said Tish. "Of course, it never occurred to him that Matt Jones would hire you to get yourself thrown in jail."

Tobias paused, cup halfway to his mouth. "Damn it."

"One day," said Tish with a grin.

"Too smart," he said, shaking his head and hiding a smile behind his mug.

"But what I don't understand is why you would help Matt," said Tish. "You hate drugs."

"I do," agreed Tobias with a twinkle in his eye.

Tish glared at him. He was holding out on her. And since he really did hate drugs then whatever he was doing was not drug related. Although, she failed to see how that was possible.

"I'm cleaning the jam cellar," she said.

"Just as well," he said. "I don't remember what's down there and Eleanor wants to store jam in it."

"Eleanor makes jam?" Eleanor was Tobias's girlfriend, although neither would admit to it.

"Apparently," he said. "I try not to inquire too closely about these things."

"It's jam, Granddad. What's there to inquire about?"

"It's never about the jam," said Tobias, sagely. "When a woman starts talking about her girlfriends and projects and suddenly it involves your jam cellar, trust me, it's never about the jam."

"Do you not want her to use the jam cellar?" Tish was confused.

"Nope, she's welcome to it. I just don't want to know *why* she's using the jam cellar."

Tish frowned. Tobias wanted to know *why* everything. He hadn't met a why that he didn't want answered.

"I think I'm too tired or too young to understand this," said Tish.

"Possibly both," said Tobias.

"Possibly both," agreed Tish. She took another lion and a bear and headed for her bed.

CHAPTER 7

SUNDAY – REGROUP

"I'm feeling snubbed, Granddad," said Tish, looking out the kitchen window for the eleventh time.

"Maybe he got hung up on the ferry," said Tobias, from the kitchen table where he was reading yesterday's paper.

"Bullpucky," said Tish. "I saw his sunglasses. The man enjoys playing Miami Vice. He could have taken the police boat over."

"Well, you said they took your statement last night," said Tobias, reasonably. "Maybe he's got more important things to do than talk to us."

"You do have an alibi for yesterday afternoon, right? I wouldn't want him accusing you of murder *again*."

"Why would he a accuse me of murdering poor Penelope Drue?"

"Why would he accuse you of murdering Reginald? The man's got a few screws loose." She moved the curtain and looked out at the driveway again.

"I think you're going to have to let that one go," said Tobias, folding the paper back.

"I do not," said Tish. "I can hold that as a grudge until his funeral if I want to."

Tobias chuckled. "I'm told that carrying grudges isn't healthy. Bad for the blood pressure. Also, I'm over it. If I don't care, why should you?"

"Because you're my Granddad!"

Tobias looked at her over the edge of his paper, his eyes twinkling. "Yes, Tishkins, and you're my wee lass of a granddaughter. But some things aren't personal. Detective Spring does not go around accusing people you like of murder just because he finds it funny."

"He's two for two," said Tish, narrowing his eyes.

"Yes, between me and Nash his batting average is not very good, is it?" offered Tobias with a chuckle.

"No, it is not, and I believe he needs to do more than offer half-assed apologies to erase the black marks in the ledger."

"Did Nash get a half-assed apology?" asked Tobias, fully looking up from the paper. "Well, that frosts my cookies. I didn't get one of those. All I got was half-assed whining about evidence. Well, that tears it. Let's not sit around here, waiting on him. Let's go into town and see what's doin'.'"

"Sold," said Tish. "I'll grab my jacket."

Orcas Island was shaped more or less like a horseshoe. Tobias lived on the right leg before Moran State Park and the tiny hamlet of Olga at the very end of the island. Eastsound was located at the apex of the horseshoe and housed the majority of the island's services. The speed limit on most of the island was thirty-five, although the majority of drivers went at least forty. There had been a big kerfuffle the previous winter when speed-limit changes had been proposed before the county council. The speed limit had dropped in several locations, including, and Tish still couldn't believe this was true, Lover's Lane. Because people were out walking on Lover's Lane and therefore it was dangerous to drive so fast. Tish still snickered every time she had to use the road's name. But, in a big win for sense in government, and a loss for Ronny's ticketing rates, the speed limit had been raised in several locations. Not that it mattered. When Tobias was in the car, she followed the speed limit otherwise he said they were guilty of *conspicuous driving.*

"Drop me up at the hardware store," said Tobias as they approached Eastsound. "I want to chat up Jeffery about some stuff."

"Sure," said Tish. "I think I'm going to the grocery store though. Do you have your phone with you? You can text me when you want to be picked up."

"I'll have Jeffery text you," said Tobias and Tish nodded. It wasn't that Tobias couldn't learn to use new technology. He delighted in his spy gear catalog and toys. But he specifically seemed to dislike cellphones. She wasn't sure why. Tish dropped Tobias off at Island Hardware, and cruised into Eastsound pondering whether or not she should buy pie or if she should feel guilty about leaving home before talking to Detective Spring.

Because I don't feel guilty. Not even a little bit. I think I've been living with Granddad too long. I've fully moved to the rebel side. Not that I was ever much a line-toer.

I really do want pie.

Tish picked up a basket and threaded her way past the produce toward the deli department. Tobias couldn't cook and Tish was frequently too lazy. That meant they spent a lot of money on the ready-made meals that came from the island's tiny grocery store.

"Oh my goodness, Tish," said the woman behind the counter as Tish approached. Her name was Magda and she usually wore her gray hair long and undyed. However, recent crack downs by health authorities had resulted in a revival of the snood—a turn of the century style hair net that kept her flowing locks from flowing into the food. Tish liked it, but now had to fight the desire to talk to her in a Scarlet O'Hara accent. "How *are* you coping?"

"Um, fine?" Tish wasn't sure what to make of this greeting. It seemed excessively sympathetic for the death of an hourly employee that she'd known for only a few weeks.

"Well, you let us know if you need any help. Tobias is such a mainstay of the island. I was just crushed when I heard the news."

"What news?" asked Tish feeling that she was missing out on half the conversation.

"Well, about the dementia?" Magda looked uncertain.

"What dementia? Granddad doesn't have dementia!"

"Then what was he doing drunk and disorderly in Anacortes?"

"He was…" Tish trailed off. "How'd you hear about that?" she demanded.

"From Elayne Dorety. She said she saw it on that new blog."

"What?"

"That new Grapevine blog. Elayne made it sound like you had already taken him to a doctor."

"He's not going to a doctor," snapped Tish. "He doesn't have dementia!"

"Then he was really drunk?" Magda looked horrified.

"You know what? Just give me some of the salmon and stop talking about Granddad!"

"Well, all right. Can we talk about you dating Matt Jones? Because I am dying to know if that one is true."

"What?" Tish dropped her basket on floor.

"Elayne said you were dating, she said there was a picture."

"Son of a bitch!"

"Well, really!" said a woman, popping out of the chip aisle and dragging her four -year -old purposefully gender-neutral child with blonde shoulder length curls and brown corduroy overalls away with her. "Come along, Aspen."

Tish considered yelling that Aspen really was a girl's name after her but restrained herself.

"I am not dating Matt Jones!" Tish leaned over the counter to whisper urgently at Magda. "You cannot go around telling people that."

"Well," said Magda leaning in to meet her half-way over the counter, "first of all, that's too bad, because he's hot and I hear he's rolling in it. Well, he'd have to be, wouldn't he? In his line of work, I mean. And second of all, I'll stop saying it, but the rest of the island is still going to see it on the blog."

Tish yanked her phone out of her pocket. "What is the damn address?"

"I think it's just the Orcas Grapevine dot com," said Magda.

Tish typed it in and waited for the browser to load—the wi-fi at the store was running at 2003 speed. Finally, the page loaded and Tish scrolled past the hideous pink header graphic with the Victorian-esque grapevine and font.

Top Story – The Yearlys Make Waves

Tobias Yearly, last seen drunk and disorderly in Anacortes on Thursday morning, is apparently home sleeping it off. But with this uncustomary behavior can we really rule out an onset of dementia?

The image was one of Tobias's arrest paperwork, which while technically public record seemed shockingly rude to be posting. Tobias looked quite cheerful in his mugshot.

And it looks like Tish Yearly has been busy with more than wedding planning. Could it be that local bad boy Matt Jones is consoling Tish about her grandfather's health problems?

Below this little tidbit was a photo of Tish from the wedding the previous day. Matt had his hand on her shoulder and was leaning into her with a smile. Tish thought her own expression looked worried.

"Oh, I am so dead," said Tish.

Nash is going to lose it.

"Tobias is going to be pissed?" asked Magda.

"Well, the blog just said he's losing his mind. Wouldn't you be pissed? Also, he hates drugs! He's not going to want to hear some rumor about me dating Matt Jones."

"Well, you do look friendly in the picture," said Magda.

"Friendly," stressed Tish. "That's it. And make sure you tell everyone else that too."

"OK," said Magda with a shrug.

Tish slammed through the rest of her shopping and then hurried out to the car, desperately dialing Sarah. Sarah picked up on the third ring.

"Hey!" Sarah sounded high-energy.

Is that cheerful? Or was she doing the marketing smile while talking thing?

"Oh, thank God you picked up."

"Oh dear," said Sarah. "Who's dead now?"

"Penelope Drue. I'm really upset. I mean, I only knew her for a couple of weeks, but I'm still not sure it wasn't murder. And I can't even talk about that right now. I'm in deep shit, Sarah. Some idiot is publishing a blog called the Orcas Grapevine and saying I'm dating Matt Jones and that Granddad's got dementia. But you know what? People think he's crazy anyway. That'll die down once they forget he went to jail."

"Uh," said Sarah.

"Hey Tish," called a voice from the other side of the car. It was one of the Tims from a local construction outfit staffed by five guys—all named Tim.

"Hey Tim," she said, stowing the groceries, and pinching her phone between her ear and her shoulder.

"Hey, I heard Tobias got arrested? Is he OK?"

"Yeah, he's fine. You know Granddad—always up for an adventure."

"Oh, that's good. Are you dating Matt Jones? You're going to break our hearts."

"Tish?" said Sarah, faintly from the phone.

"All of you may only have one name, but you need more than one girlfriend," said Tish, firmly. "And no. I'm not dating Matt Jones."

"Well, all right," said Tim, "but you could do worse. He's a good guy."

"I'll keep that in mind," said Tish, with a smile and got in her car. "Seriously, Sarah," as she slammed the door to her car, "I need help. I need wine and I need a girl who knows how to lunch time drink. I know it's Sunday, but can we do a girl's night like ASAP? I could drive down. What about tonight? Or maybe tomorrow. Detective Spring might still want to talk to me."

"Um," said Sarah. "Yeah. Maybe tomorrow night? I've been really slammed at work and I've got some… people coming over tonight."

"Oh," said Tish. "Um, yeah. Whatever works for you."

I'm just having a crisis over here. No big deal. I guess if you're too busy for that then it's cool.

"The food is here!" bellowed a male voice from Sarah's end of the phone.

"Gotta go," said Sarah. "Food's here!"

"OK," said Tish, feeling shoved aside. "Call me when you're free."

"OK, bye!" said Sarah and the line clicked off before the last part of bye was even complete. Tish stared at the phone and felt like crying. She couldn't believe that Sarah had just ditched her in mid-panic attack. She hadn't even gotten to tell her about Nash. She clunked her head down on the steering wheel. This day was a disaster.

Thunk.

"Ahhh!" Tish jumped about three feet in her seat. Outside the window Nash was looking at her with a skeptical expression. She opened the car door and glared at him. "You people need to stop doing that!"

"So," he said with a pleasant smile, "I hear from three different sources this morning that you're dating Matt Jones."

"I am not dating Matt Jones!" Tish yelled.

"I hear there's photographic evidence."

"He is just touching me!"

"There's photographic evidence of him touching you?" She couldn't tell if Nash was laughing or actually shocked.

"That didn't come out right," said Tish.

"I imagine that it didn't, but I'm not really sure how it could have gone better."

"I bumped into him at the wedding yesterday," said Tish, swinging her legs out of the car. He stepped back and leaned against the side of her vehicle, arms folded, and waited for her to finish her exit. "And apparently some douchebag was taking paparazzi shots of me while I talked to him. You should go arrest that person."

"Public location. Not illegal." She eyed his lanky form and tried not to admire him. It was a losing battle.

"Sarah practically hung up on me!"

"You're just going to change the subject?" he asked.

"It's the same subject! I was trying to tell her how I am being publically stalked and that I was dating you and she rushed me off the phone for food and plans with someone else!"

"Aw, Tishkins," he said, borrowing her grandfather's nickname, but his face said it was faux sympathy.

"They also said Granddad had dementia."

"Sarah said Tobias had dementia?"

"No, that stupid blog."

"You know this wouldn't be a problem if you would just tell people we were dating."

"I am trying," snapped Tish, waving her hands in frustration. "I've been trying to tell Sarah for weeks and she won't answer the phone. And I wanted to have dinner today with you and Granddad and now there's a dead body and a blog and I hate everyone! Also," she stopped and pointed at him. "Also, it would still be a problem because then I'd just be having to explain how I wasn't cheating on you. And I would still have to defend Granddad from dementia rumors which I can't even do because—"

Nash waited eyebrows raised. "Because why?"

If I tell him it's for Matt he's going to blow a gasket.

Tish pursed her lips. "Client confidentiality. Can't."

"Seriously?"

She smiled awkwardly. "Seriously." But the word kind of trailed off and ended up as a question. "Sworn to secrecy," she added.

Is that going to fly?

Nash took a deep breath. "You know," he said, "one of the things I like about you is that you do very surprising things. I'm literally never bored."

Oh, that's so sweet.

"Unfortunately, that frequently means that I find myself wishing for a little boredom."

Oh, that's not good.

"Which is sort of the way you wish for winter in the middle of a heat wave."

Eh. Could be worse. I'll take it.

"I like that you make my life more exciting. But there's a difference between exciting and lying. And part of the reason I'm a cop is that I'm really stupid honest. I'm not built for sneaking around. I don't like it."

"I don't like it either. And I really am trying. I told my Mom. Not that she counts because she doesn't know anyone here and never talks to Granddad. But I did! But Sarah won't talk to me. And I was trying to plan a dinner with you and Claire and Granddad, but I can't seem to get two minutes alone with you and then Granddad got arrested and then the wedding, and then Penelope. I know it doesn't look like I'm doing anything other than freaking out, but I am trying!"

Nash sighed and his head kind of ducked down. "I see that you're trying. Thank you. I'm sorry about Sarah. What if Claire and I come over next Sunday?"

"That would be good," said Tish. "I just… I'm having to plan everything. I know managing Granddad doesn't look like a lot, but if I don't pay attention, he gets up to stuff like going to jail. And the business is just one long to-do list. And I can't seem to make progress on anything. I'm not really…"

I'm freaking out.

Nash lifted his head as if he'd experienced a lightbulb moment.

I said something. What did I say? Why can I never figure out what's going on in his head?

"You can make the eggplant stuff that Claire likes and I can grill burgers." He sounded very firm and decisive.

"You're good at burgers," she agreed, thrown off by his sudden change in tone.

"We'll come over at four, do an early dinner. That way Tobias can stomp off to go see George if he wants."

"OK," said Tish, blinking.

"There. Plan: done."

And… done? I thought there would be more push-back or not wanting to bring Claire or… I… done? Done.

It was just one thing off her checklist, but it might as well have been ten. She let out a sigh of relief. "OK. Yeah. OK. Next Sunday."

He nodded, with that little twist of a smile that said he thought she was adorable, and Tish thought her heart was going to burst in her chest.

How the hell did I get so lucky? Why is he so wonderful? How does he make everything better?

"I love you," Tish blurted out and then stared at Nash her eyes wide. "Shit, I said that out loud to your face." Nash leaned in, arms sliding around her waist to pull her off her feet and kiss her. Tish felt her knees go rubbery and everything else went soft and fuzzy.

"Right," he said, setting her back on her feet. "Let's see if we can't make that damn blog."

"M-wha-huh?" It was the most inarticulate noise, but it seemed to cover her feelings on the subject.

"Love you too," he said with a grin. "And for the record, I'll say it to your face or anywhere else."

"Mp!" said Tish.

That was not even a word.

Nash's grin stretched even wider. "Next Sunday. We'll be there. Meanwhile, call Detective Spring. He has questions."

CHAPTER 8
BUY THE BOOK

Tish waited until Nash had pulled away in the Sheriff's Department patrol car before trying to drive herself. She had taken a good look around the parking lot, but for once in the entire history of the island there didn't seem to be anyone around. She felt giddy and fizzy and a little bit light-headed. She didn't need him to see her miss a turn signal or something. That would just get awkward if he had to give her a ticket.

I just said I love you in the grocery store parking lot. That's fine, right? He said it back. I'm fine. It's fine. Definitely better than the time I said it to Paul and he went 'mmm, you're so special' and then ghosted a week later.

She started the car and pulled into traffic.

I said it. And then he said it. And now we've said it. And now it's just out there.

Tish waited behind a car as they waited for some crows to finish hopping out of the road.

Should I be panicking? I'm not panicking. Nash doesn't say things he doesn't mean. So he means that. And I know I meant it, so… OK. Well, we're in love. So there's that.

Tish looked at herself in the rearview mirror. She had an extremely wide, extremely dopey smile on her face.

I said 'I love you' in a grocery store parking lot.

This time she sounded smug to herself.

We're going to tell Claire and Granddad and then we won't have to sneak around anymore. Although, I believe I've been having more fun with that than Nash, but he's right it's getting old. And then everyone will know and I'll be the girl dating the hottest Sheriff's deputy in the San Juan's. So… Yay me.

Shit, we're telling Claire.

She had been intending on driving up to the pie shop at the top of the hill before heading back to find Tobias, but instead, she pulled into a parking spot on the street and went into the bookstore.

"Hey Tish!" said Cokie, from the cash register as she walked in.

"Hey Cokie."

Cokie Matthews and his partner owned the lone bookstore that served up used and new books to the island's print word addicts. Tish wound her way back through the stacks and with a cautious look over her shoulder went into the self-help section.

It was Tish's theory that all anyone really needed to be mostly proficient at a skill was to read three books on the subject. She didn't think she needed to read up on dating. She'd had dating pretty wired by the time she left high school. But relationships, real adult relationships with stable individuals that wanted to do healthy things like support their partner emotionally, were proving to be harder to master. She wasn't sure if she'd somehow missed the memo on trusting people or if her Hollywood experiences had stunted her growth, but she felt like Nash was way better at relationshipping than she was. She was figuring it out—online articles were helpful—but adding Claire into the mix had her worried. She loved Claire and she thought Claire loved her.

But she might love me a whole lot less when she realizes I'm dating her dad.

The dealing with divorce section took up most of a shelf. The kids and divorce was a solid third of that. The dating a person with kids was a total of two books. Tish took a quick flip through the first one and shoved it back in annoyance. Be patient, you won't be introduced to the kid immediately, blah, blah, blah. Clearly, they didn't know who they were dealing with. The second book was slightly more profitable with solid tips on talking to the kid—stay factual, be kind, and don't try to be a parent.

But I think I'm doing that already. I hope Claire thinks I'm kind anyway. I try never to talk smack about her mom. Not that I think Nora ever reciprocates.

Tish perused the section again, just in case there was something that could be applicable but shook her head in frustration. She was going to have to order online.

Tish backed out of the self-help section and sidled over to mysteries, hoping that no one had seen her. She felt like most of her grandfather's tips on being a private investigator went toward concealing her life from her neighbors.

To keep herself looking normal she snagged copies of *An Anonymous Girl* from Greer Hendricks and Sarah Pekkanen and *The Lost Man* from Jane Harper. She was trying to get Tobias to branch out into women writers. Not that he objected—he just wasn't ever going to pick them up on his own.

"Good choices!" exclaimed Cokie as she approached the counter. "Hey, did you hear?"

"Hear what?" asked Tish, dreading what news could possibly be coming next.

"We're going to be online!"

"What? I thought you already had a website?"

"We do, but we're adding e-books through Kobo. Pretty soon you'll be able to order print *and* buy your e-books through us."

"That's awesome!" said Tish.

I could download self-help books to my phone, support my local bookstore and Granddad would never know. Technology for the win.

"Yeah, I got Quincy Teller to help me. You know, Marv and Sandra's kid."

Tish did not know Quincy or Marv and Sandra. Somehow, everyone just assumed that Tish knew everything Tobias knew and when she burst their bubble, they got hyper-explanatory or annoyed. With Cokie, if she reminded him that she didn't know someone she'd be in for a fifteen minute family tree on the Teller family and who they had once lived next to and on and on and on.

"She's going to school over in Bellingham," continued Cokie. "Doing some sort of techy thing—with drones I think. Or maybe robots. But she says setting up the web portal, whatever that is, is going to be a breeze. I'm really excited about it."

"That's fantastic," said Tish. "Let me know when it's up and running."

"Will do. Hey, I heard from Ray Pearson that little Penelope Drue died last night. Is that true?"

"Um, yeah," said Tish, feeling her mood plummet.

"That poor kid," said Cokie shaking his head. "That poor family cannot catch a break."

"What do you mean?"

"They were in that commune over on Shaw, the Drues and his brother and then a couple of other families. And they were actually doing OK. You know, not like some communes where everyone's filthy, starving and unvaccinated." He paused to ring up her books. "No, they had a pretty good honey business and a couple of other things going. And then the government seized the property under eminent domain to put up a cell tower or some crap. Only they never put up the tower. The family sued, but I don't think anything ever came from it. Anyway, it busted up the commune and the family never quite got back on their feet. Penelope and Paxton moved over here, and the parents kept bouncing around looking for the next big break."

"Granddad said they were in Hawaii doing aquaponics," said Tish, swiping her card.

"Something like that," said Cokie, rolling his eyes. "Supposedly Dan's brother Dexter was looking after the kids here, but from where I was standing, it looked like the other way around. Dexter is a waste of space if you ask me. Never could be counted on to do anything but steal everything that wasn't nailed down."

"No job?"

"Bad habits," said Cokie, tapping the side of his nose. He ripped off the receipt as it finished printing out and put it, bookmark-like, in the top book, before sliding them across the counter to her.

"Gotcha," said Tish, taking the books. "Hey, do you know if Penelope was dating anyone?"

"Not that I know of, but I haven't talked to her much in the last couple of years. She used to come in and buy the sci-fi section and we'd chat, but once she turned eighteen, she didn't have any support from the state and I think all her money went to paying rent, so I didn't see her as much. She was a good kid."

"Yeah," said Tish, "I liked her. She was enthusiastic about life."

"Yeah," said Cokie, nodding and looking touched, "yeah, that was Pen. Enthusiastic about everything. I just… Ray said it was probably a drug overdose? Paxton, her brother, I could see doing that maybe. I heard he was dealing, but I didn't think Pen was like that."

"I don't know," said Tish. "That didn't seem right to me either."

"I'm not saying she never used, but…" Cokie shook his head. "Such a shame."

"Thanks for the books," said Tish.

"That is what I'm here for," said Cokie with a smile.

Tish had barely made it back to the car when her phone rang. She recognized the number and picked up with a sigh.

"You're too good to come out to the house now?" she asked.

"I'm too busy," said Detective Spring, sounding not the least bothered by her salutation. "I've got a stabbing in Anacortes and an armed burglary. Both of which take precedence over an accidental drowning."

"Was it though?"

"A drowning? Yes, Mitch, the coroner, confirmed on site."

"Accidental," said Tish.

"It's a reasonable question and I fully intend to look into it. So, you tell me, what makes you think it's murder?"

Tish hesitated, trying to pinpoint what was bothering her. When it came down to saying it out loud, it didn't sound like very much.

"I hired her a few weeks ago as waitstaff for Yearly Events. She was smart and had experience and her friend Azalea recommended her."

"OK. Then what happened?"

"I talked to her on Friday. She was panicking because she didn't want to lift heavy things because she had recently found out she was pregnant. She said she was excited about it, but that it was an accident. She also said she wasn't going to drink anymore. I know Nash said she had a history of drug use, but on Friday she was talking about the baby. She was also talking about working through the wedding season."

Detective Spring made a non-committal noise.

"On Saturday, she didn't show up for work. Azalea said she was waiting for a ride from her brother Paxton who had spent the night at his girlfriend's. But she never showed. Azalea called her around noon, but she didn't answer."

"How do you know she didn't answer?"

"I was standing there while Azalea left the message. After the wedding Azalea had car trouble and I drove her home and we swung by Penelope's."

"And that's when you found the body."

"Yes."

"What time was that?"

You could try reading my statement. Just a thought.

"Around five."

"Anything strike you as odd about the scene?"

"All of it. Her body was still warm. I don't know how long she'd been dead, but she wasn't… like Reginald. I could still move her."

"Yeah, full rigor hadn't set in. On-site Mitch was guessing that she'd been dead a couple of hours. We'll have to wait until we get the full autopsy report to narrow down the timeline."

"Yeah, but she was barefoot and in her underwear and tank-top.

She didn't even have a bra on. It looked like what you wear to bed. But if she'd only been dead a couple of hours that means she'd been wearing that in the middle of the day."

"She could have stayed home sick and never gotten dressed. She could have been changing. She might just have been enjoying lounging around in her underwear."

"Yeah, you're right. She could have been doing any of that," said Tish. "But it was weird."

"Noted," said Spring. "Anything else?"

No.

Tish felt annoyed. She ought to have more. "No, not really," she admitted.

"Because I agree. The stuff you just mentioned is weird. I don't like it either."

Tish was struck dumb in surprise.

"But what I'm lacking here is any motivation for someone to kill her. You have to be pretty mad to hold someone face down in a pond long enough to drown them. Also, that's the kind of thing that tends to leave a lot of mud and mess around the edge of the pond."

And there wasn't any.

"And there wasn't any. And Mitch didn't find any marks on the body to really indicate any sense of violence. He found a bump on the head, that was perimortem and consistent with slipping and falling face first into something. Say a rock in a pond."

Tish sighed.

"Or someone could have wacked her in the face and then drowned her." Tish sounded hopeless, even to herself.

"Could have. We'll know more when we get the autopsy. Look, I'm not ignoring what you've told me. I agree, something feels a little weird. But unless there's some additional evidence, I'm going to have to be guided by the autopsy report."

"And when will Mitch be getting around to that?" asked Tish sourly.

"A couple of days. If you hear anything or come up with something new, let me know."

Tish thought about being rude and then realized that for once Detective Spring was being fairly reasonable.

I just don't like that this is what's reasonable.

"Yeah, OK," said Tish, trying not sound sullen.

"Cool. New topic. You're not dating Matt Jones, are you?"

"Oh my God. I'm going to hunt down that blogger and punch him in the face."

Detective Spring chuckled. "I'll take that as a no. And good. I think you'd break Nash's heart. It's none of my business, but you should give our friend the Sheriff's deputy a nod."

"I will keep that in mind," said Tish.

"Just a suggestion. Better than that slippery weasel Jones."

"Matt's a slippery weasel?"

"He's been smuggling for at least ten years. And I don't mean dime bags. I mean serious weight. What has he been charged with? Misdemeanors. Every time we get close he's been able to weasel and bargain everything down to misdemeanors. I know people with parking tickets who've done more time. And now that weed is legal, our crazy governor is going to dismiss all non-violent marijuana related misdemeanors. That jackass is going to come out of this with a clean record!"

"Huh," said Tish. "I didn't realize that."

"Anyway, my point is, dating him is a bad proposition. I know you want advice from me like you want another hole in the head, but I'm handing out my two cents for free."

"And your two cents is: Nash?"

"Yes. He's a good guy."

"I believe I told you that when you tried to arrest him for murder."

Spring snorted through his nose. "He owned the damn murder weapon!"

"Well, fortunately for Nash, Yearly Investigations was able to prove that he wasn't the only one who had access to it."

"You know what?" he demanded clearly about to launch into a tirade.

"I'm going to date Nash," she announced.

"Seriously?" he said, thrown off his rant.

"Yeah."

"Does he know this?"

"I imagine he'll figure it out. He's smart."

"Well, good." Spring sounded confused and Tish nearly laughed into the phone. "OK, talk to you later. Bye."

She clicked off and went to buy pie before heading up to Island Hardware to collect Tobias. He was outside talking to a rough look-ing guy in a torn plaid who might have been one of the semi-home-less residents or simply a homeowner collecting materials for a week-end project. They shook hands and parted as Tish pulled up.

"Hey," said Tobias, opening the door. "Nice timing."

"Thanks," said Tish. "We need to talk."

"Whoo-doggies. What happened? Am I in the doghouse again?"

"No. I'm pissed Granddad. There's some blogger who is posting that I'm dating Matt Jones and you've got dementia."

"What's a blog?" he asked. "I hear people say it, but I don't know what it means."

"I don't have time to go into that right now. I'll show you when we get home. But the important point is that Detective Spring is not investigating Penelope's death as a murder. He's not *not* investigating it. He's just sitting on it and waiting for the autopsy report. And I couldn't even come up with a reason that someone would want to kill her. For once in his damn life he's willing to listen and I don't have anything to tell him."

"Ah," said Tobias, with a sly grin. "I can help with that. But we might need more pie."

CHAPTER 9

TISH & TOBIAS INVESTIGATE

"Granddad, what are we doing?" asked Tish as they turned onto Crow Valley Road toward West Sound.

"We're going to find Dexter Drue, Penelope and Paxton's uncle," said Tobias.

"I hear he has drug problems and can generally be described as a waste of space."

"Yeah, that's about what I hear too. But I think he'll have some insight into what's been going on with Penelope."

"I was going to talk to her brother," said Tish, slowing down behind a truck carrying an enormous load of hay. The truck slowed to a crawl and the driver extended a hand to wave them around.

"If you were nice you'd stop and open the gate for him," said Tobias, point at the gate the truck driver was clearly planning on turning into.

"If he were smart he would have brought someone with him," said Tish and kept driving.

"So lacking in island spirit," said Tobias shaking his head.

"I notice how it's me that was going to do the getting out and opening," said Tish, drily.

"Well, sure," said Tobias. "I'm old and I got the bum leg. It'd be easier for you."

"Well, sure," parroted Tish, "but I don't actually care and I'm driving so…"

Tobias gave her a healthy dose of grandfather glare.

"Being neighborly doesn't hurt anyone and we're not in a hurry."

"I'm very neighborly," said Tish. "But I don't see the need to stop and open a gate that no one asked me to open."

"I'm just saying that you could stand to get more in the island spirit of things," said Tobias, with an air of injured dignity.

"If I get any more in the island spirit I'd be hosting a drum circle this weekend."

Tobias grunted. "They hit you up too?"

"I told them it would affect my insurance or something and I'd have to charge them."

"It's America and I'm a hundred percent in favor of the freedom to do dumb stuff," said Tobias, "but I don't feel the need to host it in my backyard."

Tish snort-laughed in surprise. Then she gave her grandfather the side eye.

"What?" he asked.

"I just booked an August wedding for a gay couple."

He shrugged. "And?"

"Just didn't want you to be surprised by it."

"It ain't none of my business who marries who," said Tobias, with another shrug.

"Well, you're old."

"Hey!"

"You just said it," said Tish. "And I'm just saying sometimes your generation gets all *God sayeth* etc."

"I don't know what God sayeth. I ain't *that* old. And if he's got a problem with it then it's between him and those two fellas. I've got my own problems to worry about. I can't be worrying about other people's marriages."

"All right," said Tish, feeling pleased. Sometimes her grandfather's libertarian streak worked for her and sometimes it didn't. Today it was streaking in her favor. "What were we talking about?"

"When?"

"Before we got side-tracked by gates."

"Oh. Um. You were going to talk to Penelope's brother, which I agree with. If we're building out lists of suspects then you gotta start with the closest male relative and that *is* her brother."

"Closest male relative?" asked Tish.

"Well, a really depressing statistic on crime is that a woman is three times as likely to be attacked by a male family member or friend than a stranger. Penelope and Paxton were living in that house together, that means he had access and could potentially get close enough to her to hit before she could fight back. That makes him number one suspect in my book, but I want to get some background before I talk to him."

"Makes sense," said Tish. "But some of that applies to Dexter too."

"Definitely," agreed Tobias. "And if he's as drug addled as I hear he is, then he's potentially got the instability to attack her as well. We'll have to be on our toes."

"So where does he live? Some place near West Sound?"

"Well, that was what I was sussing out up at the hardware store. He moves around quite a bit and it appears that at the moment he's docked at the marina and living in his boat."

"Is that legal?"

"As long as the slip fees get paid, I think he's got every right to spend as much time on his boat as he wants."

"Huh. I don't think I would want to live on a boat."

"Well, fortunately no one is asking you to."

"Don't get snippy with me. I'll hide your coffee."

"I'll still have wine," said Tobias with equanimity.

"Yeah," agreed Tish. "Got me there. I'm not going to hide the wine."

Tobias chuckled as the road curved past Nordstroms Lane. A few minutes later they dropped down to water level and pulled up at the stop sign across from the water. Deer Harbor Road ran left and right and the West Sound Marina lay in front of them, a picturesque collection of boats, their reflections painted with an impressionist's brush in the dark blue water. Tish parked in one of the empty spots outside the gate of the marina and waited for Tobias to lever himself out of the passenger seat.

"Don't forget the pie," said Tobias and Tish went back to the car to bring the pie.

He did that on purpose so he could get a head start down the walkway without me.

Tish carried the pie and purposely didn't hurry to catch up, watching her grandfather's gait with a critical eye. He was managing the gently swaying dock and awkward surface well—hardly using his cane. He really was doing a lot better than when she had first arrived. Tobias slowed down as he appeared to check the slip numbers and Tish hurried to catch up as he stopped at number eight.

The boat was a dilapidated nightmare and appeared to be from the eighties. The decal of the boat's name was peeling off, turning what once had been the *Bail Out* into just *Bail.*

"What do we do now?" whispered Tish. "It seems rude to go on board. They ought to install doorbells."

"You're supposed to yell out," said Tobias. "Ahoy, aboard the *Bail Out,*" bellowed Tobias, raising his voice and reaching out to rap on the hull with his cane. Tish jumped at the cracking sound.

"You're going to put a hole in it," she said, as a chorus of barks erupted from inside the boat.

There was the sound of someone moving and then eventually a door opened and Dexter Drue staggered out onto the deck and blinked at them owlishly. Dexter was fifty-ish and pot-bellied with thinning hair. He was wearing a black t-shirt with a faded beer logo, jeans and carrying a small Chihuahua under one arm. His skin was sallow and despite the pot belly he looked malnourished and under-fed.

"What?" he demanded.

"I'm Tobias Yearly, this is my granddaughter Tish."

"Yeah. I heard about you two. Penelope was working for you

over at the wedding place."

"We have condolence pie," said Tobias and Tish glared at him.

Why don't you just offer him a slice of death pastry while you're at it?

"Thanks," said Dexter, coming closer to the railing of the boat and looking down at them—inspecting the pie. "I'm actually pretty pissed off. I don't suppose you brought condolence bourbon?"

"Sorry," said Tobias. "Just pie. What's got ya biting and scratching?"

"Besides the fucking fleas? The damn cops say I can't have the death certificate until after the coroner's done and even then it's going to go to Paxton. Paxton can go to hell. He's already getting the money."

Tish found her hands curled around the edges of the pie in white knuckled fury.

I will not smash this pie into his face. I will not smash this pie into his face. I will not smash this pie into his face.

"What money?" she asked, smiling her most Stepford Wife smile.

"Damn lawsuit finally came through for the commune. The Drues are all getting a payout. Oh, wait, not all of the Drues. Just the ones on the deed and apparently my idiot brother didn't think to include me."

"But of course, as her former legal guardian you're entitled to a piece of her estate," said Tobias with an easy smile.

"Goddamn right I am," said Dexter. "The cops can suck it. Then that bastard Nash had the nerve to ask me where I was all yesterday. Like I'm going to tell him."

"Well, sure," said Tobias, "never talk to the cops. But you do got an alibi, don't you?"

"I don't need an alibi!" He seemed outraged. The dog yipped and then nipped at his hand as he squeezed it too tight. Dexter dropped the dog and folded his arms over his chest. "Poor Pen did something stupid, dinged herself on the head and drowned in the pond. I talked to Paxton. It ain't no murder plot. I don't got to tell nobody nothing. And I sure as hell ain't going to be telling the cops I was…"

He paused and frowned at Tish.

"Hey, ain't you the one doing the horizontal mambo with Matt Jones?"

"Uh…" said Tish. "No. Definitely not."

"Well, you can tell him from me that if he thinks he's going to mess with the Drue family, he's got another think coming."

"What does that mean?" asked Tish, glancing at Tobias. He flexed his shoulders in a miniscule shrug.

"Paxton ain't gonna be scared away just cuz Matt Jones thinks he owns this island."

"Scared away from what?" asked Tobias.

"Why don't you ask her boyfriend?" demanded Dexter, jerking his thumb at Tish.

"He seriously is not my boyfriend," said Tish. "We ate dinner together one time. That's it."

"Really? When?" asked Tobias.

"While you were convincing Detective Spring to invade the island when we were trying to keep Nash out of jail."

"Oh, right," said Tobias.

"What you want to keep him out of jail for?" demanded Dexter. "That jackass harasses me and my friends all the time. Like I'm just going to roll over and tell him who's cooking meth."

The little dog at Dexter's feet began to growl.

"Uh…" said Tish.

I don't think I've ever quite factored in that dating Nash might make people less likely to talk to me.

"It was an unrelated incident," said Tobias. "Gotta go where the case leads you."

"Yeah, well, it should have led you to letting that pig rot in jail." Dexter stepped back and slammed the door in their faces.

"Well—" Tish began, but the door opened back up and Dexter

stepped out.

"I'm keeping the pie," he said, leaning across the small expanse of water and snatching it out of her hands. Then he slammed the door again.

"Could have gone better," said Tobias.

"Could have gone worse," said Tish.

"True. Come on, let's head back to town. You know," said Tobias, stumping back up the dock, "it's a good thing that blog didn't say you was dating Nash. Then no one would be talking to us."

"I think you mean none of the low-life meth heads," said Tish.

"I mean all the good sources of information," said Tobias, opening the car door.

"Yeah," said Tish. "He was just a fountain of facts. But he didn't exactly come up with an alibi."

"No, he did not," agreed Tobias, settling into his seat. "Let's go home. I feel the need for a fried egg sandwich and a Quincy MD."

"Matlock will think you're cheating on him," said Tish, starting the car.

"I'm branching out. I found a DVD box set of Quincy at the Exchange," said Tobias. "Meanwhile, I'm suddenly wondering just who *is* cooking meth on the island."

"You mean it's not in your files?" asked Tish, sarcastically, as she opened her door.

"They move around too much," said Tobias. "The drug scene is constantly in flux. Also, meth kills. So the attrition rate of cooks is pretty high for me to keep serious tabs on."

"Granddad," said Tish with a sigh. "Sometimes you worry me."

"Well, if it comes down to it," said Tobias as she got in the car, "sometimes you worry me."

"Me? What'd I do?"

"You…" Tobias eyeballed her. "Work too much," he said at last.

"Well, I'm trying to start a business," said Tish. "I've got to work to get it going."

"Yeah, but it seems like you've been going since winter. Hardly see you. And while you may not be dating Matt, it does seem like you used to enjoy dating someone. People are going to start thinking I keep you locked in the attic or something."

"We haven't got an attic. And I see lots of people all the time. I'm just not going out a lot because of the business."

He's going to nail me for lying later. I shouldn't have said that.

"Uh-huh. What happened to Greg? Why don't you call him up and make him take you out on the town?"

"Greg hasn't called since…" Tish tried to remember when. Greg Swenson was an FBI agent who she'd dated for about a minute and a half. He was gorgeous, but, although she never would have said it to his face, she had always privately thought he looked a little bit like the FBI edition of a Ken doll. He had also, although he had never said to *her* face, felt uncomfortable with her choice to live on Orcas instead of moving back to Seattle and getting a 'real' job. "November? Greg's a great guy, but he got sidelined by that task force he was assigned to and my living on Orcas made it hard on him. I liked him a lot, but I'm not going to call him up just because I could use a weekend away. I can do my own weekend away if it comes down to it."

"Well, you're only young once Tishkins. Remember to slow down once in a while."

"Granddad," protested Tish with a laugh. "If I'm driving you, then, trust me, I'm going slow."

"Well," he said, "we don't want to be conspicuous."

CHAPTER 10

MONDAY - DRAMATIC THREATS

Tish and Tobias sat in the A-1 diner and watched Amber give her boyfriend the cold shoulder. The morning had been slow and Tish had spent most of it avoiding bookkeeping and trying to figure out what she was supposed to be doing in specific with her morning and in general with her life. Tobias had eventually insisted on going into town just for something to do. Which Tish characterized as suspicious, but didn't question it. And now their favorite waitress was carrying on a private argument in a very public way. Amber was verging on nineteen and was practically a garden gnome compared to Tish. Amber maybe made it to five-foot-one on a good day and wore her curly hair short and bleached blonde. Tish always felt like a giant in her company. Her boyfriend, the hapless, twenty-one-year-old Kyle who constantly smelled of weed was watching from one of the diner stools at the counter with a morose expression.

"Well, Yearlys," said Amber with a smile, "what can I get you today?"

"Coffee, I guess," said Tobias. "And you could tell us what Kyle's done this time."

"Oh, he knows what he did," said Amber, bitterly. "How about you Tish?"

Tish checked her watch. It was almost time for lunch, but she wasn't sure she wanted to settle in for the full Tobias lunch which could take up to two hours. "Are we here for gossip or lunch, Granddad?"

"I'm here for the coffee," said Tobias, cryptically. "But you could have lunch if you want."

Tish translated that to mean he wasn't planning on staying all day.

"I'll take the turkey sandwich and a cup of the soup," said Tish.

"You got it," said Amber. "It'll be out shortly." She pasted on a purposely cheerful smile and sauntered past Kyle, who looked lower than ever. Tobias caught Kyle's eye and waved him over. Tish scooted over on her side of the booth to make room for him.

"How'd you screw the pooch this time?" asked Tobias when Kyle sat down.

"It was not my fault," said Kyle, brushing brown bangs out of his eyes. The haircut, clipped on the sides and long in the front, was clearly intentional, but seemed to involve a lot of bang flipping.

"Didn't say it was," said Tobias.

"All I did was go to Tori's birthday party on the mainland and suddenly I'm the bad guy."

Tish tried to remember who Tori was. She vaguely thought from Amber's ramblings that Tori was a girl of about Kyle's age that was currently at college up in Bellingham.

"You went to a college party?" asked Tish.

"Well, I mean… It wasn't… It was Tori's birthday party."

"But you didn't take Amber?"

"Amber was working and the party was at a bar, so she couldn't go anyway."

"Ah," said Tobias. "And since it was in Bellingham and it was late, maybe you… stayed over at someone's house?"

"I crashed at Tori's, but a lot of people did. I wasn't the only one," said Kyle.

"Right," said Tobias. "Got it."

"It was not like that! I went, I saw some people from high school and then I came home in the morning. I don't see what the big deal is!"

"Really?" asked Tish. "You don't see the big deal?"

"Nothing happened!"

"Not really the point," said Tish. "You made Amber feel left out and acted like you were single."

"I…" Kyle shifted uncomfortably in his seat. "I didn't mean to!"

"So tell her that," said Tobias. "Just say sorry and that you'll try not to be such a dipshit next time."

Kyle looked from Tish to Tobias and back. "I don't think girls really work that way, do they? I mean, can you just go around saying sorry for stuff and bam everything's fixed?"

"Depends," said Tish. "Mostly on whether or not you're actually sorry and whether or not Amber likes retribution."

Kyle appeared to be calculating Amber's need for revenge.

"Well, while you're pondering that," said Tobias. "Why don't you tell us about Paxton Drue."

Kyle sighed. "I heard about Penelope. That's such a bummer. I always liked her. She was a year above me, but was always nice. Paxton's a couple years older than her. He's an asshole. Deals a lot of meth that he gets from his uncle. Mr. Sunshine tried to put the kibosh on that, but it never really took."

"Mr. Sunshine?" asked Tish.

"Matt Jones," said Tobias, as if he'd always known this information. "He's got a personalized license plate that says Sunshine."

I reviewed the files last year and that was not included. But. Fine. I am letting it go. I really need to find someone to build me a database I can search and update easily.

"Uh-huh. Well, K." asked Tish. "But what's Matt got to do with it?"

"Well, you know Matt… makes certain trips."

"We've all heard," said Tobias drily.

"And that requires some people with boats and sometimes it requires people with extra space in their sheds or wherever. But there's only so many people on the island that will rent out that kind of space and they tend to also be the people who rent out space to other types of people."

Tish glanced at Tobias. He also appeared to be working through the vagaries of Kyle's speech.

"Matt was using the same storage space as the meth heads?" asked Tobias after a minute.

"Shhh," said Kyle, looking around the restaurant. "But yeah. Except Matt doesn't like that. Meth draws too much attention because meth heads are stupid. But Matt doesn't use island space often enough to have a lock on the market. So people gonna do what people gonna do."

"So Matt tried to crack down on the meth dealing?" asked Tish. "When was this?"

"Some time last year. And it wasn't the dealing so much as making sure anyone that stored his stuff didn't also store other stuff. And Paxton got pissed because it screwed up some deal for him. Anyway, they hate each other. Penelope tried to stay out of it. She and Paxton argued about it a lot. She said that meth was not the same as pot—which is true—and that meth was harmful to the human condition. Paxton told her to shove the commune bullshit out her ass."

"Paxton sounds like a real winner," said Tish.

Kyle shrugged. "He's not as bad as he sounds, and I mean… sisters. They're annoying. Anyway, Pax and Pen settled on an agreement where he didn't bring it in the house, and she stopped bitching about it."

"Azalea said Paxton kept drugs in the house," said Tish, with a frown.

Kyle shrugged. "I'm just telling you what I heard from Pax. Plus, Zales always thinks the worst about everyone, so she probably just assumed."

"Hm," said Tish. "Do you know who Pen was dating?"

Kyle looked surprised. "I didn't know she was dating anyone. But I mean, we didn't hang that much what with the competing business interests, so I'd probably be the last to know."

Seems unlikely, considering that he gossips more than the proverbial old wife. Although, come to think of it, you're the only one who hasn't asked me about that stupid gossip blog. Now why is that?

"Have you seen that new blog, Kyle?" Tish asked, narrowing her eyes at him.

Kyle gave a total stoner chuckle. "Oh. Yeah. That's some good stuff right there. I just about peed myself laughing at that. Don't tell me you're big mad on that. Whoever posted that clearly doesn't know you." Tobias looked like he had some questions about that statement, but Kyle spotted Amber and started to get up. "Amber's coming back. I gotta jet."

Tobias gave him a look that was the sort of pin you to a wall stare that only an old person could manage.

"I'm gonna apologize, but I can't do it here. She's working. And I don't need to hang around and get the angry eyes."

"Yeah," said Tish. "Meanwhile, can you do a quick survey and find out who Dexter Drue is helping cook?"

"Sure," said Kyle, one leg out of the booth. "As long as the names aren't going back to the cops. I know you and Nash is all friendly-like."

"P.I.'s promise," said Tish, holding up her right hand, earning a skeptical look from her grandfather.

"Cool. K. I'm gonna bounce. See ya."

"See ya, Kyle," said Tish.

Amber arrived as Kyle was leaving. "I cannot believe he just left," said Amber, slamming down Tish's soup.

"I sent him out to do something," said Tish. "Sorry. He said he was sorry about not taking you to the party."

"Like I would be caught dead at Tori's party anyway," said Amber, pouring Tobias's coffee. "She's one of the skanks who hooked up with my ex."

"Ah," said Tobias. "This becomes clearer."

"Does it?" asked Amber, looking at him in confusion.

"Never mind that though," said Tobias. "When do you think

Mrs. Palmer is likely to come through here?"

"She usually comes in after her shift at the clinic," said Amber. She looked up and checked the clock above the diner counter. "Should have been here already, I think. She'll probably be in soon. Back in a bit with your sandwich, Tish."

"Who's Mrs. Palmer?" asked Tish, taking a spoonful of the crab bisque.

"Social worker," said Tobias. "She works a couple of days a week up at the clinic. That's mostly therapy and what not. But previously, she was the case worker for Penelope and Paxton. I thought I'd chat her up and see what she can tell us."

Tish nodded. "How do you know that used to be Pen's social worker?"

"She was the only one on the island there for a while. Stands to reason it was her. Now I think we've got three for all of Island County, but I think they operate out of Friday Harbor."

Tish ate her soup and contemplated telling Tobias about Nash. She wished he would at least explain why he had such a thing about her dating him.

"Granddad," began Tish.

"Amber's waving at us. Go see what she wants."

Tish dutifully got up and went over to the counter. "Mrs. Palmer just called. She's running late for the ferry and put in a to-go order. I said Tobias wanted to talk to her, but she says she's really in a hurry, so if you want to chat you'd better meet her at the curb."

"Uh, OK," said Tish. "Um, I'll roust Granddad."

"They're getting her order ready now. I'll meet you out there."

Tish followed Tobias out to the curb and tried not to feel like an idiot as she stood on the curb next to Amber. It really didn't seem like it should take three of them to deliver one bag of food.

The A-1 was housed in a brown sixties-style building with a low-pitched roof and a strange block of a sign rising from the peak. The place reminded her a bit of a Looney Tunes cartoon, although the owners had done their best to make it more Northwest-y with a decorative kayak strapped to the outside, a tree-stump bear carving and a driftwood bench.

Tish had just decided to go back in and finish her soup when a gray Mercedes pulled up to the curb.

"Hey Amber!" chirped a woman rolling down the window.

"Hey Mrs. Palmer! Total is $17.81 and this is Tobias Yearly. He wants to talk to you about poor Penelope."

Mrs. Palmer handed over a card and Amber began the process of swiping it through a device attached to her phone.

"Poor Penelope," said Mrs. Palmer, focusing on Tobias. She was probably north of fifty and softly losing cohesion of shape. She had round hair, a round figure and round glasses. "I just heard! I'm so devastated."

"Hey!" Someone down the block yelled and Tish looked up. A twenty-something guy was striding angrily down the sidewalk. He had dark spikey hair and an angular face. "You!" He pointed angrily at Tish. Tish straightened up and so did Tobias.

"You're Tish Yearly, right?" he demanded as he drew closer.

"Yeah," said Tish. "Who're you?"

"You need to shut your damn mouth!" he barked.

"Paxton!" snapped Mrs. Palmer. "You watch your mouth!"

Paxton pulled up short, looking at Mrs. Palmer like a deer in the headlights.

"Now, you apologize to the young lady," commanded Mrs. Palmer.

"Mrs. Palmer! She is telling people Penelope was killed and that she was..." his voice lowered to a whisper, "pregnant."

"Oh dear," said Mrs. Palmer. "And how does that make you feel?"

"Damn angry," he said, his voice going back up.

"And is this the most constructive way to deal with that anger?"

"She is questioning people!"

"Well, maybe if you had a conversation with her you might be able to find out why she was doing that. Or you could express how you find that hurtful. Or you might learn something new. But you can't do any of those things unless, you stop, assess, and take a moment to calm down."

"I don't have to take a moment," snapped Paxton, pivoting back to Tish. "You need to shut up," he said, stabbing his finger toward her chest. "Penelope's dead and you ain't helping."

He turned around and stormed off the way he'd come.

"His anger management is still a work in progress," said Mrs. Palmer with a soft cluck of the tongue. "But it's nice that he's expressing himself."

"Is that what you call it," said Tobias.

"Now, Tish, is it? Dear, I understand that you have family obligations," she looked around Tobias, as if he wasn't there. "But really you can't let care management slide into enabling."

"What?" asked Tish.

"Here's your card, Mrs. Palmer," said Amber, shoving the credit card back into the woman's hand.

"I'm sure your grandfather is having a hard time," continued Mrs. Palmer, "but you can't let him give others a hard time because of his condition. If you need assistance, you need to reach out. We have some really good groups up at the clinic and Friday Harbor. We even have some phone-in options."

"What?" said Tish again.

"She thinks I got the dementia," said Tobias. "Thinks you're humoring me and letting me question people cuz I slipped a cog."

"Oh! Thanks. I wasn't getting that at all," said Tish.

"OK, I have to go," said Mrs. Palmer. "But seriously, dear, do call. We can help."

The car window rolled up and the Mercedes pulled away.

"That did *not* go how I thought it would go," said Amber.

"Ditto to that," said Tobias. "Come on Tish, your soup is getting cold."

CHAPTER 11

CURBSIDE SERVICE

Tobias did not appear to be the least bit phased about the blog post and rumors of his impending mental collapse. Even after she'd shown him the blog on her phone, he'd still seemed mostly interested in the fact that someone could post instantaneously but didn't have to let anyone make comments like on the dratted Facebook. Tish, on the other hand, found that she was getting more annoyed, not less.

There's got to be a way to track the owner of the website. I would ask Sarah, but…

"And how did this person get the mug shot?" asked Tobias, scrutinizing his picture on the phone.

"I don't know," said Tish tiredly. "Probably a public records request."

"Gonna have to figure out how to do that," he said, poking at the phone.

Tish would have added more commentary, but Tobias had been spotted by a contingent of gray hairs that wanted his opinion on something. Eventually Tish had given up waiting inside and was now standing back outside the A-1. Somehow, although it wasn't yet two, it had already been a very long day.

She took a few calming breaths and tried to figure out why she was annoyed.

Maybe it was because today should have been a glorious day of personal laziness. It should have been a day where she kicked back on the couch and snuggled with Coats while watching lame cat videos on her phone and eventually got up to do all the accounting crap.

And Penelope ought to be picking out diaper bags and making plans for the future.

Tish didn't understand how other people dealt with death. There was no right or wrong way, she supposed. And she knew that she did a lot of avoiding, but she didn't understand how the world didn't come crashing to a stop when someone died. There ought to be some sort of pause button that allowed the bereaved to scream into the void for a while before rejoining the world. She didn't understand how her mother had managed to keep chugging along making school lunches and going to work after Dad had died. And she didn't understand how her grandfather kept doing things that had to remind him of Reginald. How did Paxton Drue find the energy to yell at strangers? Or maybe that was his way of dealing with the fact that there was still crime scene tape around where his sister's body had been found and he would see it if he looked out his back door.

I understand that. Death makes me mad.

Mad and tired.

"Oh my God, Tish," gasped a voice, and Tish turned startled to see Azalea approaching with Tate in tow. "I just heard that Paxton totally yelled at you. Are you OK?" Azalea had her hair down in what Tish thought must be her weekend look—the curls had been sprayed and forced into regimented ringlets that reminded Tish of the time she'd done a stage production of *Pride & Prejudice.*

"Um. Yeah," said Tish forcing a smile. The speed of island gossip was astounding. "I'm fine. How'd you hear about that?"

"Marty was driving by," said Tate. He was pale and red-eyed. Tish thought he looked hung over. "He said he could hear Paxton through the window."

"You have really upset Paxton," said Azalea. "What are you going to do?"

"I'm not going to do anything," said Tish, who found the question impertinent and nosy.

She probably didn't mean anything by it.

"Look," said Azalea, her voice sounding clipped and harsh. "I didn't want to say anything before, but I wish you hadn't said what you said yesterday to the cops. Penelope was my friend. She is not some sort of dramatic story for you to be the heroine of."

"Is that what you think I'm doing?"

"I'm not trying to be rude," said Azalea. "But everyone knows that you and Tobias like to play the big city big shots and solve crime or whatever. But I don't think you should go around spreading rumors about Penelope. I really think you need to stop your little investigation."

"You think her death was an accident?" asked Tish.

"What else could it be?" demanded Azalea.

"Well," said Tate, "considering that Paxton just threatened Tish, I'm kind of wondering if maybe she's got a point."

Azalea gave Tate a look that said there would be words later.

"All I've done is tell the cops the truth," said Tish. "When I talked to Penelope on Saturday she was making plans for the future. This wasn't a suicide and the fact that she was in her underwear in a duck pond is bizarre. I liked Penelope. I may not have known her as long as you, but I want to make sure that she doesn't get brushed aside and forgotten."

Azalea's face had a pinched unhappy look.

"You have to do what you think is right," said Azalea. "But I just wish that you could maybe have a little more respect for Penelope and sympathy for her family."

"I do," said Tish. "That's why I want to find her boyfriend."

"She didn't have a boyfriend," snapped Azalea. "There were no boyfriends and you definitely need to stop spreading that rumor too."

"It's not a rumor," said Tish. "On Friday, she told me point blank that she was pregnant, but that she wasn't telling anyone yet because it was really early. That's how I know she wasn't drinking or doing drugs. She was excited about the pregnancy."

"Penelope would have told me if she was pregnant," said Azalea. "You have to stop telling people that."

"I've only told it to you and the cops," said Tish. "But I will continue to not mention it if that's what you want."

"That's what I want," said Azalea.

"Great," said Tish, with a fake smile. Azalea stared at her pointedly as if waiting for her to leave.

It's a free sidewalk and I'm the boss. You leave.

Tish stared back. Finally, Azalea gave a huff of annoyance and detoured around Tish to continue down the sidewalk, dragging Tate with her.

Tobias came out of the A-1 with a toothpick in his mouth. "Maybe if we just stand here long enough, everyone we want to talk to will come to us," he suggested.

"What if I'm wrong," said Tish. "What if Penelope just slipped on duck crap, hit her head and drowned in six inches of water?"

"While in her undies in the middle of the afternoon after not calling in sick or going to work all day?"

Tish made a helpless gesture. "Her best friend didn't know she was pregnant. Everyone says she wasn't dating. Her brother is pissed and clearly didn't know either. And… what if… what if I'm just conditioned to think every dead body I come across is murder?"

Tobias scratched his eyebrow and appeared to think about that. "Possible I suppose," he said at last. "However, it would seem to me that maybe having found a couple of dead bodies already you've got some experience in the area and know when things are hinky."

"It was easy with the others," said Tish. "Things were obviously hinky from the get-go. What if I'm messing with people's lives because I'm just determined that things *have* to be weird?"

"You never trust yourself," said Tobias, shaking his head.

"Why would anyone trust me?" asked Tish. "I never went to college and I've failed at literally every career I've ever tried."

"Failed might be putting a very distinct slant on things," said

Tobias, drily. "From where I'm sitting you've walked willy-nilly into whatever job you wanted and gotten it just for the asking."

"Hey, I work very hard!"

"Yes, you do. You put in hours of research and practice and then generally figure it out just enough to figure out that you don't want it. Similar to your boyfriends."

Tish gaped at Tobias.

"That is a very… hurtful thing to say."

"It's not a criticism," said Tobias. "Most people don't put in half the effort you do. It's just that I can see how some people might be a tad annoyed that you can do whatever you want, possibly the very thing that they want, but then just drop it like it's yesterday's news when you get bored."

"I really wanted to be an actress. But there comes a time when you either make it or you move on. The signs were clear. I wasn't going to be able to make a living as an actress, at least not a good one, and that was not good enough!"

"Yes, I understand," he said nodding. "That one you cared about. But your other *careers*," his tone propelled the word into the sarcasm hall of fame, "professional organizer, marketing, restaurant hostess—it's not like you cared about any of those. You didn't fail. You walked away. And I'm getting a tad tired of your woe-is-me-I'm-a-failure-to-launch attitude. You're a tough girl who's been out there fighting the world since you were eighteen. Don't pretend like you haven't got a real keen sense of when a situation is off. Stop selling yourself short."

Tish stared at Tobias and tried to figure out whether or not she should cry. And if she should cry, why she should be crying.

"I don't like your pep talks," she said at last. "I'm going to the bookstore."

CHAPTER 12
INSTINCTS

Tish didn't go to the bookstore. She walked angrily down Prune Alley and dashed off a text.

GRANDDAD WAS JUST VERY HONEST WITH ME AND NOW I MAY BECOME AN ALCOHOLIC.

She took more long angry strides and tried to think of all the ways in which her grandfather was wrong. Because he was definitely wrong.

Other people have expertise in something. And credentials. And all I've got is… I used to be an actress.

Her phone rang and with relief she instantly swiped to the green.

"Tobias said you might become an alcoholic?" asked Nash.

"No! I might need to take up heavy drinking because I can't deal with his pep talks."

"Oh. That makes way more sense. What was he pepping you up about? Because I have to say he gave me a pep talk once on the subject of my divorce and it was like being slapped in the face with caviar. It's dished up with compliments, but it's still fish eggs. I don't know that I need that much honesty in my life."

"There should never be that much honesty in anyone's life."

Nash chuckled. "What was he brutally honest about today?"

"He said…" Tish slowed down and then stopped, scuffing her toe on the grass growing out of a crack in the sidewalk. "I get bored easily and I also undervalue myself."

"Hm," said Nash, in a way that made Tish strongly suspect that he agreed with Tobias. "He told me I overly cling to ideals when reality is beating me over the head. You know, with a cheating spouse."

Tish laughed and then groaned. "I don't think I undervalue myself. I am awesome. I know I'm awesome."

"The awesomest," said Nash.

"It's just that if I'm so awesome how is everyone ahead of me?"

"What do you mean?"

"Everyone is all married and college and career and I'm back here being like… I think I finally found a job that would be cool to do for a longer period of time. But I'm not even sure that…"

"That what?"

"I stopped being an actress. I was definitive about it. I chose to quit. And I've figured out Yearly Events. I'm committed to that. I think it's going to be good. But is that who I am? If I'm not an actress, who am I? I don't have a thing yet. I thought by now I would have a thing. And I don't. Because I'm behind. Maybe Sam's right. Maybe I should do a sweat lodge."

"I understand," said Nash. "Maybe not the part about the sweat lodge, but I get the other stuff. After I got divorced, well, no. By the time I actually got the paperwork I was OK, but during the divorce I was just confused. I'd built a lot of my identity around being a husband and giving that up was really hard. I wanted to give it up, but it's hard being someone new. Although, for the record, I am enjoying being someone new."

"Me too! I like being this person! I know you and Sarah don't see it, but I'm a lot more relaxed than I used to be." There was a sputter on the other end of the phone. "I am. Being in LA was constantly being obsessed and on a hamster wheel of freaking out about tiny stuff that in retrospect never mattered. And here, I mean, maybe I'm wrong, but here I think I'm worrying about stuff that does matter. And I like helping people. In LA it felt like no one really did that. And I like that here I can help. At least I think I'm helping. It's just that, in general, I don't know what I'm doing. And I feel like I'm behind."

"And that's stressful," he said. "I get it. Although, I should point out that life is not a race. There is no ahead or behind."

"Maybe," said Tish. "But there are definite winners and losers."

"Then you're winning," he said.

"It sounds so factual when you say it. Do they give you training on that at the police academy?"

"Yes. It's an hour long seminar on how to sound like Jerry Orbach on *Law & Order*. But seriously, why give yourself another option? Humans are neurologically wired to create narrative. And if you're going to tell yourself a story anyway, why would you tell yourself a shit story? You're the hero of your own story. The hero's journey has enough drama without making some up."

"I find it soothing that you use narrative arc and the hero's journey to make your points," said Tish. "And also, incredibly attractive."

"Secret librarian powers," he said. "I know. It's sexy as hell."

So sexy.

"Want to go out to dinner tonight?" she asked.

"Can't. Working."

"Want to meet up and make out behind the ice cream shop?"

"Yes, but not gonna. Want to go for a run before my shift?"

"Oh, that sounds nice. Meet you at Mt. Constitution in like an hour?"

"Works for me. Love you."

"Love you too," said Tish, as she hung up with a smile.

He didn't talk about me being bored easily. Is that because it wasn't worth mentioning or because he didn't want to mention it?

Tish cut through the walkway between Prune Alley and North Beach Road and went into Now and Zen.

Talia Granger was working on a display of… Tish wasn't sure what they were. Dangling crystal thingies of indeterminate purpose. Talia Granger was late forties and had the slightly leathery texture of someone who spent too much time in the sun, or as Tish had come to find out, a tanning bed. Talia had a tanning bed in her basement and claimed to use it to fight seasonal affected disorder and the vitamin D deficiency that plagued the Northwest.

"Hey Tish," said Talia looking up. "What do you think?"

Tish surveyed the crystal's dangling from an old Madrona branch. The usual curling bark had all been stripped away from the branch to reveal the startling orange underneath and the crystals reflected rainbows on it. It was beautiful. She still wasn't sure of the purpose, but it looked great. Talia seemed to be waiting for a response, but Tish wasn't sure how to comment without revealing her complete lack of knowledge about what it was supposed to be.

"It looks really artistic," Tish said at last.

"Thanks! What can I do for you today?" asked Talia looking slightly nervous. Ever since the time she had nearly gotten Tish killed Talia always looked slightly nervous around Tish.

"You've got all of Reginald's recipes, right?"

Reginald's will had been specific. His house, land, and cowboy style revolver had gone to Tobias. The contents of the house went to his son. The garden gnome with his pants down went to Elayne, one of their annoying rivals at Bridge. And all of his recipes had gone to Talia, his chief rival in local baking contests, with the instructions that she share them with whoever wanted them.

"Yes," said Talia. "I've been working on typing them up and I'm going to be putting them in a cookbook. Cokie even said he'd sell them at the bookstore once I get done. I was kind of thinking that I'd put all the proceeds toward a scholarship in Reginald's name toward a culinary school or something. What do you think?"

"Aww," said Tish. "I bet Granddad would contribute to that. He'd be really touched."

Talia looked relieved.

"But speaking of Granddad," began Tish.

"That blog is full of crap, right?" Talia cut in. "There's no way he's got dementia, right?"

"Oh, yeah, totally. I can't go into it, but yeah, Granddad's fine. Well, you know, he's Granddad, so…"

"He's just as much of a jackass as ever?" suggested Talia.

"I did not say that. Although, I must admit that today I'm resonating with it."

Talia chuckled.

"Anyway, I was wondering if any of Reginald's recipes were tagged for Granddad and if I could have a couple?"

"Oh, there's a whole section of the recipe box labeled *Tobias*. What are you looking for—soup, casserole, meat, side dish?"

"Side dish, maybe? I'm trying to persuade him on a topic and I figured I might as well put him in a good frame of mind."

"Ha!" Talia looked amused. "Yeah, here," she grabbed a receipt pad from the counter and handed it to Tish. "Write down your email and I'll send you a couple."

"Thanks," said Tish. "I don't suppose you know who is behind that stupid blog do you? It's really starting to bug me."

"Give it a day or two and someone else's personal life will be up," said Talia, with a shrug. "Although, I was staring at that photo of Mrs. McAllister and her rooster and something *is* weird about it."

"What do you mean?"

"I think whoever took the photo must have been up a tree. I drive past her place on my way home and it's not like there are any sidewalks. Whoever took the photo would have stood out like a sore thumb if they'd just been standing there. So I figure before I do anything gossip worthy I'm going to check the trees."

Tish laughed. "Sound advice," she said. "I'll keep that in mind." She finished writing out her email address and handed the pad back.

Do I really want to do this?

"Talia…"

Talia squinted at her. "Something else on your mind?"

Oh, what the hell.

"Do you think that Granddad and I try and push our way into people's business so we can be the heroes of dramatic stories?"

Talia burped out a surprised laugh. For a moment she seemed

speechless and then laughed again.

"No, sweetie. I think Tobias pushes his way into people's business because he's a nosy old fart and then he drags you along for the ride."

"In his defense, I can be nosy too," said Tish.

"Well, sure. You *are* a Yearly. But I remember what happened to Reginald. What I think is that Tobias wasn't about to let anyone get away with killing Reginald and you weren't about to let anyone hurt your grandfather. Maybe it was dramatic, but I guess it usually is when someone tries to kill you. What's this about? Little Penelope Drue?"

"Yes. Sort of. That and I think I'm having a quarter-life crisis."

"You should do a sweat lodge," said Talia. "Those are great for really sorting your stuff out. Really clears the head. I've done a couple. It really helps to learn to still your mind and let the little voices you've been ignoring for far too long come to the forefront. I trust my instincts so much more now and I've really come to understand that everything is connected."

"Granddad said I should trust my instincts too," said Tish, choosing to ignore the other crap.

"Well, possibly this is a first, me agreeing with Tobias, but yes. You have to go where the spirits lead you. Ignoring them will only lead to unhappiness."

"It's not that I'm ignoring them exactly," said Tish. "It's more like a bunch of people think I'm wrong."

"Spiritual blockers," said Talia nodding, sagely. "Ignore them. They fear that your spiritual dawning will reveal their darkness. Also, I'm pretty sure I told you to stop investigating Reginald's death because I was scared you'd find out what I'd done."

"That is a very good point," said Tish. "Fear is the mind killer."

From the uniquely eighties adaptation of Frank Herbert's sci-fi classic Dune directed by David Lynch.

"Yes it is! I should crochet that on a pillow."

I'm not going to tell her.

"Sounds awesome. I bet you would sell a ton. OK, well, thanks Talia, that was quite helpful."

"Glad I could help," said Talia, smiling. "I'll email you those recipes," she called as Tish left the store.

Tish went back to the car where Tobias was waiting and reading one of the novels. Tish settled into the driver's seat and started the engine.

"I do not get bored easily. I get bored by things that aren't a challenge. And I do trust my instincts. I'm just insecure about lacking credentials to prove that I can do things."

Tobias looked up from his book with narrowed eyes.

"Called Sarah?"

"No. I can come up with answers on my own."

"Called Nash?"

Tish glared at him. "Yes, but only because I want to go for a run when we get home."

"Uh-huh," he said.

"Also, I ran into Talia Granger and she says that she's typing up Reginald's recipes for a cookbook and if she sells them she thought she'd put the proceeds toward some sort of scholarship fund in Reginald's name."

"Aw, that's a nice thought," said Tobias, looking touched. "Did she need help with anything?"

"I think she's still in the typing phase, but she said she'd talked to Cokie and he was up for selling them at the bookstore."

"We have a nice island," said Tobias.

"I don't think it's ours exactly," said Tish with a laugh.

"Close enough," said Tobias. "You're going out for a run when we get back?"

"I told Nash I'd meet him up at Mt. Constitution in an hour, so we'd better hustle."

"I don't hustle," said Tobias. "After seventy there's just continuous motion—no sprints. But that'll be good. I'll get time for another episode or two of Quincy."

"Oh, I'm sorry. Am I impeding your television watching?"

"Well, yes, but I don't mind. It's important to leave time for loved ones."

"Which one of us are you referring to—me or Quincy?"

"Ha! By the way, this book is a good one," he said waggling one of her more recent bookstore purchases before tucking it back in the glove box. "This gal can really write. We'll have to go somewhere on the ferry so I can read more."

"Or you could just take it in the house with you."

"Didn't we just cover how I'm behind on my Quincy?"

"Sorry. Don't know what I was thinking."

"And I'm the one that's supposed to be losing it," he said, shaking his head.

"The blog really doesn't bother you?" asked Tish.

"Nah," he said. "Can't control what people think. Besides, sometimes it helps to have people think I'm nutty."

"Or sometimes they might ignore you because they think you're crazy."

"They do that after sixty-five anyway. It's a bit infuriating, but it is a fact of life. People will give you their seat on the bus, but they won't listen to a damn word you say. If they get really annoying I stamp on their toe with my cane accidentally on purpose. It's amazing how someone's ears perk up when their toes hurt."

"You're so bad," said Tish, with a chuckle.

"That's true," he agreed.

They made it home and Tish ran upstairs to throw on workout clothes and then dashed back out to the car to drive up to Mt. Constitution. Once in the parking lot, she looked around, trying to spot Nash's lanky form. He might drive over, but he was more likely to run up the back trails from his house. She walked up to the bluff and looked out over the vista of trees below her. During the summer it was usually jammed with tourists, but on a Monday afternoon in early June she had it almost entirely to herself. The only vehicle in the parking lot was a mint green moped, but no one appeared to be nearby, which meant someone had probably wandered down the trail a bit.

She checked her watch. Nash was late. They were going to have to run fast if they wanted to squeeze in a jog *and* a make-out session. On impulse, she ducked into the stone tower at the top of the mountain. Built as part of an EPA project the tower was styled like a medieval castle and gave a stunning panoramic view of the islands. Tish jogged up the stairs and went out on to the deck to admire the view. The wind was chilly and she zipped up the neck on her pull over and promptly snagged her hair. In exasperation, she pulled out her pony tail and shook out her hair, preparing to re-pony.

The view was astounding and for a moment she felt like Rapunzel or Juliet or any other fair maiden who had been stuck up on a balcony. Only Romeo was running frightfully late.

"O Romeo, Romeo, wherefore art thou Romeo?" she called, placing a dramatic hand to her forehead. Then giggled to herself. There was a rustle at the edge of the trail and Nash came out of the woods and came to stand below her.

"You called?" he asked, laughing.

"Deny thy father and refuse thy name; or, if thou wilt not, be but sworn my love, and I'll no longer be a Capulet." Tish swooned dramatically over the wooden fencing ringing the parapet.

"Shall I hear more, or shall I speak at this?" said Nash, striding forward and grasping the rough blocks of stone.

Shakespeare pop quiz!

In a panic, Tish tried to remember the rest of the speech.

"'Tis but thy name that is my enemy;" she said leaning over the wall to watch him climb. "Thou art thyself, though not a Montague. What's Montague? It is not hand, nor foot, nor arm, nor face, nor any other part belonging to a man."

Nash climbed steadily up the wall as Tish gave her most impassioned interpretation.

"O, be some other name! What's in a name? That which we call a rose by any other name would smell as sweet; so Romeo would, were he not Romeo call'd, retain that dear perfection which he owes without that title. Romeo, doff thy name, And for that name which is no part of thee, take all myself."

"I take thee at thy word," said Nash, reaching the top of the wall. He grabbed wooden boards and stood on one of the extruding wooden beams to stretch up to her face. "Call me but love, and I'll be new baptized. Henceforth I never will be Romeo."

Tish knew it was all silliness and pretend, but that couldn't stop the smile that spread across her face as she leaned down to kiss him. He was the most amazing of human beings. She gave him the best kiss she could without endangering his life and just like the first time they had kissed she felt everything go *zing*. She pulled back, feeling as if the world were buzzing. Then she realized it really was buzzing.

A drone was hovering by the tower, the little turbines whirring, a camera firmly pointed at them.

"Bravo," yelled someone and she could hear a faint clapping from below them.

Still clinging to the wall, Nash gave her a look. "These things never happened with my ex," he said.

"That is why she's your ex," said Tish tartly. "Come on. Up and over. Let's go confiscate some footage."

But by the time they returned to the parking lot, all they saw was the mint green moped driving the switchback road down the mountain.

"I can jump in the car and have a high-speed chase," offered Tish.

"Unsafe and illegal," said Nash, giving her a sour look.

"Well," said Tish, "then I guess our secret is no longer secret."

"You don't look very concerned about that," said Nash, turning to her suspiciously.

"I'm really not," said Tish, stepping closer to him and sliding her arms around his neck.

"This is not jogging," he murmured, as she nibbled his earlobe.

"Not even close," she agreed.

CHAPTER 13

TUESDAY - THE RETURN OF SPRING

Tish woke up to the sound of something thumping a wall downstairs. There was another series of bangs and Tish tried to picture what Tobias was up to. Tish resided in the same bedroom that had always been hers when she came for childhood visits. She had removed the applique butterflies from the wall and invested in a closet organizer, but it was still the same buttercream yellow and she still slept under a quilt her grandmother had made. She supposed she was going to have to redecorate at some point, but she had enough on her plate trying to start a business. There was another thump from downstairs.

Moving a body?

No likely scenario presented itself, so she got up and went to the bathroom. She brushed her teeth and tried to decide if she wanted to go downstairs and help with whatever disaster was going on down there.

No, not really.

There was another crash and then her door was nosed open and Coats slunk into the room.

"Knocked over the umbrella stand, didn't he?" she asked. The black lab eyed the top of her bed and then looked back at her. "Not a chance big guy. You can't hide in here. I know knocking over the umbrella stand is usually your job, but you're going to have to go down and face it like a big boy." Coats looked at the bed again. "I'll go with you. If it looks bad, we'll both come back up here and snuggle."

Coats let out a gusty sigh as she pulled on a pair of sweats and followed her to the door.

Downstairs, the umbrella stand was indeed knocked over and the front door open. Tish poked her head out and seeing only her grandfather's truck backed up to the front stoop, closed the door and righted the umbrella stand.

"Granddad?" she yelled.

"In here!" he yelled back.

She went into his den. It contained the La-Z-Boys, the afghans her grandmother had knitted and the big boxy TV that still connected to the VCR. In front of the wide natural stone fireplace, Tobias had set up two large white boards.

"I remembered that I had these down in the emergency shed," said Tobias, looking enormously pleased with himself.

"You discovered you had an arts and crafts emergency?" asked Tish and Tobias grinned.

"Darned tootin'. I decided that since we're not as familiar with Penelope as we were with some of the participants in our other cases, that we should take a little more scientific approach to things. And on the TV they always have case boards with pictures and red string connecting things. Although, I don't really think we need the red string."

"Pretty sure that's just the set decorator feeling like they should contribute," said Tish, pretending not to notice as Coats climbed up into the forbidden Lay-Z-Boy.

"Sounds right," Tobias agreed. "But I think it would help us to work out a few things visually. So I've got one board for suspects and one board for the timeline." He tapped each board proudly with his cane. "You go fetch the pictures from the printer and I'll start writing stuff down."

"Can I get breakfast first?"

"Well, if you want to be lazy about it, then you go right ahead."

"Going with lazy," said Tish, turning around and heading for the kitchen.

"Find where I've left my coffee while you're at it!" he bellowed after her. Tish waved her acknowledgement and continued on to the kitchen.

Twenty minutes and some cereal later Tish was much more inclined to participate in the group project. She reheated the coffee in the microwave and then snagged the pages from the printer. Tobias looked like he'd been printing things off social media again, but the photos were mostly decent. Tobias had labeled the boards and found the blue painter's tape, so Tish set to work taping the photos under the right names. Penelope went at the top and then Matt Jones, Dexter Drue, and Paxton Drue in a line next to the word suspects.

"I really don't think Matt killed Penelope," said Tish, stepping back to look at the board.

"Neither do I," said Tobias, "but we have a strong report of friction between him and the Drues."

"Between him and Paxton," corrected Tish. "I don't see a motive for him killing Penelope."

"Neither do I, but he may have gone to talk to Paxton and things got heated with Penelope. And you can't rule people out just because you like them."

"It sounds vastly out of character," said Tish. "And, also, he was at the wedding. Penelope's body was cool, but still… you know… moveable. Which means, that most of the island has seen the photographic evidence of his alibi."

Tobias grunted and looked thoughtful.

"I mean, we'll have to hear what the autopsy report says," Tish continued, "but I was guessing Penelope was killed a couple of hours before we arrived, which would be toward the end of the wedding and Matt was one of the last to leave with one of the groomsmen. I think they were friends. They helped pick up a little and round up any of the lost and found items before leaving."

Tobias grunted again and made a tick mark on the timeline board. Tish glared at the suspects board and then moved all the suspects closer and drew a blank box next to the three men.

"Who's that for?" asked Tobias. Tish wrote under the box and stepped back.

BABY DADDY.

"Good call. Although, I'm not sure we need to phrase it like that. You said Penelope was excited about the baby, but that doesn't mean he was. We need another line," he said waving at the bottom of her board.

"What for?" she asked.

"Potential witnesses or sources of information. You got that snippy friend of hers, Rhododendron."

"Azalea."

"Whatever. Then you got Mrs. Palmer. We need to find out who else Penelope hung around with and talk to them."

Tish wrote down the names and then added: TATE DONOVAN + BAND.

"Who's he?" asked Tobias.

"Azalea's boyfriend and his band. The drummer seemed pretty familiar with Azalea and she and Penelope were best friends, so I bet they'd have some insight into who Penelope was hanging out with."

"I'll let you talk to them," said Tobias. "They sound like the kind of people who'd make me want to start handing out the knuckle sandwiches."

"Probably," agreed Tish. "They do tend be very aggressive hat wearers."

"I like hats. I approve of hats. You know what I don't approve of?"

"Fashion?"

"Ironic hats. Just wear a hat because you like a hat. Don't get smart. Don't try to get clever. Just admit that you wish you were a Dick Van Dyke chimney sweep from *Mary Poppins* and wear the damn hat. Acting like you're cooler than your own hat is ridiculous, because trust me—you ain't."

"I am not cooler than my own hat," said Tish, nodding and reaching for her phone. "Words to live by." She flipped open the Twitter app, typed in the latest Granddad quote and hit *tweet*.

"All right," she said turning back to the board. "We're agreed that I'll handle the band. I'm going to see them again this weekend anyway for the next wedding. So if I don't see them before then I'll chat up the bass player who makes inappropriate comments."

"He makes inappropriate comments?" asked Tobias, looking affronted.

"Possibly. Or possibly he's just a bass player. It's not a thing. I just have to figure out how to be the boss lady. Haven't quite figured out how to do that. Probably need to watch more Helen Mirren movies or something."

"She's a pretty lady," said Tobias. "That's a good role model."

Tish tried to parse that statement.

Is she a good role model because she's a pretty woman? Is pretty what makes someone good?

Tish decided that possibly the two statements were unrelated and to ignore the whole conversation.

"Anyway, what do we have on the timeline?" she asked.

"Well, there is where I feel like we're woefully behind," said Tobias, tapping on the board with his pen. "What do we know about her day?"

"Azalea said she talked to her in the morning before work, but after she'd already driven by Penelope's house. She said that Penelope had said Paxton spent the night at his girlfriend's and she was waiting for him to get home to get a ride from him."

"OK, so what time was that?"

"Around eight-thirty? Definitely before nine. And then I heard Azalea leaving her a message around noon. Then the last guest left around three and Azalea and I left a little before five."

"That's right, it was a lunch wedding. Seemed weird." Tobias dutifully filled in the times and abbreviated details on his board.

"She wanted to get married outside and in June the hottest time of the day is lunch time. Plus, it meant that everyone could get back on a ferry without problems."

"Uh-huh. So that means you found the body at about five. But you think she was probably killed around two or three."

"Maybe," said Tish with a shrug. "It's not like I know a lot about rigor mortis or anything. I just know she wasn't like…" She trailed off, not wanting to say *like Reginald*.

Tobias nodded, his face serious, but not offended. She had the feeling he knew exactly what she had skipped over.

"Add Paxton's girlfriend to the list of people we should talk to."

"Good call," said Tish and wrote it in.

"So somewhere between nine and say two is our window of opportunity," said Tobias. "Which is kind of a big period of time. And then we still don't have a motive. What time did guests start arriving?"

"At eleven," said Tish. "So I guess that does leave a little time for Matt."

"Nope," said Tobias. "I met him at the Orcas Hotel at ten and had a coffee with him. Tidied up our business and then he left. Didn't realize that he was heading up to the wedding though."

Tish reached over and wrote under Matt's picture.

Alibied by Yearlys.

"He could have slipped off and done it when he was supposed to be at the wedding," said Tobias.

"Could have, but he would have had to work pretty hard at it. Leaving in the middle of the wedding would have been pretty conspicuous. Plus, there still isn't a motive."

"True," agreed Tobias. "All right. We'll let the alibi stand unless we get different information. Now let's—"

The doorbell rang and Tish looked at Tobias in surprise. "Are we expecting anyone?"

"Not that I know of," he said.

"Well, I guess we'll answer it," said Tish and went out to the hall. She opened the door and looked at Detective Spring's back. He was standing on the porch frowning at Tobias's truck.

"Moving furniture?" he asked, turning back to her.

"Granddad had a craft project. What's up?"

"Got news," he said. "I'd better come in. Also, did he really say *You are not cooler than your hat?*"

"It was a diatribe on the subject of ironic hats and we don't discuss Twitter in the house," whispered Tish fiercely.

"Got it," said Spring. "Probably for the best." Tish eyed him suspiciously. "So can I come in or what?"

"Fine," said Tish, sourly.

She led him into the den. "Granddad, the fuzz is here."

"Quick, hide the expensive liquor and cheap women," said Tobias automatically.

"Just the cheap ones?" asked Tish. Both Tobias and Detective Spring gave her a look. "Asking for a friend," she added. Their looks didn't get any better. "Fine. Don't let the girls play. What's up, Peter?"

"Peter?" asked the Detective skeptically. "We're moving to first names now?"

"Well, it seemed like it would annoy you," said Tish. "Do you want some coffee?"

"No thanks. You two already raise my blood pressure enough. I see you've got my work started for me." He gestured to the boards on the fireplace.

"We were about to," said Tobias. "You got some oars to stick in the water on the subject?"

"I do," said the detective taking out his phone and snapping pics of the boards. "The autopsy's not done, but Mitch had some concerns so he had a rush put on the sample of the water from the victim's lungs and a sample from the pond. Results are conclusive: the samples are not a match. Penelope Drue didn't drown in that pond."

Tish sat down in the La-Z-Boy. "But…" It was all she could

think to say.

"Where was the water in her lungs from?" asked Tobias.

"Tap water," said Detective Spring. "Bathtub, sink, etc. I was just up the at the Drue's place serving the warrant. I've got CSI's crawling all over the house. But it's been a few days. Not sure what we'll find."

"Someone killed her and moved the body out to the pond," said Tish. "That's what we're saying, right?"

"Yeah," said Detective Spring. "That's what we're saying."

Tish turned the idea over in her mind. None of it made sense.

"But why?" asked Tish and Tobias at the same time.

"Now you really are a double's act," said the detective. "What do you mean? Didn't you already think she was murdered?"

"Well, yeah," said Tish. "But why move her out to the pond?"

"You already killed the girl," said Tobias. "What difference does indoors versus outdoors make?"

"It makes the underwear make sense though," said Tish.

"Yeah, but if the killer had left her indoors it probably would have been more likely to be ruled an accident," said Tobias

"Maybe the killer didn't want anybody to know he'd been in the house?" suggested Tish.

"I suppose she could have been moved from a totally different indoor location," said Tobias. "And then just dumped at the pond. We only have Azalea's word for it that Penelope was at home."

"Lividity indicates she was probably at the pond for a fair amount of time," said Detective Spring. "Whoever moved her moved her pretty quickly after death. I can't guarantee that someone didn't move her from another location, but it seems unlikely."

"What's lividity?" asked Tish.

"When the blood settles in the body after death," said Tobias looking thoughtfully at the timeline.

"We'll know more when Mitch releases the final autopsy report and when CSI gets done at the house. In the meantime, why don't we go over who you've talked to and what you know?"

"Why do I get the feeling he's sponging off our legwork?" asked Tish.

"Because he's sponging off our legwork," said Tobias. "But as long as the job gets done, I guess it don't matter who gets the credit."

CHAPTER 14

WEDNESDAY – MR. SUNSHINE

Tish bumped her way down the ramp from the ferry to the dock and tried to plan her day. She had a haircut appointment at a salon in Seattle, but her real idea had been to phone Sarah and try to get her to come out to lunch. But if she was going to do that, she really should have phoned Sarah this morning. Only she hadn't.

Chickened out.

Her every effort at connecting with Sarah lately had ended in being shunted abruptly off the phone. And even their rambling instant message chats had petered out except for periodic rants about work from Sarah and Tish's grumbling about Terry the flower vendor. She couldn't help but feel that it was more than just Sarah being busy at work—it felt deliberate.

She's ditching me. But why?

Tish tried to come up with something she'd done to piss Sarah off, but couldn't come up with anything more than the usual Tish-i-ness.

Maybe she just got tired of me.

Tish wound her way up the hill and through Anacortes to the freeway on ramp and paused, waiting for the merge light to tell her to launch herself into traffic. Three cars up—in glorious, bold and, above all manly, yellow—was a Ferrari advertising its owner's wealth and power. Tish could never quite see the point of fast cars. It was Seattle after all. It wasn't like anyone was going anywhere at top speed. But maybe they were really fun to drive. Maybe they were like having a really attractive, but shallow, significant other—half the fun was making other people jealous even though at the end of the day all they did was go to the grocery store.

That is why I am the luckiest girl on the planet. My man is handsome, smart, and supportive. I got the Tesla of boyfriends.

Tish followed the Ferrari onto the freeway and then into the fast lane. It was definitely a speed monster, but I-5 ate speed monsters for breakfast. That and the Ferrari driver apparently knew he was driving a ticket magnet. He might have the ability to change lanes and add speed at the drop of the hat, but he was keeping to the speed of traffic. Tish found herself following the Ferrari toward the steadily growing plinths of the spires of Seattle in the distance and after another few miles she realized that the plates were personalized.

SNSHINE

Mr. Sunshine. Funny how no one mentioned that Matt Jones' personalized plate was attached to a Ferrari. I guess watches aren't his only splurge.

Tish checked the clock on the dash, as Matt changed lanes, apparently heading for an upcoming exit. She'd left a whole ferry earlier than she needed to, something she was a little bitter about. The ferries had moved to a reservation system with blocks of reservations being made available a month, two weeks and two days in advance of a date. However, what everyone on the island had discovered was that the online system almost always booked out within seconds, particularly in the summer. However, what the website failed to communicate was that there was almost always room for anyone who showed up and risked riding "stand-by". The website also failed to mention that if someone called the ferry office directly and waded through the recordings to a real person that a reservation could be achieved even on most of the "sold out" ferries. But when Tish had made her reservation, she'd been feeling full on Millennial and hadn't wanted to talk to a real person, so she'd settled for the random reservation she'd been able to make online. Tish checked her rear-view mirror and then eased over into Matt's lane.

Time to practice my tailing skills.

Matt took the Seneca street exit and Tish, keeping three cars behind him, did the same. Driving in Seattle was always a challenge. The stoplights were frequently posted off to the side instead of being strung across the street. One-way streets crisscrossed the city and invariably whatever the way the street was going it was the opposite of the way Tish wished to go. And even if she managed all the other problems, the sheer crush of cars made driving difficult. And now she had the added challenge of trying not to be spotted.

Matt wound his way through the city with Tish trailing behind until he finally pulled into the underground parking garage of an office building. Tish drove past and pulled into the first spot she saw down the block. She grabbed her phone and checked the address. The building housed an accountant, a real estate agent, and a law firm. Tish tapped her nails on her phone case and tried to figure out what she wanted from this encounter. After a few more minutes she got out of her car and walked down the street to the nearest not-a-Starbucks coffee shop. Then she ambled back and went into the parking garage while she perused the websites of the businesses in the building. She checked her pants for any scratch making rivets and then parked her butt on Matt's Ferrari.

Tish was sipping her coffee and ogling puppy photos on Instagram when Matt returned twenty minutes later.

"Patricia," he said, coming to a stop a few feet away and folding his arms. She thought that was as much to hide the folder of paperwork in his hands as to express his annoyance.

"Matthew," said Tish, hearting one more photo.

Boop for your nose. Yes, you little bundle of fluff. Yes.

"How's the incorporation process going?" she asked, looking up.

"Son of… He told you."

"Nope. But there's a lot riding on me figuring it out. And it looks like I will be cleaning out the emergency shed after all."

Matt laughed. "All right, fine. *How* did you know?"

"Well, with the changes in the law on marijuana and the Governor's declaration of leniency that means that all your priors are about to get wiped out, right? That means that you're sitting on a fair amount of cash and are suddenly eligible to do something... legitimate?"

He gave a reluctant nod.

"This building has a lawyer, an accountant, and a real estate agent. You strike me as someone who has your money man already picked out and real estate agents will come to you. That just leaves the lawyer and these ones specialize in business law. You were schmoozing for investors at the wedding. What are you looking to do? High-end pot shop?"

"The uber-eats of pot," said Matt. "Place your order on-line. Pick up at the designated time. I'm still looking into delivery options."

"You can't use USPS and you would expose drivers to liability, not to mention robbery. Ooh! Locker boxes. That's why you were talking to the Amazon crowd."

Matt sighed. "Tobias said you'd figure it out."

Tish giggled. "Meanwhile, I still haven't figured out why Granddad needed to go to jail."

Matt shrugged. "I have a silent partner. Then this opportunity fell in my lap. We've been talking about dissolving the partnership, but I needed it dissolved ASAP without upsetting anyone. I needed to assure my partner that he was getting his fair share without any fuss. Only he's inconveniently taking a short vacation due to an unrelated matter courtesy of the Island County Corrections Department."

"So Granddad delivered the message," said Tish nodding. "Is everything going to work out?"

"Looks that way," said Matt, with another shrug.

"Good," said Tish. "Meanwhile, I feel like I should warn you that Detective Spring may be coming to harass you."

"Really? For what? I haven't even sneezed in the wrong direction in the last three months. I've been too paranoid."

"Penelope Drue's death," said Tish.

He came over and sat on the hood with her. "I thought that was an accident?"

"Murder," said Tish, shaking her head.

"You couldn't get me a coffee too?" he complained. "I feel like I shouldn't be forced to discuss murder without beverages."

"If we share coffee the Grapevine is going to say we're getting hitched or something. I can't afford that kind of friction."

"And why not?" asked Matt with a knowing grin. "Would some particular Sheriff's Deputy get annoyed?"

"Yeah, but Ronny's a putz, so I ignore him."

Matt laughed. "Why don't you just admit that you've got the hots for Nash and at least give him a shot?"

"I did. We've been doing shots since winter. I've just been scared to tell Claire and Granddad."

Matt threw his head back in a full throated laugh, drawing the attention of a gaggle of suited employees coming out of the elevator into the garage.

"Come on, let's grab lunch. You can tell me all about everything."

"I'm not dressed for a Ferrari," said Tish. "I need tighter pants and heels for that."

"There's a place around the corner. Decent sandwiches. No Ferrari necessary." He opened the door and tucked the folder of papers under the seat. "Come on." He jerked his head toward the street, as he locked the Ferrari, and Tish shrugged.

"All right, but you're buying. I'm a struggling business woman now. And if you're going to pump me for information then I expect bribes and considerations," she said following him to the exit.

"Who's pumping who here? You're the P.I. who turned up on my car."

"Well, you're not exactly hard to tail, Mr. Sunshine," said Tish.

"The car tends to stick out."

"Seriously, are you sure you don't want to go into a life of crime?"

"Aren't you the one trying to get out? Come to the light side, Mr. Jones."

"But the dark side has more fun."

"You mean the dark side has Ferraris," said Tish, as they walked out onto the sidewalk. Since it was Washington and it was only June it was overcast but bright and Tish put her sunglasses back on.

"Trust me," said Matt. "They are the same thing. So, you and Nash. That's a thing."

"It *is* a thing. Which is weird because I don't usually do things, but I think I'm into it."

"Good for you," said Matt, in what Tish thought was a surprisingly supportive way. "I mean I also find that weird, because I also don't do things. But they seem good for other people."

Tish laughed. "Yeah, that's what I told Pen about babies."

Matt pulled up short. "Wait, Penelope was pregnant?"

Tish grimaced. "Yeah. Not that her family wants that spread around. But she seemed pretty happy about it."

"Damn," said Matt, frowning. "I can't believe… Penelope was always too good for that family. She should have gotten off the damn island after high school. I ran into her two or three months ago listening to some band at a bar in Anacortes. She came over and said hi. She was on a peace keeping mission because Pax and I had a minor disagreement and she wanted to assure me that Pax had a big mouth and not much more. I didn't give a shit, frankly. I told her she needed to ditch Paxton and head out on her own, but she said couldn't do it. Also, that Paxton was going to clean up his act and they were going to be a good family again. I tried not to outright laugh in her face. Communes warp people. Give you a warped idea that we're all in this together."

"We are," said Tish. "No one gets out of this life alive."

"Yeah, but you don't have to haul your brother's stupid ass the entire damn way. Paxton Drue is marginally smarter than their idiot uncle Dexter, but he's a screw-up. He's not bright enough to keep himself out of trouble. Penelope didn't need that in her life."

"Being on your own is hard," argued Tish. "It takes a lot resilience to go it alone. It isn't fun. Screw-ups may be annoying, but they're familiar."

"You sound like you've got experience."

"You're speaking to the girl who lived with her cokehead cousin for nine months and managed to not notice."

Matt laughed.

He's laughing at me. Just straight at me. Not even pretending.

"In my defense, I was working a lot and we were rarely home at the same time, but yeah. He managed to weasel out of the coke charge, but I think he's currently in on a DUI and some other warrant. My aunt is managing to blame me because… Yeah, I don't even know. But let's just say I'm not going to a lot of family gatherings lately."

"Sorry," he said. "But that's my point. You ditched his ass and you're happier for it."

"Yeah, but my point is that if Paxton wasn't bringing his shit home and they were running on different schedules, Penelope probably had a pretty easy time ignoring it. Maybe she should have left, and maybe she would have with the baby, but leaving is a lot harder than it sounds."

"You managed it."

"I got evicted, fired, and I moved in with Granddad. The decision got made for me. I'm only managing to avoid my aunt and her drama because…" Tish considered why she was managing to duck her mom's requests to show up. "Well, honestly, it's because I don't actually care and I'm kind of a bitch."

"Being a bit of an asshole does help when it comes to looking out for your mental health and self-preservation," agreed Matt.

"Sandwich place."

He took an abrupt left and grabbed a door, holding it open for her. Tish proceeded inside and found herself in a true delicatessen with a meat counter, shelves of products and five cramped tables.

"Let me guess," she said, looking around. "I feel like a Reuben is in our future."

"Nah, it's owned by a Hawaiian guy. Get the pulled pork."

"Sounds great."

They placed their order and found a table. They were a little before the lunch rush, so they had the place to themselves.

"OK," said Tish, arranging the ketchup and salt and pepper to her satisfaction. "What were we talking about?"

"I think we were arguing about the existential angst of separating oneself from loser family members. And also discussing Penelope and Paxton."

"Right." Tish paused and couldn't find a re-entry point. "I forget which side I was arguing on."

"Doesn't matter. We're both right. Anyway, you were saying that Spring might be paying me a call?"

Tish sighed. "Maybe. Sorry. You were on our suspect board for a minute, but Spring showed up before I could take you down."

"Was I? Oh. Gee. That's nice of you?" He looked torn between confusion and amusement.

"It's fine," said Tish apologetically. "You have an alibi. So it just depends on how big a jerk he wants to be."

"Do I have an alibi?" he asked blinking.

"Yeah. Us. You saw Granddad in the morning and then you came to the wedding. And everyone on the damn island has seen the photographic evidence of where you were all afternoon."

He grinned. "Sorry. Was Nash totally pissed?"

"He was mildly annoyed, but mostly because we haven't gone public. Not about you."

"Oh, good. Because if I get all legal, I'm totally buying my mom a new place on Orcas. I'm tired of the dump she's living in and she won't let me get her someplace new. And the last thing I need is Nash turning up to make my life miserable."

"I don't think he will. You know, unless someone calls you in for building without a permit or noise pollution or illegal chicken impregnating."

"I don't think I want to know who's been impregnating chickens."

"Mrs. McAllister's rooster."

"That is such a relief."

Tish laughed. "See the things you miss out on by living on the mainland?"

"Clearly. Who do you think the mystery blogger is? I've been thinking about this for a bit. I really don't remember anyone with their phone out or a camera. I mean it only takes a second to snap a picture, but... I just don't remember anyone paying that much attention to us. And despite you following me today, I generally do have a pretty good sense of when someone is stalking me."

Tish was about to respond when the counter guy arrived with their plastic baskets filled with over-stuffed sandwiches. Tish took the opportunity to pull open the Grapevine on her phone and stared at the photo again.

"I think they were standing pretty far away," she said staring at the picture. Matt scrutinized the picture and crunched his pickle.

"You don't think it's just low-res for the web?"

"No," said Tish, scrolling down. "The other photos look perfectly crisp. Although, Talia's right, this one with Mrs. McAllister looks like it's taken from above."

"Well, depending on how far away they were standing, that's going to take an actual camera," said Matt. "Phone cameras have shitty zoom."

"Yeah," agreed Tish, setting her phone down and taking a bite of her sandwich. She chewed reflectively and then looked up to find

Matt smiling. "What?"

"When I met you, I think I severely underestimated just how much of a P.I. you were. I thought you were just helping Nash."

"Granddad's the P.I.," said Tish. "I own an event business. I just help out from time to time."

"Uh-huh," said Matt, taking a bite of his own sandwich. "You know what I like about Tobias?"

"His utter refusal to think inside the box?"

"That too," he agreed. "But I like that he collects for Orcas."

"What do you mean?"

"Orcas, as I'm sure you've noticed, is its own little ecosystem. And Tobias is what I'd call a gardener. He loans money. He gives advice. He pulls in people that he thinks would be useful to the island."

"You think he's planting me in the garden?" asked Tish skeptically.

Matt shrugged. "I don't think he's recruiting specifically. I think it's convenient for him to make it convenient for you. But I think it's good. Orcas could use more problem solvers."

Tish chewed her sandwich and thought about it.

Matt's right. He's just not right about which one of us Granddad is planting.

"He does do that," she said at last. "But the event business was my idea. If he had his way we'd have a tiny P.I. office in Eastsound and be running around in un-ironic fedoras."

"Well, you are not cooler than your own hat," agreed Matt.

"You cannot tell him that I tweet about him," said Tish. "He would be *so* mad."

"He's not going to hear about it from me," promised Matt. "I love Words from Granddad. How else will I find out what my generation is doing wrong?"

Tish giggled. "Right? Some days, I literally cannot type fast enough."

They finished lunch and Matt walked her back to her car.

"Tish," he said, as she unlocked the door.

"Yeah?"

"Thanks for doing this."

"It's lunch," said Tish, "and you paid. Not sure what I'm getting thanked for."

"It's… I can tell my transition is not going to be as smooth as I would like it to be. I appreciate that you and Tobias are treating me like…"

"Like a normal human being whose weird ass problems aren't all that unusual?"

"Yeah, that. I appreciate it. I don't know why you're doing it, but I appreciate it."

"You just said Granddad collects for Orcas," said Tish. "What do you think he's doing with you? We don't need more vacationers and part-time residents. We need more people with money who understand what the real Orcas is all about. If you are on the right side of the law that makes you available to help with things on the island."

Matt stared at her and then shook his head. "Damn Yearlys," he said.

"Granddad's ex-CIA," said Tish. "What? You think he's *not* going to set up a coup and overthrow your government? I mean… come on. Stop thinking small."

Matt laughed. "See you next time I'm on the island. Say hi to Nash and Tobias for me."

"Will do," said Tish.

CHAPTER 15
BUSTED

Tish leaned against the railing of the ferry and watched the Orcas dock grow ever closer. Then she looked back down at her phone. Sarah's smiling face burped out a speech bubble in the text field.

HEY! SAW YOUR POST FROM THE SALON. YOUR HAIR LOOKS GREAT. SWING BY THE OFFICE AND WE'LL GET THOSE DRINKS.

Tish typed in a response, deleted it, typed in another one.

The garbled voice over the intercom announced that docking was imminent and that all drivers should return to their cars. Tish did as instructed, leaving her message unsent.

She waited her turn to disembark trying to pick the perfect time to turn on the car engine. It was a pointless game, like any of the other ferry games she played. When to leave the house for the ferry line. When to return to her car. When to start the car. They were all the ferry system's equivalent of tilting at windmills, played to keep the mind busy and fill it with the empty satisfaction of having won this round. Never mind the endless rounds that were yet to be played.

Distractions from thinking about real problems.

Tish glanced at her phone. She needed to say something to Sarah, but what? She felt like she ought to demand an explanation, but an explanation for what? Being busy? She had no real evidence, just the nagging feeling of having been abandoned. Her car came off the grate and onto the street with a bone jarring thump and she gunned her poor Toyota to get it up the hill. She wound her way past the Orcas Hotel and saw Tate Donovan gloomily trudging up the road toward the San Juan Rideshare sign—the officially sanctioned hitchhiking spots of the San Juan's. Tate had a thin rocker build with wavy brown hair, hazel eyes and the ability to grow the perfect amount of stubble. He'd also managed to procure just the right number of tattoos on one arm to look like a rebellious flouter of social conventions without looking like someone who couldn't be brought home to daddy. Although, at the moment, instead of walking with his usual rocker swagger, his shoulders were hunched miserably and his head was down.

She slowed and rolled down her window. "Hey Tate. Need a ride?"

"Um…" He looked around. "Yeah. Thanks. Just into Eastsound."

"Sure," said Tish. She scooped her ferry novel off the passenger seat and tossed it into the glove box as Tate got in.

"Thanks," he said, buckling his seat belt.

"No problem. Azalea ditch you?"

"No… Marty was supposed to pick me up. He's just running late. We're supposed to practice tonight. Go over the set list for this weekend."

"Oh, thanks! You got a mention in Mimi's review, by the way."

"Mimi?" Tate looked confused.

"Last weekend's bride. She posted a review on our Facebook page. We got five stars. You got mentioned."

"Oh. Great. That's great."

Tish took another look at Tate. He was looking less trendily photogenic than usual.

"You doing OK, Tate?"

"Yeah. Yeah," he said, quickly. "I'm fine."

A little too quick on the response time to be believable.

"Are you sure?"

"I'm just a little under the weather, I guess," he said. "Don't worry. I'll be fine for the gig."

"I'm not worried about the wedding," said Tish.

Well, I am, but at the moment I'm worried about you.

He looked at her with a miserable expression.

"I'm sorry Azalea yelled at you about Penelope. I know you're just trying to help."

"I really liked Penelope," said Tish. "The idea that someone would want to hurt her kind of makes me want to barf if I think too hard about it."

"She loved everyone," said Tate. "Do you really think someone would do… *that* to her on purpose?"

"Um," said Tish. "Yeah, I do. I know Azalea and Paxton don't want to hear it, but her death wasn't an accident. Detective Spring served a search warrant on Paxton yesterday morning."

Tate went pale. "Really? They really… The police are really serious about it?"

"Yeah," said Tish. "I know it's upsetting that I'm poking around and talking to people. But they're going to hate it even worse when it's the police."

Tate looked through the windshield, seemingly at a loss for words.

"No one I've ever known has died before," he said, finally.

It won't be the last.

Don't say that out loud. That is not a useful thing to say.

"They leave little holes in your life," said Tish. "Like someone punched out pieces of your jigsaw puzzle. They never really get filled in properly. The picture never looks quite the same after they're gone."

That probably wasn't useful either.

"Sorry, didn't mean to get super philosophical or anything," she added.

"You sound like Penelope," he said with a smile. "She really believed all that commune-one-with-the-universe stuff."

"I don't know about one-with-the-universe," said Tish. "But I've lost some people and I guess it's made me realize that even the people I wasn't particularly close to really matter."

Tate looked like he was thinking, but he didn't respond and Tish wanted to fill up the empty space, but remembered a maxim from one of her acting classes.

Silence is the hardest art.

So she turned on the radio and pushed the gas pedal to make the car chug a little past the speed limit. It seemed possible, as her car trundled up to speed, that Matt might have a point about Ferraris.

A few minutes later Tate's phone popped with a text. "Marty will meet us in Eastsound," said Tate, texting back. "You can drop me up at Ray's Pharmacy."

"Sure," said Tish. "I need to pick up some stuff for Granddad anyway."

"I don't know how you live with old people," he said, shaking his head. "I had to spend the weekend with my Grandma last year and it was horrible. Everything smelled like morning breath and Folgers."

Tish was surprised into a laugh.

"Granddad brushes his teeth," she said. "Although, I admit that there is a distinct aroma of coffee in the morning and he does tend to make it blacker than the pit of my soul. But it is at least real coffee."

"That probably helps," he said.

Tish parked the Toyota in a spot at the little 1960s strip mall and got out. Tate did the same and stretched his arms over his head as if they'd been driving a long time.

"Tate," said Tish, chasing the nebulous feeling that there was more wrong than Tate just being down, "is there anything…"

"Tater!" yelled Marty, roaring into the parking lot in an ancient Land Cruiser. "Move your ass, singer boy!" The bearded bass player's vehicle exuded the burnt smell of ancient engine and overlaid with pot and Tish tried not to shake her head in an overly Tobias like fashion.

"Thanks for the ride," said Tate and bolted for the Land Cruiser.

Tish took her time at the pharmacy picking up odds and ends

and a prescription for her grandfather before heading back out to the parking lot, only to see Paxton Drue bent over her car's windshield. His spikey dark hair looked less spiked than normal, but he seemed to have made some sort of strange statement in the clothing department by wearing an Izod shirt in aqua blue and a pair of boat shoes under a pair of brown work pants. It didn't seem in keeping with his personality, but Tish decided not to judge.

She walked up behind him, expecting him to turn at any moment, but he didn't. He seemed utterly intent on crafting a very angry note on the back of a paper sack.

"I'm a birch?" asked Tish, looking over his shoulder.

Paxton yelped and leaped in the air.

"That's a T!" he yelled, spinning to look at her.

"Oh," said Tish looking at the note again. "That does make more sense."

How did Mrs. Palmer handle you? Let's see... She talked like the two of you were on the same side. Let's see if I can do that.

"You're pissed about the search warrant, aren't you?"

"Yes!" he yelled.

"Did they find your drugs?" asked Tish, trying to look her most sympathetic.

"No, Pen never let me keep shit in the house. Everyone knows that! They just tore up all my stuff and practically accused me of killing my sister."

"That sounds really horrible. I'm sorry!"

He gaped at her. "You can't just say sorry!"

"Why not? It's not like I'm happy about being right that Penelope was killed. And it's not like I want you to be a suspect. It's not personal. Look, just tell me where you were on Saturday and we'll be able to take you off the suspect board."

"If I didn't tell the cops, I'm not telling you!"

"Why not? I can't arrest you, but I can vouch for you. You should tell me. I can help."

Paxton glared at her, then he grabbed her hand and slapped his bag with the note on it into her palm. "Drop dead, birch."

"Well, that could have gone better," said Tish, as Paxton stomped away.

"Could have gone a lot worse," said the pharmacy clerk, poking her head out of the store. "I had the cops on speed dial. I don't know how you stay so calm."

"I just pretend I'm in a movie," said Tish.

Paxton was funny just then. He was really mad and then he stopped to be funny. I think Mrs. Palmer is right—his anger management is a work in progress, but he actually is expressing himself.

Tish took the note and got back in the car. On impulse she snapped a picture of it and sent it to Detective Spring. Before she had even made it out of the parking lot there was a text back.

Who is this person and why do they think you're a tree?

With a groan, Tish realized she'd accidentally texted Sarah instead of the Detective.

Sorry, wrong person. That was supposed to go to Spring.

Tish put the phone down and prepared to drive.

Wait, someone is threatening you again? And since when do you text Spring?

Well, if you ever talked to me maybe you'd know.

Tish dropped the phone and stared at it in horror. She couldn't believe she'd just hit send on that. She waited for Sarah to respond, but the phone remained dark and silent.

"I wish we could all get along like we used to in middle school. I wish I could bake a cake filled with rainbows and smiles and everyone would eat and be happy," said Tish to the empty car.

Mean Girls, 2004, starring Lindsey Lohan before things got weird.

With a sigh, she pushed forward and got the car into traffic, heading for home. She meandered along the main road, hoping that Sarah would text her back, but she didn't hear anything. She pulled into the half-circle driveway and saw that Tobias' 1980s beat up pick-up wasn't in its usual spot. She was about to go inside when she heard the crunch of tires on gravel and stood on the porch waiting for her grandfather's vehicle to round the curve. Instead, she saw the Sheriff's Department Grand Cherokee. Tish dropped her pharmacy items on the porch and went around to the driver's side.

"Hey, beautiful," he said, rolling down the window.

"Hey!"

"Love the hair."

"Why, thank you for noticing," she said, giving her hair a pat.

"Well, the text saying *be sure to notice my hair* was quite helpful," he said, with a grin. "Although, I would have noticed anyway. I can finally see your face." He reached through the window and flipped her now much shorter bangs.

"I was kind of turning into an English Sheepdog or something," agreed Tish. "But, changing topic."

"There's something vitally more important than your hair?"

"Well, obviously my hair is of top importance, but I do want to cover a few other things."

Nash chuckled. "Me too. What's on your list?"

"Paxton Drue thinks I'm a birch." She held up her note.

"You know for sure he left this?" asked Nash, carefully not touching the bag.

"Caught him leaving it. I was going to text a picture of it to Spring. Should I do that?"

"Yes, absolutely. Did Paxton threaten you otherwise?"

"He told me to drop dead. But I didn't feel overly threatened."

"That's because your threat button is broken."

"It is not! I know threats when I get hit in the head with them."

"Kind of my point, since if you actually get hit it's no longer merely a threat. Text it to Spring. Meanwhile, I've got a line on our green moped aka the drone pilot. I might be able to track it, and the driver, down tonight."

"Why, Mr. Nash! Are you misusing police resources?"

"Considering that the moped had no license plate, no I am not. I am diligently doing my duty as an officer of the law."

"Sexy," said Tish.

"You know law and order does it for you every time," he said, with a cocky grin.

"What can I say? I'm a very predictable criminal," she said.

"But cute," he said, leaning out of the window. "Criminally cute."

Tish giggled and stretched up to kiss him.

"You'll fill me in when you find out about the moped?"

"You bet. You're texting Spring?"

"Yeah. I want to talk to Granddad about it too. I need a second brain to hash it out."

"When the first one won't cooperate, go get a spare," he said, restarting the Bronco.

"Well, the first one never cooperates, so I have to," said Tish and Nash laughed. "Anyway, call me later?"

"You got it," he agreed and leaned out the window again.

Tish kissed him again and waved as he pulled away. She put her hand down and looked at the note.

"Looks an awful lot like *birch*," she said, shaking her head.

There was an ominous creak of hinges and the side gate opened.

"Looks an awful lot like someone's been lying," said Tobias.

CHAPTER 16

GARDENING WITH TOBIAS

"Your truck's not in the driveway," blurted out Tish.

"Drove it around back to clean out some things. Which I know you think I can't do. But I can," snapped Tobias. "Also, that isn't the point. The point is that you're putting the moves on Nash!"

"I am not!"

"You kissed him!"

"Yeah! Because…"

He waited, eyebrows raised.

"We're dating, OK? We've been dating since Christmas. I didn't want to tell you because you're always going on about how dating the divorced is a bad idea. I was planning on telling you this weekend. I invited him and Claire over for dinner on Sunday. We were going to tell both of you then."

"Patricia," said Tobias, and Tish knew she was in deep shit, "don't you dare tell that little girl you're dating her father."

Tish gaped at Tobias. Of all the reactions she had expected, that hadn't been one of them.

"No," said Tish, uncertainly. "I think it's going to be fine. Claire likes me."

"I've seen the two of you together. She idolizes you. Thinks the sun shines out of your tuchus. She's going to be over the moon."

"Well, is that so bad?" asked Tish.

"Oh, it's peachy keen right up until the two of you break up," said Tobias, stomping up on to the porch and slamming open the door.

Don't throw my worst fear in my face or anything.

"That's not… Why do you think I've been waiting? I don't want that to happen."

"Great," said Tobias. "Then break it off now before anyone gets hurt."

"What? Granddad…" Tish trailed along after him, following him into the hall. Tobias lowered himself onto the bench and pulled off his rubber boots, chucking them violently into the basket by the door.

"You mark my words, Patricia, this is nothing but foolishness."

"Granddad, what the hell have you been smoking? Nash and Claire are great. It's not his fault his stupid wife cheated on him. People get divorced. It's how it is. What's so wrong with that?"

"Not a damn thing. Nash is a solid individual and mainstay of the island."

"OK," said Tish feeling lost. "So why can't I date him?"

Tish looked at her grandfather and realized that he wasn't talking. Then she realized why.

"It's not him, is it? It's me. You don't want Nash to date *me*."

Tobias sighed and rubbed his bushy eyebrows.

"What's wrong with me?" she demanded.

"Nothing's wrong with you. You are a brilliant and lovely young woman."

"But?"

"But you're not really island material. We all know it."

I'm trying to have a response to this and right now all I'm thinking about is asking him what he was actually cleaning out with the truck.

"What the hell does that mean?"

"You got fancy ideas."

"Yeah, I'm trying to build a high-end event business and that means that I have to have fancy ideas. I can't just put it together with shoestrings and duct tape. And yeah, I know that comes off as a little arrogant, but it's the kind of thing that gets high-paying clients and that means that I can pay my servers and everyone else a decent wage. So if *not island material* means doing things legally and with style, then yeah, that's me."

"And that is great. I'm very proud of you. You've worked really hard to make that happen and the island will be all the better for it. And when you want to sell the business, I'm sure it will continue to be an excellent employer for years to come."

"What do you mean—when I sell the business? Seriously, what the hell are you smoking?"

"Tish, pumpkin…"

"What? Seriously, what?"

"You're going to get bored. You're going to get bored and go on to the next adventure. And then Nash and Claire are going to be heartbroken all over again. The island doesn't need that."

"Is that why you've helped me and gave me money? You thought I'd build a business the island needed before I left?"

"Well…" said Tobias and then shrugged. "Let's just say the thought had crossed my mind. And if you abandon the business then well, you hired some people and you've renovated Reginald's and all of that is good. And if it actually works out and you sell it, well, even better. The island could use another employer. But I don't think it's fair to mess with Nash and Claire."

"And you think I'm the kind of person who would hurt them like that?"

"Not on purpose. But we've all gotta chase our own bliss. And this island is mine. It's also Nash's. But Tishkins, you're a big city kind of girl, and you know it. I'm not trying to be mean, Tish. I know you like Nash and it's perfectly obvious that he likes you. That's why I've been trying so hard to discourage you. I just think pursuing anything with him is a recipe for disaster."

I'm really used to him being right about people. Is he right about me?

"Granddad," said Tish, then stopped.

In improv the answer is always "yes and". That's my opportunity to change the story. But I don't think I can yes this. How do adults manage interpersonal conflict? What would Mrs. Palmer say about how I express my anger?

"Granddad," she started again, "I really want to discuss this in a way that doesn't involve yelling, but at the moment all I really feel like doing is yelling. So I'm going to go away and cool down. And when I come back I really hope that you'll have had an opportunity to reconsider how you feel because I am dating Nash. I love him and it would be very unfortunate if you disapproved of my relationship. I'll see you in a few hours."

Tish turned and walked out the front door and out to her car.

"Tish," called Tobias, standing in the doorway.

"Your prescription is on the stairs," said Tish, unlocking her car. "Also, I picked up a DVD of the Rockford Files Season One I thought you might like. I'm going to Olga for dinner. Don't wait up."

CHAPTER 17

ETERNAL CIRCLE

"Wine," said Tish, throwing her purse down on the glossy yellow oak of the Olga bar. "Now."

"We have a very lovely—"

"Red. Don't care what kind. Large glass."

"It's going to be one of *those* kind of shifts," said the bartender shaking her head. "Does half the island have girl problems or what?" The bartender looked about forty with a full henna tattoo down one arm and a nose ring. Also, Tish couldn't help noticing that her eyebrows were absolutely to die for and her make-up looked YouTube worthy.

"I have grandfather problems," said Tish.

"Oh, yeah. I saw on the Grapevine—you're Tish Yearly. My grams went absolutely cray cray toward the end. I mean, she was really sweet and never got mad at anyone, but she kept forgetting to put on underwear. And no one needs to see that."

"Granddad's not crazy. He's an asshole."

"Oh. Didn't he get arrested for being off his meds, though?"

"No, he got arrested for being drunk and disorderly at like five in the morning."

"But he's really old!"

"Yeah, that means he has lots of experience at getting drunk and being a jerk," said Tish.

"Oh. Well, I suppose that's true," said the bartender, pushing a glass of wine across the bar to her.

"Your eyebrows are amazing," said Tish. "Are you using a filler or…"

"Oh, thanks! Indian string technique with powder filler. I'm doing an online beautician course and I have to test on myself."

"Need any test subjects? Mine are starting to look like I'm Big Foot's one true love."

"Oh, my God, yeah, like totally. I'm Rose." She offered a hand to shake and Tish took it.

"Tish Yearly," said Tish. "Also, I'm not dating Matt Jones."

"Oh, bummer. He's hot."

"I'm dating Deputy Nash."

"Yummers! Can I do, like, full face and take pics?"

"Probably," said Tish with a shrug. She'd done lots of modeling in return for services in LA. It had always been a fun way to get what she needed. She had rather thought she'd aged out of that, but on the other hand…free eyebrow shaping.

Tish took a handful of peanuts from the dish and looked around the bar. "So who's crying into their beer?"

"The boys out on the patio. One's going on and on about breaking up and his friends are seconding that a little too hard, if you know what I mean. I think she must be a total Yoko Ono."

"Yoko… Is it Tate and the band?"

"Uh, yeah. I think so. They're switching between playing songs, trying to name the band, and trying to buck him up for doing the deed with the girlfriend."

"I was voting for Trendily Photogenic as a band name," said Tish and Rose laughed. "But I don't think they're going to go for it. What are the top choices?"

"Donovan's Reef, which I don't get."

"Tate's last name is Donovan and Donovan's Reef is a John Wayne movie circa 1963 directed by John Ford, who also directed like… a hundred and fifty movies."

"Huh," said Rose.

"I think they should steer clear of references only the elderly and the terminally film obsessed will get. What else did they have?"

"Um… The Reefer Addicts."

"Ah," said Tish. "Now I'm seeing the appeal of Donovan's Reef."

"There were like eight other pot puns. And then they had The Broken Vows." Tish snorted. "The Speak Nows. Papa's Shotgun. And I think Divorced by Eight."

"Ha! That's funny, but they cannot have that one. I absolutely forbid it."

"I don't know. That one was trending pretty high. If you actually care, you might need to go vote."

Tish groaned. "I don't want to talk to them. We don't speak the same slang. Half the crap they say just sounds like nonsense words."

Rose laughed. "Yeah. I hear you. I have a nineteen-year-old. The stuff is contagious. But if I'm using it then you can be sure that he is not."

"Oh, great! You are here! Rose, beer me!"

Tish looked up in surprise as Kyle arrived at the bar with a burst of energy.

"Hey Kyle," said Tish. "Were you looking for me?"

"Well, not really. I just tied up down at the dock and I was going to call you and tell you to come buy me beer."

"Why am I buying you beer?" asked Tish, eating more peanuts.

"Because I'm your C.I.!" He looked cheerful about this.

"I was only on *Law & Order* for like five minutes as a dead body," said Tish. "I don't know what that means."

"Confidential Informant. Get with the vocab. Jeez."

"I am hip to your jive, man," said Tish. Rose and Kyle both stared at Tish. "What? I live with a seventy-nine-year-old. It's what I've got."

"Well, what I've got is where Pax and Dex were last Saturday," said Kyle smugly. "Beer, Rose?" he asked, looking at Rose in confusion.

"Yeah, beer covers a broad spectrum, Kyle. I'm going to need a little more and also a please."

"Oh," said Kyle, looking disappointed. "In the movies they just say beer and they get beer. What's on tap right now?"

"I've got a couple of nice IPAs. And Odd Otter's Ottzel Quatzel Pale Ale is good. They just won best pale ale in Washington. I've got some stouts in the bottle if you're looking to go darker."

"I'll try the Odd Otter, please and thank you," said Kyle. "That sounds intriguing."

"You're a real connoisseur," said Rose drily.

"She's still bitter about the time I puked all over the men's room," said Kyle, confidentially to Tish.

"It was a year ago," said Rose from the end of the bar where she was pouring the beer. "And you puked on the hand dryer which means it smelled for an entire weekend every time someone used it."

"I can see how she would be annoyed," said Tish.

"But I've matured since then. Sorry, Rose," he called down the bar.

"You're practically a man of the world," said Tish.

"Well, I don't puke on stuff anymore, so I figure that's a definite sign of maturity."

"I find that I agree with you," said Tish. "Although, I am very surprised by that."

Kyle flashed a grin. "Understandable. OK. You want the low down?"

"Give me the dirt," said Tish.

"So Paxton's seeing this girl, Anna Gulliver, over in Friday Harbor and he was there all night and then caught the nine o'clock ferry home in the morning."

"The nine? How the hell was he planning on getting home in time to give Penelope a ride to work?"

"Probably wasn't. He's a jerk. What are you going to do? But I talked to Barry, and I told him I was asking for you and Tobias, and he says he for sure saw Paxton's shitty car on the nine."

Tish grunted. Barry worked for the ferry system and while he looked like a massively overweight fifty-something who probably didn't think beyond his own nose Tish knew for a fact that he could frequently be found in Seattle during protest season holding up picket signs for immigrant rights and had good memory for all the regulars that floated through the ferries and which island they belonged to. In short, Barry was smarter than he looked and his word was reliable.

"OK," said Tish. "Then where did he go?"

Kyle looked around as if gauging who could be eavesdropping. Spotting Rose helping another customer in the restaurant and satisfying himself that the no one else was in earshot he continued. "Well," he said lowering his voice, "word is that he and Dexter are cooking a new batch with Miles Singer over in Deer Harbor and that's what they were doing all morning. So then, I asked around to see if anyone had seen the three of them and you will never guess what I found out."

"You are correct. I will not guess," said Tish.

Kyle waited.

"No, seriously, I'm not guessing."

"You take all the fun out of it," said Kyle. "So it turns out that Dexter and Miles were probably cooking. But Paxton was running crew on a Northwest Classic Daysailing trip. They're a tourist outfit that does day trips on sailboats."

"Wait... Paxton has a legit job?"

"Yeah! I know! How crazy is that? I talked to the owner. He says Paxton signed on last month and has been prompt and courteous for every trip he's been booked on. He says Paxton told him his girl and his sister were getting on him and he wanted to clean things up."

"Well, good for him," said Tish. "What about Dexter?"

"Dexter and Miles popped out for a sandwich up at The Deer Harbor Inn around one, but I can't find them after that."

"Hmm," said Tish. "And when did Paxton get back from his

sailing trip?"

"Around three," said Kyle. "Not sure where he went after that."

"Hmm," said Tish.

"Hmm? That's some really great information and all I get is a *hmm?*"

"That is really great Kyle, thanks."

"You're looking thoughtful," said Kyle, sipping his beer. "Is that good thoughtful or bad thoughtful?"

"It doesn't give either of them an alibi," said Tish.

"Were we expecting it to?" asked Kyle. "Aren't they the prime suspects?"

"Yeah," said Tish. "Ish."

"Well, who else you got?"

"Exactly my point. I really wish Granddad hadn't decided to be a jerk just now."

"I thought he wasn't cracking up? Don't tell me he really has dementia."

"No, he hasn't got dementia! He's just being a jerk because he caught Nash and I kissing."

"What?" Kyle stood up, knocking over his bar stool and nearly spilling his beer.

"Cool your jets, hep cat. It ain't no thing."

"What? Just what? Also, where's my phone! I'm totally texting Amber."

"Whatever," said Tish.

"Like, seriously, are you and Nash a thing?" he demanded, his eyes glued to his phone as he typed.

"Yeah," said Tish. "We're a thing. And Granddad's pissed about it because he thinks I'm likely to wanker off to the mainland and ditch out on Nash and Claire."

"Oh," said Kyle, looking up from the phone. "But you're doing a whole business thing. Does he think you're just going to walk away from that? I mean, I have friends who are super pumped about it.

Jordan, who's on your valet crew is really excited to have a job that pays pretty good and gets him tips."

"He did really well last weekend," said Tish. "I'm glad to have him."

"Yeah, but I mean… You can't just pick up and leave a business. What's Tobias thinking you're going to do?"

"I don't know. Either he thinks I'm going to flop or he thinks I'm going to just decide to go follow my bliss somewhere else. But… whatever he thinks, he thinks I shouldn't be potentially breaking Nash's heart."

"That is…" Kyle breathed out through his nose. Then, shaking his head, he righted his barstool and sat back down. "You can't get hung up on what *could* happen. I deal with this all the time with Amber. Her last boyfriend cheated on her, so she's constantly tweaking that I'm going to. And yeah, sure, theoretically I could. I have no intention of doing that. I love Amber. But if you miss out on what's awesome now because theoretically something bad could happen in the future then you'd never leave the house. You can't get hung up on the stuff that might happen because it's just as likely to *not* happen."

"I hear you," said Tish. "But what worries me is that Granddad has a better than average score on guessing what *will* happen."

"OK, yeah, but… He's also old," said Kyle as if that was the answer to everything. "And I mean… Old people. What do they know?"

Tish laughed. "Thanks Kyle. I appreciate the words of advice."

"See?" he said, raising his glass in toast. "I'm all mature and shit."

Rose came back behind the bar in time to hear that comment and snorted in derision.

"I really am," he protested. His phone lit up in a flurry of texts. "Amber wants to know how long you've been dating, and if you've told Claire and Tobias, and if it's serious."

"Well, obviously Granddad knows and we're telling Claire this weekend. And I think it's serious. But I guess you'd have to ask Nash on that one."

Of course it's serious, but I am a good girlfriend and I don't speak for my significant other. I'm not Azalea or anything.

Kyle swiped out a new response. "She seems very excited about this. But I have to say, and don't be offended, I personally am not a fan. People are going to think because I'm friends with you that I'm Team Nash now. It's going to be a problem."

"Nah," said Tish. "You're my C.I. remember? Confidential is the keyword there. The coppers will never know."

Kyle grinned. "Your old people slang is hilarious." His phone burped again and he beamed at the message. "Hey Rose, Amber is coming out after her shift. Can you put us on the list for a table?"

"Yeah, sure," said Rose, with a shrug, loading up a tray full of glasses. "Oh, ask her if she's got any of those earrings I liked last time she was in."

"Sure," said Kyle, texting automatically.

"Earrings?" asked Tish, as Rose disappeared back out to the floor.

"Amber's been taking some jewelry classes over on the mainland. She's getting really good. Check this out." He pulled his sleeve off his wrist and displayed a leather cuff with an interesting metal-work medallion in the middle.

"That's cool," said Tish. "I didn't know she was doing that."

"I think she's really talented," said Kyle. "She was showing me how to make molds and melt metal and stuff. It's crazy! She says she wants to get a bit better but then she might start doing craft fairs and looking for shops to carry her stuff. I say she's good enough already, but she says the competition here on the island is really high."

"It really is," said Tish, nodding. "But it looks like she's on her way. That's really cool!"

"Side hustle," said Kyle with a careless shrug, but still looking pleased. "You know how it is.

"Yeah," said Tish nodding. "Everybody's got one."

"Table will be ready in about twenty minutes," said Rose coming back. "Oh, and Tish, if you're serious about not having Divorced by Eight as the band name then you'd better go put the smack down on them. They were seriously considering it."

"Oh God," said Tish, rolling her eyes.

"Divorced by Eight?" repeated Kyle looking confused.

"My wedding band thinks they're clever. I'd better go tell them that no one is hiring a band called… any of the things on their list."

"Good call," said Kyle, laughing.

"Back in a bit." Tish took her wine and purse and trudged out to the patio.

The band was sprawled at one of the long tables which was awash in glasses and musical instruments. They looked like they were settling in for the night.

So much for band practice. This looks like drinking practice.

They looked up as she approached. Their half-wary expressions reminded her of raccoons with two fists in the dog kibble—they thought they were going to get yelled at but they weren't about to stop. "You cannot have Divorced by Eight," she said surveying the group.

Marty, grinned unrepentantly, still strumming gently on his guitar, but the rest of band looked somewhat cowed.

"Well, I suppose you can do better?" demanded the drummer, who like all drummers everywhere had tattoos and a subversive air. He was also tapping with his drumsticks on every flat surface like an ADD monkey.

"Uh, yeah," said Tish. "How about Something Blue, The Marry Makers, The Tied Knots, and of course, No Sax Before Marriage?"

"Ooh!" exclaimed the trumpet player.

"No!" said the entire group.

"There's the literate version," continued Tish, "Lords of the Rings."

The band groaned.

"So we *can't* have the James Earl Jones Experience?" asked the keyboard player plaintively.

"No," said Tate. "That's not even a wedding pun." His eyes were at half-mast and the table in front of him had three empties. He looked wasted. He must have started drinking the moment he hit the door—she hadn't left him that long ago.

"I mean, I like it," said Tish. "But I'd expect Tate to be a bass with that name."

There was a chorus of nods.

"Oh," said Tish, struck by inspiration, "Till Death Do Us Party."

"That's... not bad," said Marty, looking thoughtful.

"But does it have legs?" demanded Tate, rocking back in his chair and then clutching the table for support. "Can we use it anywhere else?"

"Ah," said Tish. "Well, if you want to use it outside the wedding circuit then you need a name that sounds philosophical and deep."

"Yeah," said the keyboard player, "but you shot down the James Earl Jones Experience."

"That's not deep," said the drummer. "That's just you watching Star Wars while high too many times."

"Facts," said Tate.

"Eternal Circle," said Tish.

There was silence from the band. The drummer ran a little drum roll on the table and then tinged a stick off a water glass. "I like that," he said. "It's got musical references."

"I can tie it back to Johnny Cash in a heartbeat," said the trumpet player. "And Johnny Cash is always cool."

"It works for weddings," said Marty, "but it doesn't necessarily *sound* wedding."

"I'm kind of into it," said Tate nodding. "We should try it out this weekend."

That's if you can remember it in the morning.

"Great," said Tish. "So I can go back to drinking wine at the bar and not have to worry that you're going to name yourselves The Prenups or something equally stupid?"

"Ooh!" said the keyboard player.

"No!" exclaimed the rest of the band.

"Yeah," said Tate, with a drunk persons laissez faire attitude toward the really important things, "it's fine. Noah will remember because he doesn't drink and you can—"

"Tate Donovan!"

They all turned to look at Azalea standing in the doorway between the restaurant and the patio.

"What are you doing? We decided that you weren't going to drink anymore and that you were not going to be *practicing* here anymore."

"No *we* didn't," said Tate, lurching to his feet. "We didn't decide anything. You said crap and I didn't tell you to stuff it."

"Tate!"

"No, seriously," he slurred. "There *was* no we. There *is* no we. There will not be a we in the future. You don't love me. You just love having someone to boss around. Well, Penelope's dead and I'm not doing it anymore, so you're out of luck."

"Tate!" gasped Azalea. "You don't mean that."

"Yeah," he said. "I do. I should have done this months ago. We're breaking up."

"We are not breaking up," snapped Azalea.

"You don't get to make that choice," said Tate. "This is my choice." He slapped his chest, the heavy smack of his palm against his t-shirt and flesh emphasizing his words. "Mine. And I don't want to be with you. I want you to leave me alone."

Azalea made a little squeak of outrage and surveyed the group as if looking for back up. Everyone, including Tish, avoided eye contact.

Azalea made an inarticulate growl of rage and stomped her foot.

"You will change your mind when you are sober and then you will have some serious groveling to do!"

Then she pivoted and ran out of the bar.

Tate collapsed into his chair, his hands visibly shaking. "Don't let me change my mind," he said, turning to Marty. "I know I always say I'm done with her, but I'm serious this time. I can't go back. I can't."

"You got it, bro," said Marty, throwing an arm around his shoulders. "You can crash at my place. Hand over your phone."

Tate took out his phone and handed it to his friend. Tish decided it was her moment to get out while no one was looking and walked quickly back to the bar taking a healthy swig of wine as she went. Kyle was cozily ensconced with Amber at a table on the far side of the room so she went back to the bar.

"Crisis averted?" asked Rose.

"Well," said Tish, "one of them, anyway."

CHAPTER 18

BARROOM DETECTION

Tish ordered dinner at the bar and fiddled with her phone while waiting for her food. At last, even social media stopped being able to fill her brain and she reluctantly texted the photo of Paxton's note to Detective Spring.

WHAT THE HELL IS THIS?

Tish looked at Spring's response and tried to formulate an answer.

IT'S THE NOTE PAXTON DRUE WAS LEAVING ON MY CAR WHEN I FOUND HIM IN THE PARKING LOT EARLIER TODAY.

That seemed succinct. She hit send and waited. Then realized it was too succinct.

ALSO, I HAVE SOURCES THAT SAY PAXTON DRUE WAS ON THE NINE AM FERRY AND WORKED UNTIL THREE AT NORTHWEST CLASSIC DAY-SAILING. DEXTER WAS PROBABLY COOKING METH WITH MILES SINGER UNTIL AT LEAST ONE IN THE AFTERNOON.

Moments later her phone rang.

"Sources?" demanded Spring, when she picked up.

"Sources," agreed Tish.

"And these sources are…" he prodded impatiently.

"None of your business," said Tish.

"Damn it, that doesn't help me."

"Go ask people yourself then! I can't do everything for you!"

"You're not doing anything for me. You're just handing me more questions to answer."

"Well, that's your job," said Tish. "To find out the answers. It's literally your title: detective."

"Ha ha. Back to the note. Paxton was leaving you an angry note? Did he threaten you?"

"He told me to drop dead. But that's not a threat so much as an instruction that I have no intention of following."

"You never follow any instructions. Where did he go after he got off work?"

"My sources did not indicate," said Tish. "But I think you might want to pull his phone records if you haven't already."

"I need the two of you for information. Not for telling me how to do my job!" he snapped.

"Granddad already told you to pull them?"

"He emailed yesterday. Why'd you have to teach him how to do that?"

"He already understood email. The only thing I did was give him your email address."

"Thanks for that."

"Whatever. He's right. Penelope was supposed to be at work by eight-thirty and Paxton was on the nine o'clock ferry. So if you're looking for evidence of friction between the two of them, I would look at their phone records to see if there were any calls or angry text exchanges. Although, I'm really not sure he did it."

"What makes you say that?"

"Well, I think that we can all agree that I can be really annoying."

"Definitely," said Spring.

"I'm choosing to be happy that you're agreeing with me. Anyway, he was leaving me an angry note, and he was mad, but he didn't... He didn't lose his cool. And whoever hurt Penelope well, it seems like he would have had to have been out of control angry. That's not feeling like Paxton."

"Feelings don't solve cases," said Detective Spring. "I need evidence."

"Feelings tell you where to look for evidence," countered Tish.

Spring made a derisive noise.

"When does the autopsy report come in?" asked Tish.

"Tomorrow," said Spring. "We should have a better idea of the time of death and maybe some answers to a couple of other things. I was going to come out to the island and poke around. You going to be home?"

"Yeah, I've got to start set-up for this Saturday's wedding, but I'll be around."

"Great," said Spring. "Try not to piss too many people off between now and then."

"I never try to piss people off," said Tish. "It just happens."

"Yeah, I mean, genes, what are you going to do?"

"I'm hanging up," said Tish.

"Uh-huh. See you tomorrow."

"Bye," said Tish, firmly. She clunked the phone down on the bar and glared at it.

"Here you go," said Rose, sliding a plate of salmon under her nose.

"Thanks," said Tish. "Hey Rose, you read the Grapevine, right?"

"Yeah. It's the most interesting thing to hit the island in months."

"Who do you think is behind it?"

Rose looked thoughtful and then pulled her phone out of her back pocket and called up the blog.

"Well, it's only been up and running for a few weeks. And the stories are kind of all over the island."

"When do they get posted?" asked Tish, around a mouthful of fish. "Like what days and times?"

"Doesn't look like there's a pattern," said Rose. "All days, random times. I only found out about the blog from my kid. Now that he's home from college for the summer all he does is surf the web. I would be more annoyed, but at least he has the decency to send me cat videos on the regular."

Tish laughed and then stopped. "College," she said, pausing with the fork half-way to her mouth.

"Yeah. He's got about a month of farting around the house and then he's got an internship down in Tacoma. I don't know where he's going to stay while he's down there though. Hopefully, he can couch surf because I'm not paying for an apartment."

Tish reached for her phone and looked at the photos from the blog again.

"Knows how to put together a website," said Tish.

"Who doesn't?" asked Rose, rhetorically.

"Do you?" asked Tish. "I know all those ads make it look like it's dead easy, but I assure you it's not. So we've got someone who is tech savvy, familiar with the island, moves around unnoticed, just started up recently. Likes taking photos."

"That could be anybody," said Rose.

"No, it really can't. The number of people at that wedding who know or care to take a picture of me and Matt was pretty small. The band was on stage. The servers were busy. So who took the photo? Someone with camera equipment."

"But that's everyone at a wedding," said Rose.

"No," said Tish shaking her head again. "It really isn't. Also, it's someone who can take photos from strangely high angles."

She took another bite and then grabbed her phone again, flipping through her contact list until she found Neil Cho.

Hey Neil. It's Tish. I meant to ask, your assistant last weekend, did she do drone shots of the wedding?

Tish ordered another glass of wine and went back to eating while she waited for Neil to respond. Outside the sun was setting and painted the entire interior of the restaurant in the glorious hazy yellow that made the sealed oak glow.

"Oh my God," exclaimed Amber practically tackling her in a hug. "I'm so happy for you!"

"Wha?" said Tish, trying not to spill her wine.

"You and Nash. It's the best. You two are so epically cute together. I've been 'shipping you for months."

"Oh. Um. Thanks?"

"I really believe in the power of the mind to influence the universe," she said seriously. "I'm taking credit for this."

Tish laughed and then tried not to. Taking other people's quasi-religious wackery seriously was the hardest part of living on Orcas for her. "Sure," she said and smiled.

"Hey, is Kyle really helping you investigate stuff?"

"Yeah," said Tish. "Why?"

"It's just, he's really pepped up about it and I was hoping he was really helping and you weren't just pretending he was helping."

"No, he's really helping."

"That's awesome. Because he is super smart. But he's dyslexic, you know. So he always feels like he's not as smart as everyone else. Or at least that he can't ever prove it. And it's really cool to see him feeling like this."

I didn't know that. And now I feel like kind of a jerk for flipping him as much crap as I do.

"He's really helpful. He was helpful when they tried to arrest Nash too," said Tish. "I know he always complains about being on Team Nash, but I'm glad Kyle's our friend in spite of the badge."

Amber beamed. Kyle arrived, flicking a toothpick around in his mouth. "Ready to roll, babe?"

"Yes!"

"You'll give me a call if you need me to poke into something else?" asked Kyle looking at Tish.

"Yeah," said Tish. "I will. I'm still formulating next steps, but I'll be keeping you in mind."

"Awesome!"

"See you guys," said Tish and Amber waved.

Tish's phone vibrated on the bar with an alert.

YEAH. SHE GOT SOME GREAT SHOTS!

There were two more texts, this time with photos from the wedding both elevated and panoramic.

THOSE ARE AWESOME. WHAT WAS HER NAME AGAIN? SHE'S BACK
HOME FROM COLLEGE FOR THE SUMMER, RIGHT?

QUINCY TELLER. SHE'S REALLY INTO THE DRONES AND TECH, BUT
SHE'S A PRETTY DECENT PHOTOGRAPHER. I'LL BE USING HER ALL SUM-
MER.

*And she's helping build out the website for the bookstore. Gotcha mystery
blogger.*

THAT'S GREAT NEIL. THANKS.

Now she just needed to prove that Quincy Teller drove a mint
green moped and all the dots would connect. Her case wasn't entirely sewn up, but Tish went ahead and ordered a celebratory chocolate
mousse. She was taking the first bite when the band staggered in
from the patio. The drummer was supporting Tate and everyone
looked somber.

"Thanks for helping," said Marty, as the group passed.

"I'm not sure I helped," said Tish.

"Tate thinks you're helping. He thinks you're going to find who
killed Penelope and somehow that means he can break up with Azalea."

"Those are connected?" asked Tish, in confusion.

"I don't know, but it's like he thinks if you're trying to do the
right thing then he should too? I really don't get it. But whatever it
is, thanks for doing it. I'd kind of given up on his being able to break
up with her. I figured we'd just have to wait for her to get bored with
him. But this time I think it's actually going to take."

"Is he going to be OK if they're both at the wedding next weekend?" asked Tish and Marty shrugged.

"We'll figure it out. We'll just keep him on the buddy system."

"I'll keep her on table rotation and away from the gazebo," said
Tish.

"Sounds like a plan," said Marty. "See you Saturday."

Tish's phone pinged again, and Tish looked at it.

YOU AT THE BAR? I'M PARKED DOWN AT THE DOCK. COME MEET

ME IF YOU WANT TO KNOW WHO OUR DRONE PILOT IS.

Tish grinned. Nash was going to be so annoyed that she'd already beat him to it.

CHAPTER 19
ALGAE BLOOM

Tish paid her tab and wandered the short distance down to the dock parking area, which was basically just a grassy strip at the head of the steep stairs down to the dock. The barest yellow haze on the horizon was all that was left of sunset and Tish enjoyed the quiet susurration of the waves rising up from the beach blending with the sound of wind in the evergreens. Nash was leaning against his Bronco looking like some sort of noir film, high-lighted in stark contrast by Olga's one and only lamppost.

"Hi," he said straightening up, and walking the few steps to meet her. "You left Tobias at the bar, right?"

"Left him at the house," said Tish, sourly.

"Everything all right?"

Tish looked up at Nash and decided that she wasn't ready to get into it. "Probably. I'll tell you later. What's up?"

"Well, I found you a present," he said, leaning down to kiss her.

"A present?"

He turned and gestured to a scooter nearly tucked into the underbrush.

"I believe the driver is down at the dock," he said, looking smug.

"And I believe the driver is Quincy Teller," said Tish.

He stopped looking smug. "Dang it! How'd you know?"

"I went to the Olga Bar," said Tish. "You'd be amazed how much you can get done with wine and a cellphone." Nash laughed. "I also prevented some egregious band names, talked to Detective Spring, and after doing some texting, have come to the conclusion that Quincy is the mystery blogger behind the Grapevine."

"Are you sure? Because if she's the blogger, why isn't our awesome footage on the Grapevine?" demanded Nash. "We had Shakespeare, climbing and kissing. That's a gossip blogger home run."

"I'm not sure drones have audio capability, so it probably missed most of our awesomeness" said Tish. "But I'm definitely going to ask her about it because she really is the blogger."

"We'll see," he said, skeptically.

"Yes, we will," said Tish, and stuck out her tongue at him.

He grinned and gestured for her to lead the way down the stairs. The stairs down to the dock were well weathered wood with peeling traction pads on each tread. Tish navigated the stairs with one hand firmly on the rail and was happy when the dock light finally overcame the wealth of shadows. The dock was a narrow gray strip of hardi-plank with four currently empty slips—two to each side—and a weathered lantern on a post at the end.

Quincy Teller was sitting at the end of the dock, absorbed in her equipment. In the dark, she was hardly more than a lump of dark sweatshirt illuminated by the green glowing screen in her lap and the stark LED light from above. They were between tides and the dock and water were relatively still, so Tish thought their footsteps on the planks were quite loud and obvious, but it wasn't until they were a few feet away that Quincy looked up, clearly startled.

"Oh shit," Quincy said.

Quincy Teller was in her late teens or early twenties, in a hoodie and jeans with thick brown hair that she had wedged into a ponytail. The hair, from the looks of it, was having none of this nonsense and was making a break for freedom, but the ponytail was valiantly clinging on. She looked up at Nash and Tish like a very guilty puppy.

"Hi Quincy," said Tish, in the tone she used to let Claire know that she was on to her and that Claire ought to just confess now. "How are you tonight?"

"Fine," quavered Quincy uncertainly.

"Finding more people to write lies about on your little blog?"

she asked folding her arms. "Or just getting drone shots of the coastline?"

"Luminous algae bloom," said Quincy holding up her screen.

"How nice," said Tish, in a tone that would have frozen tap water.

"Look, I'm really sorry about the Matt Jones thing. But it got me so many hits on the blog! I didn't even know the Orcas population was that big!"

"Thanks to you every person I know is now concerned that Granddad has dementia."

"It's a matter of public record," said Quincy, sullenly. "Anyone can find that stuff."

"Having dementia is not part of the public record. You made that part up. And not everyone goes looking and certainly not everyone feels the need to share it with all of his neighbors and acquaintances. Do you know what happens if a judge decides that instead of paying his fine that maybe he needs a psych evaluation and to place him under court care?"

"Oh," said Quincy. "I didn't think about that."

"No, you also didn't think about the fact that posting that I was seeing Matt might negatively impact my relationship. In fact, I'm getting the impression that you didn't think at all. You just like feeling more clever than everyone else on the island."

"Well, I am," snapped Quincy. "Everyone lies on this stupid island and I'm tired of it. There's so much fakeness that I thought it would be good for people to hear the truth! And I can do that. I can do that and no one even knows it's me."

Tish bent down and looked Quincy in the eye. "I know," she said, quietly. "And it took me less than a week to figure it out."

Even under the strained lighting conditions Tish could see Quincy go pale.

"Now then," said Tish, straightening up. "Hand over the footage from the tower and I will not tell anyone what you're doing. You will also come and apologize to Granddad and show him how to do a public records search."

Because he wants to do that and I'm too lazy to figure it out.

"I can't give you the footage," said Quincy.

"Can't?" repeated Nash, sounding stern.

"I have a YouTube channel under my real name and I use it for my really cool drone footage," squeaked Quincy.

"Speak up, young lady," said Tish.

Damn, I sounded just like Granddad.

"I already uploaded it there," said Quincy, her voice rising for a moment before quickly dropping to a whisper. "It has fifty thousand views."

Holy crap.

"It has what?" demanded Nash.

"Fifty thousand hits," repeated Quincy.

"Holy crap," said Tish. "When did you upload it?"

"Yesterday."

"Holy crap," said Tish again.

"But it's just drone footage, right? Who would want to watch us make-out?" asked Nash.

"Drones can't do audio. Can they?" asked Tish, suddenly feeling Shakespeareanly embarrassed.

"I had a mic on the tower because I was going to do some voice over. I went back after you left and got it. The whole thing looks and sounds great. It's my most viewed clip ever."

"Holy crap," said Nash.

"Uh, yeah," said Tish.

"I know!" exclaimed Quincy. "It's so awesome. I only have like five thousand subscribers so it must be going viral."

"I'm going to have to call my mom and tell her I'm dating some-one," said Nash.

"You haven't told your mom?" demanded Tish.

"She's been on vacation," he said.

"For five months?"

"No, it just… Can we talk about this later?"

"I'll still come over and show your grandpa how to do the public records search though," offered Quincy.

"Uh… Yeah," said Tish. "That'll be fine. Maybe this weekend sometime."

"Sure," said Quincy.

"Meanwhile," said Nash, "stop posting things without people's permission. And if you're going to post, you'd better be damn sure they're true!"

"Sorry!" Quincy shrank down into her hoodie. "But the footage was really good!"

"That's not an excuse!" barked Nash.

"Sorry!" exclaimed Quincy again.

"I…" Nash looked at Tish and gestured to Quincy in disbelief.

"Yeah, I know," said Tish. "Remind me to have a talk with Claire about copyright and privacy laws. I didn't think I would have to yet, but they start so young these days. I guess it is better that she learns about it in the home though."

Nash gave her a look.

"No one appreciates my humor," said Tish.

"I would have laughed," said Quincy, "but I don't deal well with confrontation and I'm kind of freaked out right now."

Tish sighed. "I'm going back to the bar for more wine. Show up this weekend or I will rain down fiery retribution upon you and you will know my name is the Lord when I lay my vengeance upon thee, etcetera."

"You'll go Sam Jackson on my ass. Got it," said Quincy, nodding.

"What?" asked Nash.

"Pulp Fiction, 1994, Quentin Tarantino directing Samuel Jackson," supplied Tish. "The fake Bible quote."

"Ah," said Nash. "Right. Ezekiel 25:17. That always annoyed me."

"It's fake?" asked Quincy, looking surprised.

"Dead give-away is the mix of tenses," said Nash. "It shouldn't use *you* and *thee*."

"Huh," said Quincy.

"All right," said Tish. "And on that note, we'll leave you to your algae bloom."

Tish tugged Nash back toward the stairs. They didn't speak again until they were back at the parking area.

"Fifty thousand hits," said Tish, when they reached the Bronco. "Sheesh. I think that's more people than saw most of my movies. Possibly combined."

"I think that's more people than have ever seen me ever," said Nash. "Now I'm extremely uncomfortable that someone is going to judge my kissing technique."

"I judge you on that all the time," said Tish. "And you are totally winning."

Nash snorted. "Are you sure sending Ms. Peeping Tom over to Tobias is a good idea? I mean, I know we said we were telling him this weekend, but don't you think we might need to give him a day or two to recover?"

"He'll have had a day or two," said Tish and she couldn't keep the bitter note from creeping into her voice.

"What do you mean?"

Tish took a deep breath trying to decide what to say. "Granddad was around back with Coats and saw us kissing, so you know… cat's out of the bag."

"Is he super pissed at me?" asked Nash grimacing.

"Uh, no. Turns out you're fine. The real reason he doesn't want us to date is that he thinks I'm not good enough for you."

Nash barked out a surprised laugh and then realized that she wasn't laughing. "What?"

"Apparently he's fine with divorced people, and parents, and kids, and all the other crap he's been going on about. Apparently, he just doesn't think I should date you."

"Uh… what?"

Even under the harsh lighting of the Olga streetlight, Tish could tell that Nash was somewhere between flummoxed and flabbergasted.

"He thinks I'm going to get bored and then move on to the next adventure and leave you here. Apparently, I'm not *island material*."

"Oh," said Nash.

Tish waited for more, but nothing seemed to be forthcoming.

"Oh? That's it?"

"Well…"

Tish found herself backing away from Nash, trying to put more space between them.

"*Well* and *oh*? That's all you've got to say? You agree with him, don't you?" She knew her voice had become harsh and angry, like it always did when she didn't want to cry in public. "Is that why you haven't told your mom?"

"No!"

"Then why haven't you? I told *my* mom. I've told lots of other people."

"You have not."

"I told Detective Spring. I told Kyle and Amber. I told Matt. I just told Quincy. And now I've told Granddad. Which is what I thought you wanted. Only it turns out maybe not so much and you've just been guilt tripping me for the fun of it."

"No, that is not it! I didn't tell my mom because she can't keep a secret to save her life and I knew she'd blab it to Claire."

"OK, great. You have one reason. Now tell me you don't really agree with Granddad."

He opened his mouth, but no words came out.

"And there we go. That is just awesome."

"What do you want me to say? Yeah. OK? Yeah, sometimes I worry that you'll get bored and move on. It's not like your track record is great for sticking around. I don't like the idea of being your Plan B. And I love you and I love being with you, but I've kind of had to make myself OK with the idea that it might not be forever."

Tish stared at Nash. Her mind flipped through contingency plans of what to do. What was the solution? How was she supposed to prove to him… Tish stopped.

No. I'm not doing this. I don't do this.

"Then I think you should break up with me," she said.

"What?" Nash looked like she'd slapped him.

"I can't spend the rest of our relationship trying to prove that I'm serious about this. I can't and I won't."

"Tish," he reached out and she shook her head and backed up.

"No. I have to be… not here."

She turned around and walked back up the street. She heard Nash start to follow her and then heard the crackle of his radio and the garbled voice that ended with Nash's call sign. She didn't stop, but he did.

CHAPTER 20
SLOW DANCE PLAYLIST

Tish drove toward home and then realized that she didn't want to go there either and instead pulled into Reginald's. She wondered when it would start to just be Yearly Events instead of Reginald's. Probably never for her and Tobias. She parked the car and slowly climbed up onto the porch. She felt beat up. Like the time she'd been to six step aerobics classes in a row to try and lose five pounds for that one audition. She couldn't even remember what the audition had been for now. At the time it had seemed so vital. She had been thinner in LA. But she was stronger here.

She got to the front door of Reginald's and frowned. The motion light swept on and revealed a dark blot of something on the front door. Tish approached cautiously and eyed the disgusting mound of what looked like roadkill possum on the front mat. Someone had used the poor creature's blood to write STOP on the front door.

Tish let out a long sigh.

Because this is what I need tonight.

"Thanks Paxton. You couldn't just stick with *drop dead*? You thought roadkill would really send the message home?"

Could have been Dexter, I suppose. It's nastier than I would have expected from Paxton. So... probably Dexter.

Reluctantly, Tish threw her purse back in the car and then went around to the side of the house where the garden shed housed all the tools. She collected a shovel and gloves and a couple of the compostable food waste bags. She wasn't sure she should or could compost the poor possum, but she didn't think she could just fling it into the woods either. It somehow seemed disrespectful.

She scooped up the remains of the possum and then sighed again. The doormat was toast. She'd been thinking about getting a new one that was more cutesy and less functional anyway, but didn't want this to be the reason why.

She bundled up the remains in the bags and then gingerly carried it over to the garden shed. Then she went back for the doormat. After a moment's thought, she tucked them both into a cardboard box and put them into the trash can.

I can ask someone what the appropriate thing to do with them tomorrow.

Tish returned to the house and unlocked the door and then went into the kitchen for a sponge and a bucket of soapy water.

STOP.

Does everyone in my life have the same opinion? Stop doing that one thing. Or that thing. Or this other thing. Stop doing what you're doing. Stop being what you're being.

She tidied up and put all her equipment away. And found herself leaning on the sink and staring down the drain. She knew that drain from the inside out. She'd helped the plumber put the sink in place. She looked around the kitchen. She knew what every wall looked like behind the drywall and paint. One of the studs even had her initials carved in it. For once though, the familiarity didn't feel comforting. Instead, the house felt claustrophobic. Tish grabbed a blanket from the hall closet and went out back to the firepit.

Behind the house, Reginald had put in a patio with an arbor and a firepit. Tish had brought her own style to it with new furniture and a candle chandelier and romantic strings of lights. But it was Reginald who had plumbed the firepit for gas so that it lit with the flip of a switch. Tish was looking forward to an evening wedding where she could put out a s'mores buffet. Tish grabbed the remote and got the candles going with their realistic looking faux flicker and hit play on the slow dance playlist. It seemed reasonably depressing. There was probably at least one song on it she could cry to.

Tish sat on a lounge chair and stared out at the property. She was looking forward to a lot of things here. Or at least she had been.

Were they right? Did she get bored? Except, bored wasn't what they meant. Even when they were being mean they were both pulling their punches. They thought she gave up on things.

Am I the kind of person who gives up?

Tish leaned back and stared up at the stars. At least here she could see stars. She could leave Orcas. She was fully aware that the mainland and a real job were what waited for her if she failed. She'd updated her resume at least three times in the last nine months, but each time she'd managed to pull out a miracle to get the business back on track. Usually with the help of Tobias, Nash, or Sarah. She'd put so much work into this business. She'd thought that they'd all had her back, but she was out here on her own. Sarah was AWOL. Tobias was helping her because a business helped the island and Nash was being adventurous and having a fling with someone that he thought wasn't serious about him. And all of that hurt so bad she ought to want to cry. Instead, she just felt stomped flat.

Deflated.

She'd been so proud of herself for making so much progress and now that the business was finally taking flight, she was... Well, terrified, but elated too. And she had thought that they would be proud of her too.

Only they never thought I was going to go further.

Tish wasn't sure she was the kind of person who went further either. They were right—she never had in the past.

But I want to.

Tish pulled the blanket around her tighter and wished she'd been smart enough to bring a bottle of wine out from the kitchen.

I was counting on them to be the wind in my sails. I was believing because they were believing. If they don't believe I can do it. Do I?

Tish looked out to the gazebo that she'd spent an entire week pressure washing and painting. The fresh white paint and gold accents made it glow in the moonlight like a fairy house. She thought of the plumbing and electrical work she'd done in the kitchen. The business plan. The website. The trade shows she attended. She thought of Bowen, and Terry the florist, and the band, and all the people who had told her how happy they were to have jobs at Yearly Events. They all believed in the dream. Did she?

Hell yes, I do.

Yearly Events was a damn good idea. And maybe someone with more experience could be running it better or more efficiently or with fewer mistakes, but she was making it happen. She had made all of this happen. She had willed it into being. She had been lucky to have Reginald's beautiful property to start with, but that had been Reginald's dream—to leave a little piece of himself, and Orcas, behind and to make it last. That dream had seemed worthwhile to her and that was what she was doing. Damn them if they couldn't see that.

Tish sighed and settled back against the cushion that, like every other decision she'd made about Yearly Events, was a careful balance of style, durability, and cost. She'd dithered for three days over these cushions. They were good cushions.

This is my place. My dream. And I will make it happen whether they believe in it or not. I really wish they did believe, but this is happening with or without them.

Tish closed her eyes and tried to breathe away the tight feeling of tears in her throat. She woke up several hours later to the sound of a text alert. She picked up her phone and tried to make her eyes focus. The dew had set in and everything was damp and cold.

I WANT TO TALK TO YOU, BUT ROGER BURR FOUND WHERE IS WIFE HID THE SHOTGUN AND SHOT SOMEONE'S COW. I'M TIED UP HERE UNTIL AT LEAST TOMORROW MORNING. I DON'T WANT TO PUT THIS IN TEXT. I WANT TO TALK TO YOU, BUT I'M OUT OF OPTIONS. I DON'T WANT TO BREAK UP. I'M SORRY. PLEASE CALL ME TOMORROW.

Tish stumbled to her feet and went into the house, flipping off the fire as she went.

So much for the hope that he'd come swooping in to apologize as soon as he was off shift.

She read the text again. At least it included an *I'm sorry*. How much did she want to belabor this? What were her feelings on retribution?

WE CAN TALK TOMORROW, BUT YOU MADE ME FEEL LIKE YOU DON'T BELIEVE IN ME OR IN US. THE WHOLE POINT OF TELLING GRANDDAD WAS SO THAT WE COULD START BEING REAL. IF YOU THOUGHT I WAS GOING TO LEAVE, WHY BOTHER? WHY ARE YOU BOTHERING NOW?

The response was almost instantaneous.

BECAUSE I LOVE YOU.

As if that was the answer to all of her questions. She read her own text again. Maybe it was. She tapped in a reply and hit send.

I'LL CALL YOU TOMORROW. I'M TOO TIRED TO DO THIS RIGHT NOW.

Tish stumbled into the spare bedroom and stripped off her clothes, watching the phone for a response. Crawling into the bed, she stared one more time at Nash's text. Finally, she typed in a final message.

I LOVE YOU TOO.

Then she turned her phone to silent and put it face down on the bedside table.

CHAPTER 21

THURSDAY – THE TIMELINE

Tish woke up feeling hung over despite not having been drunk the night before. Maybe she was getting too old for falling asleep on lawn furniture and having that be OK. Eventually, she struggled out of the bed and into the shower, taking a moment to admire her caulking work on the shower surround. The plumbing had been one disaster after another and now there wasn't a fixture in the house that Tish hadn't seen on the inside and out. Once out of the shower, she started the coffee pot brewing and pulled some left over noshables out of the fridge for breakfast before sitting down with her binder.

But first there was the reconsideration of all of Nash's text from the previous night.

As apologies go it wasn't exactly top notch. It didn't address her main points of complaint. But on the other hand, it seemed like it was more of an appointment to apologize later, rather than an apology itself.

Which could be fine if there is an actual apology later.

Tish started on her checklist of event items. First there were the email confirmations to the bride and groom with cheerful exclamation points about seeing them in a few days.

I don't like the idea of being your Plan B.

Tish considered Nash's words from the previous night. Did she make him feel like he was Plan B? She wrinkled her nose in dislike at the coffee pot. He really was not a Plan B. Truthfully, he hadn't even been a Plan *A*. Nothing about her life on Orcas was any kind of plan. She had made plans for Yearly Events, but those were concrete, tiny, step-by-step plans that lived in a box and didn't relate to any sort of grand life scheme. Mostly she was flying by the seat of her pants into the great unknown and that included her relationship with Nash. Maybe that's why he didn't feel like she was taking it seriously—she hadn't mapped out their everything like she had mapped out the business.

But not knowing what I'm doing is half the fun. Half the intensely scary fun.

Tish looked back down at the binder and tried to focus. She texted Bowen with a reminder to show up later that afternoon to start set-up and to Terry to make sure the flowers were going to be on time. Then there was another text to Terry—a reminder to remind the flower delivery guy to allow for extra ferry time.

This time when she looked up from the binder she found herself staring at the walls. The beautiful walls, hung with beautiful drywall by Nash.

OK, so I can address the Plan B thing. No one should feel like anyone's second choice. But after that, he will need to do some serious apologizing. And I will listen to what he says because I do love him and adults do that. They listen to each other and I am having an adult relationship where I don't just cut people off and go drink.

Tish stared at the drywall again.

Also, I don't want to. I want the giant stupid head to get this right because he's my Mr. Right. Maybe I should call him now?

I'M AWAKE AND MOSTLY FUNCTIONAL. CALL NOW?

STILL FILLING OUT PAPERWORK ON THE COW AND RONNY SAYS HE SPRAINED HIS THUMB WHEN HE TRIPPED IN A GOPHER HOLE LAST NIGHT, SO I'M DOING ALL THE TYPING.

Tish laughed out loud, her shoulders shaking as she ate another chocolate covered strawberry.

Poor baby must be having the worst twenty-four hours ever. Am I supposed to have this much sympathy for him while I'm mad at him? I don't think that's normal.

OK, WELL, THEN I'LL CONTINUE TO BE MAD AT YOU UNTIL LATER.

MEANWHILE, WHAT DO YOU KNOW ABOUT MILES SINGER OVER IN DEER HARBOR?

I'M NOT SURE YOU'RE ALLOWED TO PUMP ME FOR INFORMATION WITHOUT RESOLVING INTERPERSONAL ISSUES.

Tish tousled her hair and lowered her neckline, then snapped some selfies while nibbling a strawberry. She titled the best one THIS IS MY MORNING, before hitting send.

MY MORNING HATES YOUR MORNING. NOISE ORDINANCE. IL-LEGAL DUMPING. DUI. UNLICENSED VEHICLE. BOATING WITHOUT PROPER EQUIPMENT. PROBABLE METH DEALER AND ALL-AROUND JERK. STAY AWAY FROM HIM. HE'S DONE TOO MUCH OF HIS OWN PRODUCT. HE'S STARTING TO GET TO THE CRAZY STAGE.

CRAZY ENOUGH TO KILL PENELOPE?

SEEMS UNLIKELY, Nash texted, BUT MAYBE. WHATEVER YOU'RE DOING, JUST CALL SPRING FIRST, OK?

I am mad at you so I don't feel obligated to respond, but on the other hand I don't want you to panic.

ALREADY TALKED TO HIM LAST NIGHT. HE'S COMING TO THE IS-LAND TO POKE AROUND TODAY. I WANT TO BE PREPPED UP SO I CAN LOOK ONE STEP AHEAD OF HIM AS USUAL. I'M WORKING AT REGI-NALD'S TODAY. PROBABLY AT LEAST UNTIL AFTER LUNCH.

There. Now you know where to find me, but we don't actually have an appointment.

I HAVE TO GO OVER TO THE MAINLAND TO GET FOOD FOR CLAIRE'S VISIT NEXT WEEK. I'LL COME FIND YOU AFTER.

Tish looked at her phone in disbelief. Admittedly, the man was short on sleep, had probably already booked his ferry reservation weeks ago, and, yes, the Island Market was more commonly known as the Island Mark-up, but...

I am more important than the damn groceries!

I wonder if he can get me some vitamins at the Costco. Wait, no, we are not glossing over this.

WHY AM I THE ONE WHO'S NOT SERIOUS, BUT YOU'RE THE ONE

going grocery shopping?

The text left her phone before she could properly think through the ramifications. She stared at her phone waiting for a response. The message popped up that Nash was typing and then it went away again. Apparently the text was epic, because the message fluttered off and on for another two minutes.

Because Ray asked if he could come along last week and I couldn't figure out a way to tell him no without talking about us. Call me crazy, but I didn't feel like explaining to my co-workers that we were dating and fighting in the same conversation.

Tish read the message and put the phone down so it wouldn't have the *Tish is typing* message while she considered what to say.

I will be over as soon as I get back.

You'd better.

That seemed fairly clear on her feelings in a passive aggressive way.

Understood.

And that seemed pretty clear on the promise of apology. Not that it made her feel better. Less anxious possibly, but not necessarily better. She went back to her binder so she could stop checking her phone.

She had completed her visual inspection of the tables when her phone burped out a text.

Spring is on his way over. Says he has the autopsy report.

Tish eyed her grandfather's text. It was notably lacking in apologies or invitations. It was two bald statements of fact. On the other hand, it was a text. From her grandfather. That meant that he would have had to turn on his cell phone and then figure out the texting app. That felt like some level of concession right there, possibly also a miracle, or an act of God.

Be over in a few minutes.

That was also notably short on information, but it seemed like an even level of concession.

What if Spring gets there first and asks Granddad questions?

Tish hesitated for a moment and then added a second text.

KYLE DID SOME DIGGING. PAXTON WAS WORKING ON A DAY SAIL-
ING TRIP UNTIL THREE AND DEXTER WAS PROBABLY COOKING METH
WITH A GUY NAMED MILES SINGER UNTIL ONE. I TOLD SPRING, BUT
TOLD HIM TO STUFF IT WHEN HE ASKED FOR SOURCES.

Tish corrected a typo and then hit send. She might be in the
midst of an argument with Tobias, but there was no reason to let the
Yearly team down because of that.

NOTED.

*Super awesome text Granddad. Love the use of 'thank you'. Oh, wait,
not.*

Tish finished her table count in an annoyed mood and then
locked up and drove the quarter mile back to her grandfather's house.

Spring was just getting out of his unmarked cruiser when Tish
arrived, and he waited as she parked.

"You know everyone can still tell that's a police car, right?"
asked Tish.

"Not everyone," said Spring. "Just the criminals."

"I can tell," said Tish.

"Exactly my point," said Spring.

Tish eyed him. "Fine. I'll give you that one," she admitted.

"You're going to give it to me? No, I earned that."

"It's early," said Tish going to the door.

"Get your head in the game, Yearly," said Spring, clearly enjoying himself.

The front door opened, and Tish saw Tobias on the porch with
his coffee cup. "I'm tagging Granddad in," she said. "You deal with
him." She brushed passed Tobias and went into the kitchen.

"You can't tag team," complained the detective following her in.
"I don't have anyone to tag with. Where's Nash when I need him?"

"I believe Tish has already drafted him to her team," said Tobias sourly.

"Yeah, I heard," said Spring, cheerfully, and mimed a punch into her shoulder. "Good for you two!"

"Uh-huh," said Tobias. Spring caught the whiff of disapproval and looked around in confusion. "You want coffee?" asked Tobias before Spring could speak.

"Sure, but can you put some cream and sugar in it this time? I think last time I tried your coffee I was doing the jitterbug for about eight hours.

"Well, it ain't for pansies," said Tobias.

"I'm not sure it's for humans, let alone plants," said Spring.

Tobias glared at him.

"He's on a streak, Granddad," said Tish, pouring herself a glass of juice from the fridge. "We'd better be on our toes."

"Uh-huh," said Tobias, pouring another cup of coffee and shoving it at Spring. "With-its," he said, pointing to the tray of creamer and sugar on the bar.

"I *am* on a streak," said Spring, doctoring his coffee. "Come on, let's go look at your case board and talk autopsy."

Tish looked at Tobias who shrugged.

"All right," said Spring, settling into the recliner that usually belonged to Tish and pulling out his phone. Tish checked out the timeline board and saw that Tobias had added her information on Paxton and Dexter. "So first off, the coroner has reached an official conclusion of murder by drowning. However, we believe that she was first struck with an object and then held under water most likely in the bathtub based on the indentation in her skull and the evidence we collected from the search warrant and the water in her lungs—"

"How do you know it was the bathtub?" asked Tobias, interrupting.

"Soap compounds in the water in her lungs matched the shampoo we recovered with the search warrant. And we have a high degree of certainty that she was struck with this."

He held up his phone and Tish and Tobias leaned closer to look at the photo.

"All right," said Tobias. "I give. What the hell is it?"

"Ditto," said Tish.

"Oh, sorry. Try the pull-back shot." He flipped to a different picture and both Tish and Tobias made understanding noises. "It's a vintage block and tackle that Penelope was intending to use to rig a clothesline from the bathroom where she hand-washed delicate items to the tree outside the window. She'd apparently had it sitting in the bathroom for months."

"So someone clocked her with it and held her under water in the bathtub. Then they put the block back on the shelf and drug her body outside?" asked Tobias with a frown.

"That is the look of it," said Spring.

"But why?" murmured Tish, glancing back at their board of suspects. "So it would look more like it had been done by a stranger?"

"That's my guess," said Spring. "The night you found the body, Nash noted that the backdoor lock on the sliding glass door was non-functional and scratched, possibly as though someone had tried to break in. However, Paxton says the door was never locked, so he doesn't know when that happened. He says he always figured that if someone wanted to steal their crappy stuff they were just going to do it, so why have to replace doors and locks to boot?"

Tish scratched her head thoughtfully as Spring continued talking.

"We assumed he was lying because as a known drug dealer it would seem like he wanted to protect his stash."

"Except that Penelope wouldn't let him keep his stuff in the house and all his friends knew it," said Tish. "Although, now that I'm thinking about it, Azalea said they always locked the door."

"Differing reports," said Spring, nodding. "That's one of the things I'll be chasing down today. But let's get to the interesting stuff. Stuff that affects the timeline."

"All right," said Tobias, sitting down in his recliner. "What have you got?"

"Now, we don't know whether or not this was intentional, but due to the location by the pond, Penelope's body was in full sunlight for the entire day enhanced by the reflected heat of the white house and protected nature of the backyard area with the wind break provided by the trees. That kept the body temperature artificially elevated for an extended period of time."

"My time of death is wrong," blurted out Tish spinning to look at the board.

"What's the actual time of death?" demanded Tobias leaning forward.

"Somewhere between seven to eleven in the morning," said Spring, sounding smug.

"It couldn't have been Paxton," said Tish. "He was with his girlfriend all night and then took the nine o'clock ferry over."

"There's a little wiggle room there after nine," said Tobias.

"I'll be looking into that," said Spring, "and I've got someone having a word with the girlfriend. It also opens Matt Jones back up as a suspect. You didn't meet him until ten."

"It's not him," said Tish, eying the board. "He's opening a pot dispensary business. He's walking the straight and narrow. Also, he doesn't have motive."

"He might," said Spring, "if he's the father of Penelope's baby. You were right about that too. She was about nine weeks along. A guy trying to start a legitimate business might be a little bit ticked off to find out some girl he's barely been seeing got knocked up."

"He wasn't seeing her," said Tish.

"Don't have to be dating to get someone pregnant. Inquiries will be made," said Spring primly.

"Uh-huh," said Tish, which made Tobias laugh softly into his coffee cup.

Tish went over to the timeline board and started to add tick marks then she stepped back and stared at the board, while tapping her chin with the end of the marker.

"I think the window of opportunity is smaller than seven to eleven," said Tobias. "The Hydrangea girl—"

"Azalea," corrected Tish without bothering to look over at him.

"Right. She arrived at eight-thirty." Tish pointed to one of the tick marks.

8:30A.M. A. ARRIVES AT R.

Tish could now translate that to mean *Azalea arrives at Reginald's*.

"And she said she'd talked to Penelope on her way over. So we know that the window is actually somewhere between then and eleven."

"Mm," said Spring. "So we need to confirm Paxton's arrival on the nine o'clock ferry and when he arrived at work. Then find out what ferry Matt Jones came in on, although, that's not conclusive because I know he owns a boat of his own. And then nail down what's going on with Dexter Drue."

"I looked into the lawsuit, by the way," said Tobias, taking a judicious sip of his coffee. "Called up Penelope's parents. They're in Guam, not Hawaii. In case anyone is wondering. They're flying back at the end of the month for the service."

"Oh, that's good," said Tish. "I was worried that no one was going to have one."

I was going to talk to Azalea this weekend, but that was going to be awkward. Glad I won't have to.

"Paxton's working on it apparently," said Tobias. "However, the reason that Dexter Drue is not listed as a plaintiff on the lawsuit or as an owner of the commune property was that he was arrested for assaulting another commune member and ex-communicated right before they purchased the property. Then he got out of jail and apologized a year or two later, but he was only allowed back on probationary grounds. General commune consensus was that he did not do his share of the work and shouldn't get added to the paperwork. Then the government took over and everyone thought it was a moot point until the lawsuit. But they all chipped in money for the lawyers and Dexter never did. So, once again, the general feeling was that Dexter should not reap the rewards."

"I looked up the arrest record," said Spring. "It was a fight over some money that Dexter apparently stole from the commune petty cash."

"I'm getting the impression that Dexter isn't really commune material," said Tish.

"The Drues agree with you. Or at least they said something about his chakras not being open and his self-centered id still needing to develop. Which I'm assuming means the same thing."

"Dexter is my best bet right now," said Tish.

Spring and Tobias appeared to ruminate on this.

"You think he wanted Penelope's lawsuit money and then he got mad and killed her?" asked Spring.

"It's my current theory," said Tish.

"Hm," said the detective, tucking his phone away. "Well, we shall have to see what we can find out. I'm off to ask people questions. That means the two of you need to stay out of my way from here on out. No interfering in police business."

"Wouldn't dream of it," said Tobias serenely.

Spring skewered Tobias with a glare, but relaxed when he didn't get a response. Tish walked him to the door expecting some sort of last minute lecture.

"You're keeping an eye on him, right?" whispered Spring as they reached the porch.

"Keeping an eye on who?" Tish whispered back.

"Tobias! And his dementia."

"He doesn't have dementia! He's an annoying pain in the ass, but he's got all his marbles."

"Sane people don't get arrested for being drunk and disorderly on a Thursday morning! I mean, he seems fine now, but you should get him checked out."

"He had a physical like three months ago. He's fine. He had his reasons. Move on to doing something useful."

"Reasons?" demanded Spring, returning to his normal volume in full skepticism.

"Yes," snapped Tish. "Now go away."

She slammed the door and went back into the den.

"Wanted to ask about my dementia?" asked Tobias as she flung herself into her recliner.

"Yes. I'm really tired of people asking about you having dementia. Also, I found the blogger and she's going to come by this weekend and show you how to do a public records search or request or whatever."

"Well, that's nice," said Tobias looking pleasantly surprised. "Who is she?"

"Quincy Teller."

"Marv and Sandra's kid?"

Tish dredged up her half-remembered conversation with Cokie at the bookstore. "Yes," she said nodding. "I believe so."

I really need to get someone to put all of Granddad's files in a database. He may not have dementia, but I can't run a search on his memory banks.

"So she knows about computers and things?"

"Yes. Apparently. She's helping Cokie with the bookstore website and Neil with photography, so I'm going with yes, to computers and things."

"Could be useful," said Tobias, thoughtfully.

"Yes, well, she's home from college and keeping herself entertained by publishing gossip and flying drones. Also, as a result, fifty-thousand people may have seen Nash and I kissing on YouTube. FYI. I'm assuming at least one of those fifty-thousand lives on the island and may ask you about it."

"Good gravy," said Tobias, looking mildly perturbed. "Where *did* you go last night?"

"Olga bar."

"Some of my best work was done in bars. Do you really think Dexter did it?"

"There're problems with the theory," said Tish. "But I didn't want Spring to ask me anything further about Matt."

"Why shouldn't he ask you about Matt?"

"Because Matt told me that he ran into Penelope *two or three months ago.*"

"Hm," said Tobias. "That's the right time frame for Spring's theory."

"I'm aware," said Tish.

"Also," said Tobias, "one of the problems with the Dexter theory is the underwear."

"What do you mean?"

"I'm not saying our family is a pattern of normalcy."

"I don't think anyone would say that," agreed Tish.

"But I can't really imagine you standing around in your underwear in front of me. Even if we were in an argument."

"We *are* in an argument," said Tish. "We just haven't got back to it yet."

"We'll get there," said Tobias. "We're working the case right now. But my point is, the girl was in her undies. Unless he snuck up and popped her with the block—"

"She was hit from the front," said Tish.

"Right. Which means she was talking to the person and that person smacked her on the noggin. That says to me that whoever she was talking to, she was close to them. I'd give you maybe the brother, but the uncle? Doesn't seem likely. An ex-lover though? That seems probable."

"Matt didn't say anything about playing backseat bingo with her," said Tish. "He just said they talked. He said he ran into her at some bar in Anacortes and she came over and talked to him. I'm not sure he'd volunteer that information if he'd killed her."

"Agreed," said Tobias. "But it's concerning, particularly with the time frame opening up."

"Yes," said Tish.

They both stared at the board and after a moment Tish took out a phone and sent out a text.

"Texting Nash?"

"No, I'm texting Jordan who was handling the valet services last weekend. I want to know if Matt's Mr. Sunshine car was at the wedding. If it was, then that means Matt came over on the ferry and that starts to close the window of opportunity back up."

"Mm," said Tobias nodding. "That would put it down to between eight-thirty and nine-thirty to get back to a ten o'clock meeting with me at the Orcas Hotel."

"And depending on the ferry schedule we might be able to narrow it down even further. Meanwhile, what do you think about going to talk to Miles Singer?"

"The meth dealer Dexter was cooking with on Saturday? I think we should because Spring's going to start with Paxton and Dexter and Matt and probably won't make it around to Miles for quite some time."

"I don't suppose you happen to know where he lives?"

"Deer Harbor. Pulled his address after you texted."

"Great. Can we argue now?"

"If you want to. But I'm not sure what the point would be since you're going to date Nash no matter what I say."

"Yes, I am!"

And no, I'm not telling you that Nash and I are fighting.

"And it probably isn't any of my business what two adults do anyway."

"No, it isn't!"

"All right then."

Tish stared at Tobias in fury.

"No! No, not all right then. I want you to be happy for me, damn it!"

"Oh. Well, that seems a bit of a stretch."

"When do I not do things that are a stretch? Seriously. You think I'm going to quit, but when have I quit? Yeah, I quit acting, but that wasn't because I didn't love it. It was because I failed. I tried and I failed."

"You didn't fail," said Tobias sensibly.

"I couldn't fully support myself at it. And it wasn't getting better. So yeah, I quit. I quit one thing. And now it's like you think I'm a quitter. I work really hard and I make stuff happen."

"Yes, you do," he agreed.

"And I genuinely think I can succeed at this business. And even if the business fails, I don't see why that means my relationship will fail. Nash is a wonderful human being and he will love me even if the business bombs."

"But will you love him if the business bombs?"

"Yes! I mean, it would super suck if…" Tish trailed off and stared at Tobias in frustration. "No. You don't get to do that. I'm not playing hypotheticals where we argue about whose version of the future is more right because that's a conversation that I will never be allowed to win. You aren't right about this. And even if you are, that's not something you get to dictate. Nash and I are adults. It's not like we haven't had those same fears, but we think it's worth the risk. I love him and I'm sorry if that doesn't align with your master plan, but you need to get the hell over it or I'm moving out."

Tobias took a sip of his coffee and rubbed his chin, giving off the scritchity, static-y sound of stubble being disturbed.

"Well?" demanded Tish, when the silence had gone for a while.

"I'm pondering."

"Trying to figure out how to admit you were wrong without sounding like it?"

"You are your grandmother's child. I swear, I don't see how you're related to me at all."

"Orneriness," said Tish.

"Oh, well, that's true. But here's the thing Tishkins—I want you to be happy. Are you really going to be happy here on the island?"

"Granddad, no one thinks this is weirder than me, but I am happier here than I have been anywhere. I'm not saying it's perfect or that I don't periodically want to run off to the city, but there's breathing room here and space to make things happen and people seem excited to build something instead of tear it down. And even if Nash and I break up, I don't think I'm going anywhere. I like it here. Why do you think I started the business in the first place?"

"You weren't supposed to stay," said Tobias. "You have never committed to staying. You haven't even redecorated your room!"

"Well, I've been a tad busy! Also, I didn't know there was supposed to be a formal announcement. Do you want me to release a statement on the Grapevine?"

"Works for me," he said, his eyes twinkling over the rim of his mug.

"Whatever," said Tish. They sat in silence for a few minutes and Tish stared angrily at the board. "I'm going to go change. I was going to finish up a bit more at Reginald's, but it seems like we ought to beat feet over to Miles Singer's."

"Yeah, probably ought to in case Spring gets ahead of us or scares Singer into running off."

"Uh-huh," said Tish, heading for the stairs. "Back in a few."

CHAPTER 22

MILES SINGER

The home occupied by Miles Singer looked too nice to belong to a meth dealer. It was a cute little A-frame that had a cheerful blue door and, like a lot of homes on Orcas, it was set well back from the road and was hard to approach surreptitiously. Tish and Tobias parked in front of the house and stood staring. There was the general chirping of birds, but no other noises.

"We're sure he lives here? It looks… cute."

"His sister lives in Seattle," said Tobias. "It belonged to their parents. She pays for the yard and exterior maintenance. He's supposed to take care of the interior. But she never comes to visit, so I don't think she knows what he's doing."

"Nash said he violated a noise ordinance. The nearest neighbor is at least a full acre away. How loud do you have to be to get a noise complaint called in at that distance?"

"Pretty loud," said Tobias. "Nash say anything else?"

"Said he did too much of his own product and I should stay away from him."

Tobias paused and raised an eyebrow at her. "Aren't you two all shacked up and what not?"

"No," said Tish. "I don't think living together right now would be a good idea. We can't go straight from telling Claire we're dating to moving in. That's a terrible plan."

"No, I mean, you're…" He gestured in a floppy circular motion.

"On a Ferris wheel? Whirlpool? Ooh! In the dryer?"

"In the dryer? Really? No. You're a couple."

"Yes. I'm not sure what that has to do with the price of eggs, but yes, this is true."

"Well, isn't he going to be hacked off if you go around doing things he tells you not to do?"

"Probably, but that's never stopped me before."

Also, we're currently not speaking, so he's not going to know.

He stared at her some more. "And once again I feel like your entire generation is doing dating wrong."

"Well, don't you want to go talk to Miles?" asked Tish.

"Yeah, but vis-a-vis your relationship, that might not be the best plan. I mean, you shouldn't go around intentionally pissing off your loved one."

"Ah," said Tish. "See where you've got it wrong is thinking that Nash's resistance to me doing something is a valid argument. He just doesn't want me to get hurt."

"That *is* a valid argument."

"Do you think I'm going to get hurt?"

"No, or I wouldn't have brought you."

"So, is your argument invalid?"

"Of course not, but usually the romantic interest gets top vote."

"You are wildly incorrect," said Tish. "The only person who gets a vote is me. In the land of *What Tish Does* there is no democracy. It's a benevolent dictatorship run by yours truly. And Queen Me says I'm going to go talk to Miles Singer."

"Huh."

"Bodily agency and free will—ain't it a bitch when women start running their own lives?"

"I don't like the *B* word," said Tobias tartly. "It's disrespectful."

"Granddad, I love you."

"Well, I love you too Tishkins, but I'm not sure what that's got to do with inappropriate language."

"Very true. And to clarify, I do value and listen to Nash's input. He's a smart guy with lots of good information who gives insanely sensible advice. But I don't feel the need to do whatever he tells me.

And in pursuit of justice for Penelope, I extra don't feel the need."

"Well, that's reasonable," admitted Tobias. "Got to have priorities."

"Exactly. Now how do you want to do this? Go poke around, ask him questions and maybe break in if he's not there? Because I have to say, he doesn't really look home."

"That's the general idea," said Tobias. "I hope he's not here. I've been brushing up on my lock picking skills and ordered a new set. Wouldn't mind putting them to the test." He patted his jacket pocket proudly.

"Really? That's awesome. How do I learn that?"

"YouTube, Tish," said Tobias, giving her a look and shaking his head.

"Oh," said Tish.

I just got schooled on YouTube use by a seventy-nine- year old. Really not sure how that happened.

They rounded a large red cedar tree that was fat enough to probably be over fifty years old and surveyed the backyard. Tobias walked carefully on the slick brown carpet of ancient needles. Tish was pleased to see that physical therapy had done wonders for her grandfather's balance. He seemed to be managing much better than he had when she had first arrived on the island.

They turned the corner on the house and stopped. From the front, the house was neat and cheerful, but the back was a different story entirely. The backyard looked like a blue tarp burial ground for a serial killer. The lawn was brown and dead in spots and a pile of bleach bottles spilled out from under one of the tarps. There was a choking acrid stench in the air that made Tish want to cover her mouth and nose.

Taking out her phone she snapped a few pictures of the scene and then the bleach bottles.

"What're you doing?" demanded Tobias.

"The guy is clearly cooking meth," said Tish. "And if he's not then he's improperly disposing of chemicals."

"You gonna rat him out to Nash?"

"No. Because then I'd have to testify or something and we're probably trespassing. Also, I don't want to get the reputation that we're snitches or people will stop talking to us. I'm going to send the pictures to Quincy Teller and get her to post them on the Grapevine. Which should cause the police to act."

Tobias looked thoughtful. "Doesn't Nash know who she is?"

"Yeah, but she's got an email address on the blog for news tips. I'll create a new address at the library and send it from there. That will give them both plausible deniability."

"Ah. Nice," said Tobias.

"All right, let's go up to the house. See if he's home."

Tish and Tobias approached the back door. Like the Yearly home, the back of the house was made up of tall panes of glass. Unlike the Yearly home, the double paned windows had clearly not been updated from their original installation and were now cloudy and spotted with condensation between the panes.

Peering through the fog Tish could see a skinny man stretched out on an orange and yellow floral patterned velveteen couch. He was shirtless and even through the warped windows she could count his ribs.

"Are we sure he's breathing?" whispered Tish.

"No," said Tobias, raising his hand to his eyes and leaning against the glass. "Not really." Tish looked at their reflection in the glass and the prone figure on the other side. Her grandfather was wearing one of Sarah's joke Christmas presents—a Hawaiian shirt. Sarah had gifted them each with one so that they could properly play Magnum P.I.

"OK, what do we do now?" asked Tish.

"You keep a look out and I'll poke around under the tarps," suggested Tobias.

"OK," agreed Tish. "But wave at me if you find anything cool because I'll take—"

They both froze as Tish's phone began to cheerfully ring out the sounds of *Best Friend* by Sofi Tukker. Tish gave a little squeak of panic, grabbed for her phone, nearly dropped it, recovered and finally swiped to *dismiss*. Inside, Miles gave a snort, and rolled onto his side, blinking at them.

"Or I guess, now we're knocking on the door," said Tobias, glaring at her.

"Sorry," said Tish. "Sarah hasn't called me in weeks. How am I supposed to know she'd call now?"

The phone began to ring again, and Tish glared at Sarah's image on her phone.

"Well, aren't you going to answer it?" growled Tobias, stomping up to the back door and knocking.

"What?" demanded Tish, picking up. Inside, Miles roused himself and lurched to his feet.

"What do you mean, *what?*" retorted Sarah. "I'm trying to talk to you. I know you're not working right now. Pick up the phone. You don't get to be mad at me if you don't actually talk to me."

"Well, I'm sorry I don't have a very important job doing very important stuff, but I'm just out here trying to solve a murder, and this really isn't the best time for me."

"Murder? Tish, seriously, what is going on?"

"That was sarcasm, Tish," said Tobias. "You weren't actually supposed to answer."

Tish shot him an angry glare as on the other side of the glass Miles staggered toward the door.

"Well, maybe if you hadn't been ditching out on me for a solid month then you'd know. I thought you were like my partner and I had to do my entire first wedding on my own. You didn't even like my Instagram pic of the set-up!"

Miles disappeared momentarily—hidden by the wooden door.

"I did!"

"Three days later!"

"Yeah, I'm sorry, but I've had a little bit of difficulty."

"Oh, are your fingers broken?" demanded Tish, sarcastically.

"No," said Sarah, "not exactly. But—"

The back door swung open and Miles stepped out with a shot-gun. "I don't like Jehovah's Witnesses," he said and racked the slide.

"Gotta go," said Tish and hung up.

"No one likes the JWs," said Tobias, one hand going to rest casually on his hip. "Most boring people on the planet. Always ring the bell when you're trying to nap."

"No, that's Mormons," disagreed Miles.

"Them too," said Tobias.

"I like Quakers," said Tish. Both men turned to stare at her. "I hear their church is basically sitting quietly with each other. That seems nice."

"That's not..." Miles seemed thrown off by their refusal to be scared or argumentative. "Who the hell are you people?" he demanded, rallying.

"Tobias Yearly," said Tobias. "That's Tish. We live over out toward Olga."

"OK," said Miles, looking perplexed.

"We're friends of the Drues. We're worried about Dexter."

"What? Why? What happened?" Miles' eyes widened to an extreme. The whites showing around the entire iris of his eyes. "He didn't get wacked too, did he?"

"No, don't think so," said Tobias.

"You don't *think* so!" The man's eyes got even wider and his hands seemed to tense around the shotgun that he was still pointing firmly at them.

"He is fine," said Tish, firmly. "Totally alive."

Miles relaxed slightly and breathed out a sigh of relief.

"But," began Tish.

"But!" The shotgun swung her way.

"Well, we're worried that the police are going to try and pin Penelope's death on Dexter," said Tish. "Maybe you could point that someplace else?"

The shotgun drifted toward the floor but didn't move in a completely southerly direction.

"Why would they think that? Penelope was the only one who would have given him some of that damn commune money. He went on and on about it."

"Penelope had a soft heart," agreed Tish.

"She was an easy touch."

"You touched her!" Tish found herself jerking back in horror.

"No, she was easy to get money off of! I'm not a pervert!"

"Oh. That's better."

"Not a lot," murmured Tobias. "You and Dexter were hanging out last Saturday, right?"

"Maybe," said Miles. "What day is it now?"

"Thursday," said Tish.

"Oh. I been up for a few days. Um… Yeah, I called him last Friday I think because then he came over and we watched *Friday*. He crashed out in the den and then the next morning…" Miles petered out and eyed them suspiciously. "We did stuff. Who did you say you was again? Are you cops?"

"Not cops," said Tobias. "Cops have to tell you they're cops if you ask them. So you know we're not cops."

That is so not true. I can't believe he just blatantly lied like that!

"Oh. Right," said Miles nodding.

"Anyway, we just wanted to make sure that Dexter was with you," said Tish. "And now that we know that, we'll go away."

"No," said Miles, suddenly raising the shotgun. "I think you ought to stay here while I call Dexter."

"Well, suit yourself," said Tobias. "But I mean, the police are probably tapping everyone's phones. That's why we came over in person."

"Shit!" exclaimed Miles, looking around the yard as if expecting police to leap over the fence at any moment. "Leave! And don't come back!" He shoved the shotgun at them aggressively.

"Leaving!" agreed Tish and scooted backwards.

She and Tobias left the yard at what was a brisk pace for Tobias but felt far too slow to Tish. She found herself attempting to calculate how far buckshot would go without actually knowing anything about buckshot.

"Well," said Tish, as they got back in the car, "that was disappointing."

"I don't want Matt to have done it," said Tobias, easing a holster from under his shirt. Tish found herself glaring at the old 1911 pistol inside it.

Might have mentioned that you were carrying Granddad!

"I was really pulling for him to get on the legal side of things," continued Tobias. "The rivalry between him and Pax is a stretch and being the baby daddy—dang it, girl, I don't like that you got me saying that—seems unlikely. But if Pax and Dex are out of the picture, who else do we have?"

CHAPTER 23
LIES AND OTHER TRUTHS

When they returned home, Tobias pulled on his rubber boots and stomped out into the yard with Coats frisking at his heels. And after a while Tish couldn't think of anything else to do, so she went to see what he was up to. She found him around the side of the house, pulling items out of the cellar. As a child she'd always been fascinated by the cellar which was exactly like the one in *The Wizard of Oz*, with slanty little doors and stairs leading down under the house to a dank little cave of a room.

"Ah," said Tish, peering down into the dark hole. "Eleanor's jam project must still be on."

"Yes," he said, leaning on the edge of the stairs.

"Did you ever figure out why she's making jam?"

"Apparently, there is some sort of old school friend who donates jam to homeless people or something and makes a thing out of it. And Eleanor's finally had it up to here and plans to out donate her. Or something."

"I don't think you can donate homemade jam," said Tish.

"You can't," said Tobias, and then cleared his throat. "Which may be why I volunteered the kitchen over at Reginald's for the ladies to make jam in, since you've got it certified as a commercial kitchen by the State and what not. The ladies in Eleanor's group are all getting their food handler cards."

"Oh," said Tish. "Huh. Sure, I guess. Probably on a Monday or Tuesday would be best."

"I just told them they had to talk to you about scheduling. However, they need someplace to store the jam while they get the collection together. They're planning on donating about a pallet load from what I can tell and this place really isn't ready. So Coats and I have been working on cleaning out the cellar. I probably don't need moldy camping gear anyway."

"You know, it's not a bad idea. I bet I could rent out the kitchen between events to small businesses who want to do small batch edibles."

Tobias raised an eyebrow.

"What? Passive income is my dream. The more money I can get for doing less work the better. And the winter is going to be slow for events until I can commit to a remodel on the barn. I was planning on Air B-n-Bing the house, but this is another good option too. I wonder how I go about advertising it?"

"Tell Eleanor and Elayne to tell everyone else."

"Good call. I can probably tell the Economic Development Office too. They might be able to connect me to people. Want some help down there?"

"No, not really. The dog already takes up too much space."

"Yeah, but if I don't help you I have to go do my own work over at Reginald's."

Tobias chuckled. "Sorry, kiddo."

Tish sighed. "Maybe I'll come up with something brilliant about who killed Penelope while I count chairs."

"And maybe I'll come up with something while loading the truck."

They looked at each other and then shrugged. "Good luck to us," said Tish as she returned to the house.

But counting chairs was not productive and the weather had turned overcast and Tish found herself obsessively checking the forecast for the weekend. She had purchased tents on the assumption that rain was bound to happen sooner or later at one of her events, but if she needed Bowen to set them up she needed to make that call at the earliest possible moment. After chairs there was the bookkeeping and e-mails, including a very promising lead for an August wedding from a panicked bride whose venue had unexpectedly cancelled. But even accounting with the totting up of numbers and projections and the what-ifs couldn't hold her attention. She began to trudge back toward home and tried not to check her watch.

Nash should be here soon.

She felt a flutter of nerves in her stomach and took deep breaths as she walked. There was no reason to be nervous. She'd been pretty clear in person and in text. Nash was a smart guy. He was bound to say all the right things.

Her phone rang, startling her and she jumped in the middle of the road like a deer seeing a dog. With trepidation, she saw it was Nash calling. Reluctantly, she swiped right.

"Hi?"

"Tish…"

Oh shit. That's not a good tone.

"Yeah," said Tish bracing herself for the worst.

"I just missed the ferry and Ray is freaking out. I'm going to have to drive us directly to work when I get back."

"Oh."

So much for being a priority. I guess grocery shopping comes before our relationship.

"I can come over first thing tomorrow."

"Why?" snapped Tish. "I'm sure you have a vitally important home repair errand that could take priority."

"And maybe you just need more time to go interview meth dealers."

Tish froze mid-stride.

"I know you didn't talk to Granddad."

"What did you do? Go talk to Miles Springer? Didn't I specifically tell you that he was crazy and not to do that? Sarah is freaking out. She keeps going on about how you hate her. Or you're going to hate her. I don't know."

"You're both overreacting," said Tish, said stretching out her legs in long angry strides.

"She said it sounded like he cocked a shotgun! How is this over-reacting?"

"Well, gosh, that is such a lot of caring for two people who can't be bothered to show up."

"We missed the ferry because Ray insisted on waiting for his photos to be developed! This is not my fault."

"You went grocery shopping instead of talking to me!"

"Claire is going to want food! I literally have a half a block of cheese and a pack of hotdogs in my fridge because all I've been doing is sneaking out with you and working the damn night shift all month."

"You didn't have to leave the island! We have food here!"

"Since when are you a *we*?"

"What?"

"Since when are you a part of this island?"

"Since I started dating you, you asshole!"

Tish hung up the phone and resisted the urge to throw the phone down and stomp on it. It noticeably didn't immediately ring with a call back from Nash. Tish tried to stretch her neck and thought about calling Sarah.

I'm done adulting for today. I already had to talk to Granddad and do accounting. I just can't take talking to Sarah too. I'll do it tomorrow.

She turned down the driveway to home and Coats bounded out to meet her. She had just rounded the bend of the driveway when she saw Quincy Teller and her green moped pulling in from the op-posite direction.

"Hey Quincy," said Tish, going up on the porch as a few rain-drops began to slap down. "Go ahead and put it in the shed. Nash parks his motorcycle in there all the time."

"Oh, thanks," said Quincy. She opened the wide shed door and pushed her moped up the tiny four-inch ramp and into the shed. "Is now OK?" she asked nervously, coming out of the shed. "You said this weekend, but I didn't know when that meant. And then I got nervous and then I thought maybe I ought to just do it now." Coats walked over to Quincy, his tail wagging his bottom, and began to shnuffle all over Quincy's legs.

"Oh, for the public records thing. Sure. Let me go yell at Grand-dad to get out of the cellar."

"I'm already out," said Tobias opening the front door. "Don't like rain and I found wine while I was cleaning."

"Ha! How long has it been in there?"

Quincy tentatively patted Coats' ears and then rubbed them more enthusiastically when he leaned against her.

"Don't know, but I'm going with at least twenty years judging by the dates and the fact that I can't remember storing it. Although, come to think of it, your Grandmother might have done it and not told me because she was trying to clear space in the cupboards. Come on in. I've got one breathing now and I've put aside a good one for Sunday dinner with Nash."

Quincy and Tish followed Tobias into the house. Quincy hung her helmet on a hat peg and dutifully took off her boots without being told. Her ponytail situation was once again on the precipice of disaster with entire thick mousey brown locks dangling down in front of her ears.

"Quincy, do you want wine?" asked Tish, slipping out of her shoes and chucking them in the shoe basket.

"I'm only nineteen," said Quincy.

"I don't think that was the question," said Tobias, going into the kitchen.

Quincy looked scandalized.

"We won't tell if you won't," said Tish with a wink.

"Well, maybe just a little bit," said Quincy. "I'm not much of a drinker."

"Good way to be," said Tish. "Granddad, this is Quincy Teller.

Quincy this is Granddad."

"Hi Mr. Yearly," said Quincy, correctly gauging her audience's preferred nomenclature.

"How're your folks?" asked Tobias. "Last I heard your dad was up for a promotion at the APW."

"Yeah, he's head of the Emergency Management division now," said Quincy enthusiastically. "I got to go out and show them some of the drone stuff I'm doing. The Pierce County Public Works is already using drones in levy surveys and custom mini-drone boats for surface water run-off pond surveys." Quincy's face lit up in excitement. "Drones are the future, but there are so many fantastic applications that can be implemented now!"

"Well, it must have been cool to be able to show your dad what you were working on," said Tish with a smile.

"It was," said Quincy, fading back to serious and looking embarrassed to have been caught showing enthusiasm.

"Neil seemed pretty excited about some of the shots you got from the wedding," said Tish, trying to coax Quincy out of her shell. Quincy's face perked back up.

"Yeah! You want to see them?"

"I do," said Tobias, handing each of them a glass. Quincy's glass had a noticeably modest amount in it. "I wanted to see what Reginald's place looked like all dolled up. Come on into the living room. Let's look at the pictures and then Tish said there's some video of Tish and Nash kissing? Not that I need to see that, but I get the feeling I'm going to need to know what people are talking about."

"Oh, yeah, totally. It's up to a hundred and fifty thousand views."

Tish choked on her wine. "It was at fifty-thousand last night!"

"It went over big in Asia."

"I… It was Shakespeare. People really want to watch that?"

"You said it was kissing," said Tobias settling onto the Chesterfield. Coats made a couple of turns and then curled up in his dog bed beside the leather couch.

"Well, I mean, you two are hot. And people like Romeo and Juliet and the mountain looks pretty. And I have to say, my footage is amazing. I'd run like six flights on that same pattern before you showed up, so I was totally practiced up and I got the lighting just right. There's like a sunburst right over your head and you look all glowy. And then I was able to drop out the drone motor, so you only hear the audio from the mic. It looks like a scene from a movie."

"Well, it's probably better than her voodoo time traveling movie," said Tobias.

"My five minutes as the dead body on Law and Order are better than that movie," said Tish.

"Wait, that's a real movie? It sounds awesome."

"It should have been, but sadly no," said Tish. "Anyway, let's see the Shakespeare stuff and then we'll look at wedding photos.

"OK," said Quincy. She plunked herself down on the Chester-field and then looked around for a place to put her wine while she tried to manage her laptop bag. Tish grabbed a TV tray from the rack against the wall and put in front of the couch, so they all had wine glass storage space and sat on the other side of Quincy.

"Well," said Tobias, when the video stopped. "That was... weird."

"Thanks a bunch, Granddad," said Tish.

"No, Quincy's right. It looks amazing. And you and Nash look very...cinematic. I'm just not used to you looking cinematic. And I didn't realize you could quote Shakespeare off the top of your head."

"I may have had a tiny Shakespeare obsession in high school," said Tish. "I was convinced that all actors knew Shakespeare and could quote it at the drop of a hat. So I studied."

"OK," said Tobias. "But what's his excuse."

"Well, you know, he..." Tish trailed off as both Quincy and Tobias turned toward her with inquiring expressions. "He took a course in college," she said, remembering that she had been sworn to secrecy on the subject of Nash's Library Sciences degree. She wasn't sure how serious he'd been about the secrecy, but with all the recent upheavals she didn't care to find out.

"I feel like that sentence was going to go a different direction," said Tobias. "But moving on. Do you have other Orcas videos?"

"Aside from Mrs. McAllister and her rooster," said Tish, taking a sip of wine. Quincy went pink and grabbed for her wine.

"People should know," she said after a swallow. "Everyone always pretends like life's perfect here and that everyone gets along, but they don't. I get tired of everyone lying all the time."

"Hmm," said Tobias. "But that wasn't exactly truth you were spewing when you implied I had dementia was it? Maybe you were hoping to get a few more hits on your blog?"

Quincy sank down in her seat.

"Should have just stuck with posting the mug shot and the arrest report and let people draw their own conclusions. Would have upheld your truth-telling point a little better."

Quincy risked a look at Tobias and he smiled kindly.

She squinted, trying to decipher his expression. "You're not mad?" she asked after a bit.

"Oh, hell no, kid. I'm too old to get mad about the internet. Besides, don't take the mission if you can't accept the consequences."

"Mission?" repeated Quincy, a puzzled crease forming between her eyes.

"Nix, nix," Tish muttered into her glass, which made Tobias laugh.

Quincy's head twisted back and forth between the two of them like an owl.

"I don't understand," she began. "What do you mean—"

"Never mind," said Tobias. "We're going to probably say a bunch of stuff you won't understand. Hell, half the time Tish sounds like she swallowed the entire noir collection from Turner Classic Movies."

Tish found herself laughing. "I get it from you and your stupid crime novels!"

"I didn't say where you got it from. I'm just telling Quincy that she probably should ignore anything we say that sounds too confusing. Although, I have to say, before you get too high and mighty about people lying, you should maybe ask yourself why they're doing it. This is a small island. And even if you hate your neighbor you still got to get up in the morning and wave hello. Sometimes it's better to just smile and toss your rooster over the fence than to try and resolve the matter of what her husband said about our Nancy that one time and how we all know her son stole that twenty dollars out of my purse the time I left it in the car."

"Rooster tossing is not constructive," said Tish, eyeing her grandfather, skeptically.

"Didn't say it was. Said it was better than getting in a fist fight. Sometimes the lies are what keep things from going down in flames. Not everyone has Mrs. Palmer to teach them anger management."

"But don't you think it would be better to say stuff instead of bottling it up?" demanded Quincy.

"Not always," said Tobias. "I know that's an old person perspective, but think on it. Anyway, what's this pretty looking one of the beach?"

He pointed to a thumbnail image of a beach on Quincy's laptop screen.

"That is over by Deer Harbor," said Quincy, clicking play. "I borrowed a kayak and went out and took some shots from the water. I got some fantastic footage. See this cliff here? You can't get to that on foot. And this little beach. Well, obviously someone figured out how to get to it, but I kind of think the Vanagon just makes it extra Orcas, if you know what I mean."

On the screen, a couple walked hand in hand across the beach toward the vehicle. The setting sun illuminated the girl's hair, painting it purple.

No, that's not the sun.

"Tish," said Tobias, glancing up at the board and the picture of Penelope, and then leaning in to Quincy's screen.

"Yeah, I see it," said Tish, yanking the computer off of Quincy's lap. "When did you take this?" she demanded,

"A couple of weeks ago," said Quincy.

"Can you zoom it in?"

"Maybe. Not sure that we'll be able to get good enough resolution to see the people though. Why?"

"Because that's Penelope Drue. And I'm about ninety percent certain that's Tate Donovan."

CHAPTER 24
THE BOARDS

Tobias finished printing out the picture of Tate Donovan and slapped it on the board in the empty square that Tish had labeled BABY DADDY.

"Wait, I don't understand," said Quincy. She'd been following Tish and Tobias around for the last ten minutes like a lost puppy. Coats, seeing where things were headed, had already transferred from the dog bed to Tish's recliner. "What is this?" Quincy gestured at the boards.

"Murder boards," said Tobias, in his patented *well duh* tone.

"They are case boards," corrected Tish. "Suspects and timeline." She gestured to the boards in turn.

"Holy shit," said Quincy. "You guys are serious about this. I mean, like seriously serious."

"I told you we needed fedoras," said Tobias. "No one takes you seriously as a P.I. without the hat."

"But are you allowed to just go around investigating crimes on your own?" asked Quincy, sounding worried.

Tobias turned around and stared at Quincy in disbelief.

"What ever happened to rebellious youth?" he demanded of Tish.

"I blame the Democrats," said Tish, facetiously.

"Don't start, young lady," he said, wagging the dry erase marker at her sternly.

"Yes, Quincy. Granddad has his Private Investigator's license, so he's allowed. Also, you don't need to have a license to ask people questions. I do it all the time. I mean, it annoys the crap out of

Detective Spring and it makes Nash worry, but it's fine. We only get threatened every once in a while."

"Threatened?" Quincy's eyes had gone wide. "I don't think I can be a part of something where I get threatened."

"No, no," said Tobias, sounding his most reassuring. "Threats barely happen at all really."

"Percentage-wise, it's barely a blip compared to all the people that we talk to that *don't* threaten us," said Tish.

"Exactly," agreed Tobias.

Quincy didn't look reassured.

"Besides," said Tish, "didn't you just say you wanted the truth to come out?"

"Well, yeah…"

"And right now we're just talking about stuff. Who's going to know? This is all theoretical anyway."

Come on, Quincy. You know you want to solve problems and I want to use your skills for my own private investigating purposes. Come to the dark side.

"Theoretical," Quincy said slowly. "OK. But you don't really think Tate Donovan killed Penelope Drue, do you?"

"We don't know what we think yet," said Tobias, turning back to the board.

"What we know is that Penelope was about nine weeks pregnant," said Tish. "We also know that no one thought she was dating and no one knew she was pregnant. That means it was either a one-night stand or she was keeping her relationship on the DL."

"Don't go millennial on me, Tishkins," said Tobias.

"Down low," translated Quincy.

"Got it," said Tobias. "Now here we got Penelope walking hand in hand on a sunset beach with young Mr. Donovan. And you don't do a lot of hand-holding with boys that aren't yours. That makes him a shoe-in for being the father of the baby."

"And, since he also happens to be Penelope's best friend's boyfriend, there's plenty of motivation for keeping the relationship quiet," said Tish. "Now the real question is whether or not he killed Penelope."

"He might," said Tobias, "to keep the relationship and the baby a secret from Azalea."

"Yeah," said Tish, "except that last night, he broke up with Azalea in a very public way and, from what I hear from Marty, the bassist, he's been wanting to do it for some time, but hasn't had the guts to make it stick. Azalea keeps steamrolling him into taking it back."

"Last night? Good gravy, just how much stuff did you get up to last night?" demanded Tobias.

"A lot," said Tish. "I also prevented the band from naming themselves Divorced by Eight."

"That's funny," said Tobias, approvingly.

"My favorite was Till Death Do Us Party," said Tish.

"I like that one," said Quincy. "Why didn't they go with that one?"

"They wanted something they could use off the wedding circuit. Meanwhile, what do we know about Tate's timeline the day of the wedding?"

"You tell me," said Tobias. "You're the one who actually saw him that day."

"I'm trying to remember. The wedding started at eleven o'clock. I needed the band there by ten-thirty to do sound checks and make sure they were all sober in order to do the processional music. Tate called around eight-fifteen in the morning and said they were missing some sort of part for the amplifier. Don't ask me what part because I don't know and I'm not going to know. I just fill in the *Peanuts* wah-wah-wah noise when they talk about equipment."

Tobias snorted.

"But he said that the band was on the island and would be there on time, but he was taking a slightly later ferry. However, he was still convinced that would be on time and didn't want me to freak out if he wasn't there precisely at ten."

"I thought you said you wanted them there at ten-thirty," said Quincy.

"Yeah, but I told everyone a half-hour early because it's Orcas. Then Azalea showed up and said Penelope was waiting on Paxton, but that she could call Tate and get him to pick up Penelope. But I said not to because I wanted them there on time. I figured we could make it without Penelope, but we couldn't make it without the band. And then he and the band showed up in a lather at ten-twenty-eight."

"Perfect planning on your part then," said Tobias, with a nod.

"That is what I thought," said Tish, once again feeling pleased with herself.

"But I was there when they got there," said Quincy. "And they were there for the rest of the day. I've got tons of shots of them."

"Agreed," said Tish. "I really don't think he could have slipped away after that. Not that it matters since before then is when Penelope died. But then Tate and Azalea got in a fight and he left before I could tip him out. Which, crap, I still need to tip him out. Anyway, then Azalea's car wouldn't start, and I drove her home and we stopped to see Penelope and found the body."

"So, theoretically, he could already have been on the island, killed Penelope and then called and told you he was going to be late?" asked Quincy.

"Theoretically," said Tish. "Or he could have called, still managed to get on the earlier ferry, stopped in to see Pen, killed her, and then come to Reginald's."

"Or any variation thereof," said Tobias. "Basically we've got him from ten-thirty on, but we don't have any concrete evidence of his movements during the time-of-death window."

"So, how do we find that out?" asked Quincy.

"We?" repeated Tobias, sounding a shade too innocent. "I thought you couldn't be involved in solving mysteries."

"I... well... I mean, as long as we're not doing anything dangerous, I could help."

"That's nice," said Tish. "You know, it's really too bad that all of Granddad's files are still on paper. It would be so nice to read all about Tate with a simple computer search."

Tobias was giving her the eye.

"But, oh well," continued Tish. "I guess we can read through them the old-fashioned way."

"You know with some of the document scanners these days you could probably have them scanned in no time and then plug them into some sort of database," said Quincy.

"Really?" said Tish. "I didn't think of that. How long do you think something like that would take?"

"I don't know," said Quincy. "It would depend on how many files there were and how many people you had scanning and then whether or not you're building a custom database or if you were using something off the shelf."

"I don't think we know anything about databases," said Tobias. "Probably best to give up that dream, Tish."

"Yeah," said Tish, sadly.

"I could help," said Quincy. "I'm not a database expert, but I know a little programming and I know lots of people at school I could ask. I'm sure I could come up with anything."

"That would be really great!" Tish exclaimed, doing her pleasantly surprised look. "Do you think you could get it done by the end of the summer?"

"Oh, yeah, totally! But don't we need to look through them sooner to figure out stuff about Tate?" Quincy looked from Tish to Tobias and back.

"You know, it occurs to me that since I still need to tip him out for last week that I'll just text him to come out to Reginald's. I can question him then."

"Oh," said Quincy looking confused, and scratching her head so that even more hair dislodged from the ponytail.

"But I'm so glad you're going to help," said Tobias. "We've been wanting to get the files on the computer for a while."

"Sure," said Quincy, "happy to help."

"Of course," said Tish, "if you tell anyone about the files I'll tell everyone you're running the Grapevine. Some things need to stay just between us. Don't you agree?"

"Oh," said Quincy. "Uh. Yeah."

"Great," said Tish, with a beaming smile. "Now, how about a snack to go with your wine?"

An hour or so later, Quincy pulled away and Tish and Tobias waved to her from the porch.

"That was probably a little bit mean," said Tobias.

"It's for her own good," said Tish. "She needs to learn what to do with secrets if she's going to be collecting them all over the island."

"True," he agreed. Then he turned to look at her, leaning on his cane, but still managing to look her right in the eye. "You're really staying here."

"Yeah," said Tish. "I'm really staying here."

He took a deep breath and let it out again. "Well, that will be nice, but you should really learn to play bridge if you're going to do that."

"It's a weird game," said Tish. "And I'm not Reginald."

"We'll see," he said, going back inside.

"We'll see what? We can see it now. I'm definitely not Reginald. And I'm not learning to play bridge!"

I'm going to end up playing bridge.

CHAPTER 25

FRIDAY – REMEMBER HIM

Tish waited on the porch and watched Tate's truck pull up the drive.

This feels like an ambush. I'm not sure this was the best plan. But at least I told Granddad he couldn't come.

"Hey Tish," said Tate climbing slowly out of his truck and approaching the house with dragging feet.

"Hey Tate, how's the break-up going?"

Tate shrugged. His hair had slipped beyond stylish disarray into unkempt and he looked like he hadn't slept properly in days.

"Thanks for keeping my cash for me," he said, slowly climbing the three stairs up to the porch.

"Sure," said Tish, handing him the envelope with his tip. "Sorry to make you come out here. I would have just given it to you tomorrow, but I wanted to talk to you. Have a seat." She patted the chair next to her and he dropped down into as if his knees had given out.

"I'm sorry about the break-up thing. I swear I can…" He trailed off as if not sure what he could do.

"Don't worry about it," said Tish. She pursed her lips, trying to figure out how to say what she wanted to say without sounding like a complete jerk.

Time to death pastry it up, I guess.

"I actually wanted to talk to you about Penelope," said Tish.

Tate's head came up, but he didn't say anything.

"You know Granddad and I are investigating, right?" He nodded, somewhat jerkily. "And you know we've done this kind of thing before?"

"Yeah," he said nodding. "For Reginald and Nash."

"Yeah." Tish nodded in turn, trying to set up a resonant behavior pattern. People trusted other people who behaved like them. "Well, when we investigate, we tend to come across information that maybe other people might not want spread around. We're usually pretty good about keeping secrets unless they absolutely have to be told."

She stared at him, hoping he would take the hint, but he stared blankly back at her.

"Tate, Penelope was nine weeks pregnant."

He nodded, clearly unsurprised, but didn't say anything.

Tish sighed. "Tate, you're the father, aren't you?"

Tears welled up in his eyes. "We were going to tell Azalea after the wedding on Saturday. When she didn't show up, I thought she'd chickened out. I was so mad! She was dead and I was mad at her." A sob shook his frame. "She was going to move off the island to live with me. We were so happy! Why didn't I stop in that morning? What if I could have stopped it? I called her! Why didn't she pick-up?"

Tish leaned closer and put an arm around his shoulders and squeezed as he covered his face with his hands.

"It's going to be OK," she murmured.

It won't, really. Nothing will ever be the same, but at least at some point it will be better than it is now.

She muttered nonsense phrases for the grieving and rubbed his back until the sobs died down. He sniffed and wiped his nose on his sleeve.

"Sorry," he said.

"Don't be sorry for your feelings," said Tish. "You don't have to make other people comfortable with your grief. That's on them."

"You're really good at this stuff," he said.

"My dad died in a car accident when I was a kid. I didn't work through it until years later and I read a lot of books on grieving. I can recommend some if you want. But mostly, just try to remember that you have people who love you and that whatever you're feeling is all right. When did you call her?"

"What?"

"Sorry. Occupational hazard. You said you called her and she didn't pick up."

"I called on our way off the ferry," said Tate with a sniff. "So before ten."

"Thanks," said Tish. "Have you thought about talking to Mrs. Palmer up at the clinic? She's got therapy groups for a lot of stuff."

"I'd have to tell people that Penelope and I were together. It was bad enough that we were going to embarrass Azalea when Penelope was alive. She's already pissed that I broke up with her. If she finds out about me and Penelope she'll go mental. I can't do that. I can't tell anyone."

He pushed himself out of his chair, shaking his head.

"I can't. I really just can't." He rushed down the stairs, heading back to his truck.

"Tate, just wait a minute," said Tish, trying to get the singer to slow down.

"I can't," said Tate, shaking his head. "I'm not even sure I'm going to make it through tomorrow sober. Everywhere I look is some place that Penelope should be."

"I know," said Tish. "I really do know. But your friends will be here. I will be here. We will make sure you make it through."

"Yeah, you're going to be here, but so is a happy bride and groom who are going to be getting what Penelope and I will never have. And Azalea will be here. And I…"

There was a happy toot of a car horn and Terry the florist's blue Subaru came around the corner. Tish smiled perfunctorily and waved, but stopped mid-wave when she realized that Sarah was in the passenger seat. Sarah had been at the initial meetings with Terry, so it wasn't like they were unknown to each other, but Tish would not have characterized them as giving-each-other-rides type friends.

Tate took Tish's moment of distraction as an opportunity and climbed in his truck.

"Look Tish," said Tate, looking at her through the open window, "I appreciate everything you're trying to do. I really do. But I'm struggling. I'm trying to do all the right things, but I don't even know what those things are."

I want to push him. But I can't. I really can't.

"You're doing great, Tate," said Tish. "Just wake up and put one foot in front of the other. The rest will take care of itself. If you can't show up tomorrow, I'll understand."

Tate's eyes filled up with tears again. He looked like he was about to speak, but instead he just nodded and started the engine.

"Well, there goes that theory," said Tish as Tate's truck roared down the drive. She turned around and looked at Terry's car. Sarah had gotten out and was watching her. Terry had opened the hatchback and was pulling out a box of flower arrangements.

"Tish," said Sarah, sounding uncertain.

"I'm going to carry the flowers in," said Terry looking from Sarah to Tish.

"No problem," said Tish. "I've got the air conditioner going." Terry nodded and then hefting her box of flowers she hurried toward the house.

Tish turned to look at Sarah. She was standing oddly—leaning heavily against the open door.

"Did you get a ride from the ferry dock with Terry?" asked Tish, feeling perplexed. "Why didn't you just call me?"

"Actually, I saw on the Orcas Rideshare page on Facebook that she was planning on coming into town, so I got a ride with her," said Sarah, reaching back into the car and pulling out a crutch. She tucked it into one armpit and gimped around the front of the car. Tish stared in disbelief at the boot-cast that went all the way up to Sarah's knee.

"Oh my God! Are you OK? What happened? Oh my God. Stop standing up. Come and sit down." Tish twisted left and right in a panic looking for the quickest place to sit down.

"I'm OK," said Sarah. "I just can't drive. Or walk very far without one of those wheelie scooter things."

"Oh my God," said Tish again. "What happened?" She ran up to the porch and began scooting chairs around to clear a path to the lounge chair. "Do you need pillows? I can get more pillows."

"Those are fine," said Sarah, levering herself up the short flight of stairs.

"Ack! Don't go up the stairs! Go up the wheelchair ramp!"

"I'm fine," said Sarah. "I'm actually getting pretty good at stairs."

Sarah lowered herself onto the lounge chair and settled the crutch off to one side.

"Do you want something to drink? Something to eat?" Tish didn't know what to do for an incapacitated Sarah. "Should you be out in the sun? I've got a hat somewhere."

"Tish, I'm not dying of consumption. I have a broken ankle. Stop freaking out and sit down!"

"I am freaking out! Why didn't you call me?" Tish did as she was told and sat down, but on the very edge of the wooden Adirondack chair so she could leap up in case Sarah needed something.

"Um, OK..." Sarah trailed off and seemed to be staring at Tish as if hoping Tish was psychic.

"How did this happen?" asked Tish, not certain what she was supposed to be asking.

Sarah stared for another minute and then took a deep breath and swallowed hard. "OK, well, remember that event I did for work last month?"

"Yeah, the grand opening of that new building. With all the shmukity-shmucks. It got a bit in the Business Insider. Sounded like it went well."

"It did," said Sarah. "Right up until the end. Which is when the

FBI came in to arrest Mr. Patterson for fraud."

"Holy crap! Wait, do I know Patterson?"

"No, he was just one of the investors on the project. Not even a big one. He acted like a big investor, but he barely made it on the list and apparently he was running some sort of pyramid investment scheme."

"OK," said Tish, not sure where this was going.

"Anyway, Mr. Patterson saw them coming and for some idiot reason decided to flee. Only he fled right into me as I was taking down one of the banners at the entryway."

"Oh no! What happened?"

"You're holding back a laugh right now, aren't you?"

"A little bit, but I swear I can keep it in."

"Well, I was on a step-ladder and he slammed right into me and knocked the step-ladder out from under me. And then I was swinging from the banner and then I landed on Patterson and we rolled down the stairs and he landed on me and broke my ankle."

"I lied," said Tish, cracking under the pressure and beginning to giggle.

"You're a true friend," said Sarah, sounding a little angrier than Tish thought the situation warranted.

"The ankle is *not* funny and I'm *very* sorry," gasped Tish between chuckles. Tears were starting to squeeze out the corners of her eyes. "But you were swinging from a banner!"

"Not for very long!"

"Yes," said Tish, breathing in sharply in an attempt to control her giggles. "I'm so very sorry. That must have been horrifying. What happened? Did they at least get Patterson?"

"Yes, Greg arrested him," said Sarah, her voice sounded very tight and she seemed to be squeezing one of the chair pillows very hard.

"Greg, who?" asked Tish, still picturing the banner debacle.

"Greg," repeated Sarah, as if that explained anything.

Tish stared blankly at Sarah.

"Greg Swensen, your ex-boyfriend!"

"Oh! Greg!" Sarah nodded going pink in the face. "Well, that's good! How's he doing? Thank God there was someone reasonable there to take care of you. Did he get you off to the hospital properly?"

"Yes," said Sarah, going an even deeper shade of red. "And then he took me home."

"Great," said Tish again. Greg had always been a decent human being and she thought it was extra nice of him to take care of Sarah for her.

Only… it wasn't for me, was it?

"Sarah…" said Tish, finally getting an inkling of why Sarah hadn't been calling. "Did Greg ever go home again after he brought you back to your place?"

"No," squeaked Sarah. "I mean, briefly. I mean, yes, of course."

Tish began to laugh wholeheartedly this time until the tears leaked out of her eyes. "You're so pink!" gasped Tish, pointing at her friend and laughing.

"Tish!" Sarah threw the pillow at her and Tish caught it and fell back into her chair laughing harder. "Tish this isn't funny. I've been having panic attacks for weeks about how to tell you I was dating your ex. Particularly when even he admits that the two of you never properly broke up. I've stayed up nights worrying about this!"

"Oh, sweetie!" Tish reached over to hug Sarah. "I'm so sorry that you did that. Please don't do that anymore. Greg is a great guy and you are the awesomest. How could I be mad about that?"

"Really? Because my best friend in high school stopped speaking to me in college when I dated her ex two years after they broke up."

"Dumb move," said Tish, shaking her head. "Sisters before misters. Besides, if you'd bothered to talk to me for longer than five minutes in the last month, I would have told you that I've been dating Nash."

"What?" gasped Sarah, sitting bolt upright. "How could you not tell me?"

"I've been trying, but a bitch won't call me back."

"But the Grapevine said you were dating Matt Jones! I was prepping up to do an intervention! It was going to be exceedingly difficult to tell you not to date him while I was snuggling up to Greg. I just about had a meltdown."

"Oh, for crying out loud! I really need to get Quincy to take that down. Let me guess, you're worried that Granddad has dementia too?"

"Well, no. That one didn't really seem very likely."

"But dating an international drug smuggler seemed like something I was super likely to do?"

"Well," said Sarah, looking like she was mulling it over, "yeah?"

"Well, I guess that means you didn't see the Shakespeare drone footage."

"The Shakespeare… I'm so behind. I don't know how I'm going to get caught up. What about the man with the shotgun? Nash texted and said that you were mad at both of us…" Sarah trailed off. "Are you and Nash in a fight? He sounded really depressed."

"Yeah, kind of," said Tish. "He and Granddad apparently think that I'm likely to quit the business and run off to the mainland after I fail."

Sarah frowned. "I don't think that sounds right."

"Granddad may not have thought I was going to fail exactly. He thought I'd just get bored with being on the island and go chase my bliss elsewhere. He didn't think I was serious about staying."

"OK, well, that sounds like a more likely thing to think," said Sarah. "I don't think it's true, but at least that has some sort of basis in reality."

"You don't think it's true?" asked Tish, tearing up.

"No," said Sarah, looking startled. "I mean, you've been totally digging in here. And you've been so happy. I know it's sort of the exact opposite of LA. But it has a lot of the things you liked about acting. It has a really varied daily schedule. You get to be artistic and part of a large-scale project with different creative people. But it also lets you be in control in a way that being an actress never did. And you are super kicking ass. Why would you leave?" Tish gave a small wail and squished in beside Sarah to hug her. Sarah patted her in sympathetic puzzlement.

"You are my best friend!" Tish wailed.

"You're my best friend too," agreed Sarah, still sounding befuddled.

"You really validate me," Tish sniffed into Sarah's shoulder.

"I hope so? Sorry, I'm lost."

"Boys don't understand anything!"

"Well, that is definitely true." She hugged Tish tighter, then leaned back to try and look Tish in the face. "What have they been saying to you?"

"Nash said I made him feel like he was Plan *B*," said Tish, with another sniff. Sarah grimaced. "I know! That's so not OK. I really never meant to! I don't think of him like that! And then he and Granddad both thought I was going to quit the business and go back to the city."

"Why are boys so stupid?"

"I don't know!"

"Well, what did you say to them?"

"I told Granddad to stop being an idiot and he said he didn't realize I was serious about staying and then I think he got over it. Also, he texted me. So, that's pretty much like an apology. You know, for an old person."

"Totally," agreed Sarah. "I mean… he must have had to figure out how to turn on his phone and everything."

"I know!"

"What about Nash?"

"He went grocery shopping."

"What?"

"He was working when we got into it. So then he was supposed to come over afterwards. But then Roger Barr shot a cow and afterwards Nash decided it was crucial to go to the mainland and go grocery shopping because he only has cheese in his fridge and Claire is coming this weekend."

"No one has just cheese," said Sarah.

"Well, cheese and condiments," said Tish. "I ate the last of the hot dogs last time I was over."

"Holy shit, you're really dating."

"Did you think we weren't?"

"I just didn't think it was serious until you updated me on the status of his refrigerator. OK, so he did something about the cow, and then stupidly decided to go grocery shopping and then what?"

"And then he called and said that he'd talked to you and I yelled at him and he never called back. That was yesterday." Tish wiped her nose and moved back to her own chair.

"Ah. OK. Well, obviously you can't call him," said Sarah.

"Obviously."

Sarah appeared to think over Nash's behavior. "Sorry, I've got nothing at the moment. We will consider that and hope that he comes to his senses. In the meantime, we should probably move on to the next agenda item—namely the man with the shotgun."

"Miles Singer, meth dealer. Sorry. Meant to call you today, but I forgot because I discovered that Tate was the father of Penelope's baby and got distracted. Also, it's wedding prep day."

"Yup," said Sarah, "still lost."

"Tell you what—I'll bring out the napkins and the silverware. We can roll the silverware and I'll tell you all about everything."

"That would be good. I can roll silverware."

"Great," said Tish, standing up. "Back in a jiff."

"Tish," said Sarah, as Tish moved toward the door, "you're really not mad about Greg?"

"No," said Tish, shaking her head. "I'm really not."

Sarah relaxed back into the lounger. "That's such a relief."

"I know I get amped about a lot of stuff," said Tish, with a smile. "But boys aren't one of them."

"I really thought you were going to murder me."

Tish had one foot across the threshold, when Sarah's words hit into her consciousness with a smack.

"What'd you say?" demanded Tish, stepping back out onto the porch.

"I said it was a relief," said Sarah, looking up with a questioning expression.

"After that."

"I thought you were going to kill me?"

We got it wrong. We got it all wrong.

"No, you said *murder*. And that's exactly what she did."

CHAPTER 26

THE CHECKLIST

"OK," said Tish. "This is the binder. Go down the checklist. Bowen is going to be here in the next twenty minutes if my forecast modules are correct."

"What?" asked Sarah, accepting the binder reluctantly.

"I told him to be here an hour ago, so at the speed of Orcas combined with the speed of Bowen, I predict he'll be here in the next twenty minutes."

"Oh."

"Just tell him what to do. Terry will help. I have to go talk to Granddad."

"But Tish," said Sarah, looking befuddled.

"Sarah, I'm sorry to be rushing out, but I think I know who did it, and I need to talk to Granddad."

"But Tish, isn't that him coming up the drive?"

"Oh! Well, yes."

Tish watched as Tobias walked easily along the gravel road. Despite the cane, he didn't look troubled by the uneven footing or by having walked the distance over from his house. "Look at him walking!" exclaimed Tish. "He could not have made that distance comfortably when I got here. That is just fantastic. I'm going to owe that PT of his an extra goat."

"What?" demanded Sarah.

"Currently, we're paying his physical therapist in goats. He lives on Shaw in a yurt. He doesn't really want a lot of money, but he says he could use more goats. So I worked a deal with a guy over in West Sound whose goat got knocked up and I can have her kids if I give him the boat I found in Reginald's shed."

"Oh," said Sarah. "Sure. I understand."

"It's not a very big boat. It's like a little one man sailboat kind of thing. But what am I going to do with that? So I'm trading it for goats. You know what I need?

"To slow down."

"No. What I need is evidence. I need to call Kyle."

Tish dialed the phone while she waited for Tobias to get to the house.

"Sarah!" said Tobias, smiling as he got to the foot of the stairs. "How's doin?"

"Well, I broke my ankle, I'm dating Tish's ex-boyfriend, and Tish says she thinks she knows who killed her friend the waitress? I think."

"Sorry to hear about the ankle. Greg's a good guy. Is it Tate?"

"No," said Tish, impatiently waiting for Kyle to pick up. "Not Tate."

"Yeet!" said Kyle and Tish tried not to roll her eyes.

"Kyle, it's Tish. How do you feel about doing something illegal?"

"Uh, is this a trick question?"

"Sorry, forget I asked, just come up to Reginald's. I've got a top secret mission for you. I need you to break into someone's car and check their battery."

"Sounds weird, but no problem. See you in an hour," said Kyle, and hung up without the formality of actually saying goodbye. Seconds later a text popped through.

SORRY, FORGOT TO SAY BYE. BE OVER IN A BIT!

"Kind of ruins the secret agent vibe when you text *bye*," said Tish, reading the text.

"Not saying *goodbye* is just poor phone manners," said Tobias. "I commend him for making the effort. Meanwhile, your valet friend Jordan dropped his phone in the toilet and therefore never responded to your text. So he looked up our number in the phone book like a sensible young man. And he says that Matt Jones was indeed driving the yellow Ferrari last Saturday. Also, he'll be here on time tomorrow, but hasn't gotten a replacement phone yet, so email or call his mom if there's a change in plan."

"Great," said Tish. "I am really glad I hired him. And I know it wasn't Matt, but I'm glad to have the extra info."

"Did we think it was Matt?" asked Sarah. "I thought we liked Matt."

"We do like Matt," said Tobias. "But that doesn't mean he couldn't have done it. Did Tate confirm he was the father?"

"Yes. He's utterly broken up about Penelope's death."

"That's what I thought," said Tobias, looking pleased. "Been thinking about your adventures at the Olga bar. And I had a brain wave. I think we've been looking at this wrong. Got too boxed into the probabilities. Forgot to look at the emotions and the reasons why someone would kill Penelope."

"Yes!" exclaimed Tish, grinning. "We also forgot to examine where we were getting our information."

"Right," said Tobias. "But with Tate in the picture, it changes everything."

"Stop speaking in riddles!" exclaimed Sarah. "Just tell me who is dead and who the suspects are. I have to get caught up on at least one thing!"

"Penelope Drue," said Tobias. "Tish hired her as a server a few weeks back. Turned up dead last Saturday. The killer bopped her on the head and most likely drowned her in the bathtub before dragging her body outside and leaving her in the pond."

"Which I've always thought was weird," said Tish.

"It threw off the initial estimate on the time of death because she was in the sun all day. However, we now know she was killed between seven and eleven in the morning. The suspects were her brother, the meth dealer who lived with her. Her uncle, the meth cook who was hoping to get her share of the payout from a lawsuit.

Matt Jones because he had a bit of a conflict with the brother not too long ago. And, last but not least, the up until now unknown father of her child who turned out to be Tate Donovan, her best friend's boyfriend."

"But none of them did it," said Tish. "Because Penelope was dead before eight-thirty. Matt was still on the ferry. Paxton was probably in line for the ferry over on Friday Harbor. Dexter and Miles Singer were just finishing up their movie marathon or starting to cook meth. Whichever. And I think Tate must have been on the same ferry as Matt. He called Penelope at ten and she didn't answer."

"He could be lying," suggested Sarah.

"He could, but he's not. Also, it's easy to check." She pulled out her phone and dashed off a text.

Check Tate Donovan's phone records. He's the father of her baby.

"But here's the thing, I don't have any proof," continued Tish. "All I've got is random statements that might have been mistakes instead of lies. I don't know how to tie this up in a pretty package for Detective Spring. I need to get him to connect all the dots. Make sure he doesn't get fixated on Tate or Matt as the killer and then get to the real killer and not give us crap."

"Sting operation," said Tobias, calmly. "We've got Quincy now. We can probably get it on film."

"Ooh! Film!"

"What's a Quincy?" asked Sarah from the lounger.

I can't just pull phone records on your say so.

Tish sighed and glared at her phone. Detective Spring's tone still managed to come through loud and clear over text.

Fine. There's a YouTube channel. I'll send you the link. It shows Penelope and Tate walking on a beach.

Do I tell him not to look at any of the other videos? It seems like if I say not to, he'll definitely do it. Also, what are the odds that he hasn't already seen the Shakespeare video?

"Quincy Teller," said Tobias. "She does drones and other tech stuff."

"Well, that sounds like a good addition to the team," said Sarah.

WELL, THAT WOULD BE SOME KIND OF EVIDENCE AT LEAST. YOU THINK HE KILLED HER?

"Quincy should be good," said Tish, reading Detective Spring's text and starting to swipe out her response. "As long as she doesn't freak out about doing things without permission."

NO. BUT I THINK THAT'S WHY SHE WAS KILLED.

"Although, I don't know how long we'll be able to keep her engaged. She's just home for the summer from college," added Tish.

"You'll come up with something," said Sarah confidently.

"Meanwhile, how do we do this?" demanded Tish, looking at Tobias. "I'm going to have Kyle check the car. And I can probably get everyone here, but I have a damn wedding tomorrow. I'm not having a sting operation in the middle of the wedding."

"Better do it tonight," said Tobias. "Call Quincy. We'll get her to set up the cameras. I guess we can have Nash too," he sounded sour on the idea, "as long as you can talk him into not interfering."

"What about Spring?"

Tobias sucked air through his teeth. "I think he's going to want a lot of evidence and digging. If we do it his way, you just know he's going to be having a raid mid-ceremony tomorrow or something equally inconvenient. I say we alert him last minute when it's too late for him to do anything about it."

Tish shifted anxiously from foot to foot. "Well, then maybe not Nash either. If I tell him early then he'll feel obligated to tell Spring early. It's the cop thing."

"Your call," said Tobias.

"We'll call them both right before?" suggested Tish. Then she leaned over and lowered her voice. "Maybe we can make Sarah call them."

"Works for me," said Tobias, nodding.

"Hey!" exclaimed Sarah.

CHAPTER 27
STING OPERATION

Tish surveyed the living room of Reginald's house. She had paired back the majority of the furniture to a few antique chairs and small tables. The goal was not to really seat people, but to have the perfect setting for signing the wedding certificate. Tish thought she had succeeded. There was plenty of space and the built-in book-shelves were staged with low maintenance trendy knick-knacks. Tish had actually given herself a calendar appointment to change those out yearly. She didn't want the venue to get stale. The gifts table had a gold bird cage on it for cards and had been shoved rather haphazard-ly to one side when it had been moved in from outside. Tish knew it was a silly thing to obsess over when she was about to confront a killer, but she found her eyes returning to the table again and again. The sun had set and all the light was coming from the lamps. Tish had carefully stocked yellow light bulbs so that everything looked warm and homey. It also conveniently obscured the cameras that Quincy had set up. But somehow they just seemed to spotlight the gifts table.

It's throwing the whole balance of the room off.

Unable to take it anymore she stood up and went to adjust the table placement. She had almost tweaked to the right position when the front door opened behind her.

"Hey Azalea," said Tish, without turning around.

"Hey Tish," chirped Azalea.

Tish finally turned around and eyed Azalea. She was carrying a bulky green purse and dressed in tights and a cute t-shirt with sneak-ers. Her auburn curls were pulled up in the tidiest messy bun Tish had ever seen.

"Where is everyone? I thought you said it was an all-hands on deck set-up emergency?"

"Yeah," said Tish. "I lied. I just wanted you to come out here. I thought we should talk about Tate and I didn't think you'd come if I said that."

"Tate is none of your business," said Azalea icily.

"Well," said Tish, sitting down in the quaint green velvet wing-back chair that oozed Victorian charm, "he and the band are working for me, so I disagree."

"I know that Tate and I have had a little hiccup and I'm sorry it was so public. Although, I didn't realize that you had taken to socializing with them." Azalea's smile was a thin straight line with the barest upward tilt. Her implication was completely clear—Tish should not have been associating with the band. "But, regardless," continued Azalea, switching back to breezy. "I will take care of it."

"Band names," said Tish. "They were discussing some truly horrific band names. I felt the need to make my input heard. Why don't you sit down? I really do think we need to talk."

"I'm not staying because I don't believe I need to hear your input about Tate or anything else."

Azalea turned on her heel, preparing to leave.

"Don't you want your stuff?" asked Tish, without getting up.

"What stuff?" asked Azalea, turning around and looking annoyed.

Tish pointed to the box by the door. Azalea lifted the flap and recoiled at the bag of possum inside.

"I…" Azalea trailed off and looked at Tish warily. Tish waited. *Silence is the hardest art.*

"I don't know why you would think this was mine," said Azalea, at last.

"You're the only one who told me that I needed to stop. Paxton wanted me to shut up or drop dead. Dexter just wants it all to be wrapped up so he can inherit Penelope's money. Although, I'm willing to bet Paxton isn't going to let that happen. And Tate wants me to keep going. You're the only one who wanted me to stop the investigation."

"Investigation!" Azalea made air quotes around the word and snorted in derision. "Please. Why would I care?"

"Because you killed Penelope," said Tish. "She was just getting out of the bath and let you in while she finished getting ready and the bath drained. Then the two of you argued and you hit her with the block and tackle from the bathroom shelf and then held her underwater in the bathtub. What did she do—tell you that Tate was leaving you for her?"

Azalea was silent.

"You're delusional," said Azalea, her voice slightly breathy and higher pitched than normal. "I don't know why anyone ever listens to you."

"You brought her outside so that Tate would find her, didn't you?" asked Tish. "You were planning on telling Tate to go pick her up and then have him find the body. You thought he might not go inside if she didn't answer the door and you wanted to make sure he saw her. Only I said he couldn't."

"That's right," said Azalea, with a smile. "It was your fault that Tate couldn't learn his lesson. So I thought that meant it should be you who got to find Penelope's body."

"That's why you faked a dead battery on your car. So that I would have to drive you?"

"And you bought it, hook, line and sinker," said Azalea, smugly. "Who's the actress now?"

"Clearly, you. And what lesson was I supposed to learn?" asked Tish.

"Not to interfere with things that don't concern you!" snapped Azalea.

Tish stared at Azalea in disbelief. "What do you think Granddad and I do in our spare time? I mean interfering and finding bodies is practically a second job. The coroner threatened to get me a punch card."

Azalea gaped, then her face contorted in fury.

"You are just a failed actress! You think you're so smart, but you don't know anything. You don't even know how to run a wedding business! I had to show you how to schedule the servers!"

"That is because I am not, and never will be, a waitress," said Tish, with her fakest, most mean girl, smile. "Which, face it, is all *you* are ever going to be."

Azalea let out a gasp and then fumbled for her purse. "I will show you! I will show everyone!"

"Show everyone what?" asked Tish.

"That you are not that cool!"

Azalea dropped her purse finally pulling out a hand-gun and holding it unsteadily in two hands.

Ah. Well. I'm really not that cool because I thought I had her handled. And apparently not.

"Azalea," said Tish, working hard to not turn and look down the darkened hallway toward the spare bedroom where she knew her grandfather, Sarah, and Quincy must be watching on the monitors, "that is not a good idea."

"You don't tell me what a good idea is. I am the one…" Azalea trailed off panting.

"You're the one that has the ideas and the plans," said Tish. "And life would just be better if everyone did what you told them."

"Yes!"

"Living on this island must be some kind of hell for you," said Tish, sympathetically. "No one ever arrives on time. They all have their own ideas. God, you turn around for a second and someone decides to do something creative. It must be terrible for you."

"You should never have come here," said Azalea. "Everything would have been fine if you hadn't come here. It's this stupid business. Suddenly Tate thinks he could make a living as a band? No one makes a living as a wedding singer. That's ridiculous! And Penelope..." Tears were sparkling in Azalea's eyes.

"You killed your best friend," said Tish.

Azalea gasped out a sob as if Tish had sucker punched her, but then straightened up. "She betrayed me. She was *not* my friend."

"Yes, she was. She was your best friend. She loved you."

"If she loved me then how could she do that?" demanded Azalea, the gun shaking in her hands.

"Because sometimes your loved ones won't do things according to the plan," said Tobias from the hallway.

Azalea spun toward him, gun up. Tish could see in the way that he was holding his hand by his leg that he also had his pistol out, but was hiding it.

"Sometimes they do things that surprise you," said Tish and Azalea pivoted back toward her. "And they do things that hurt your feelings."

"Doesn't mean they love you any less," said Tobias.

"Yes, it does!" yelled Azalea.

"No Zales," said Tish softly. "It really doesn't. It just means you disagree. Penelope loved you."

Tears began to trickle down Azalea's cheeks. "She just made me so mad."

"I know," said Tish, standing up. "And then you find yourself yelling the most ridiculous stuff about her not liking your Instagram post." Azalea looked up, puzzled. "Sorry, that's probably just me," said Tish, shaking her head. "But the point is that you can't run from this. You can't fix this. This is one situation you can't control. Put the gun down. We'll call Nash and go to the Sheriff's Station with you."

"Speak for yourself," said Azalea, putting her shoulders back. "Just because you can't control things, doesn't mean that I can't. You're annoying and he's old. No one is going to miss either of you."

"Thanks a bunch," said Tobias, drily. He hadn't moved from the doorway to the hallway.

"Don't come any closer," said Azalea, swinging the gun back in Tish's direction.

Six feet. I'm fast, but I'm not that fast and neither is Granddad, but he's not even going to try. He's going to shoot her if she makes a move. And I really don't want that to happen.

"Azalea," said Tish, sadly, "what are you going to do? Kill everyone who disagrees with you? What about Tate?"

"Tate just needs time to realize that he's better off with me," said Azalea firmly.

"No," said Tish. "He was in love with Penelope. And once he finds out you killed her…"

"He's never going to find out," said Azalea, raising the gun.

"He's going to find out one way or another. This is being filmed," said Tobias and Azalea spun back toward him, her eyes going wide in horror. Tish took two more swift steps and Azalea backed up toward the front door trying to keep both of them in her field of vision.

"Where is the camera? Where is it?" she screamed. She began to scan the room. She headed toward the bookshelves, intent on looking for the camera. Tish reached down and picked up the decorative pillow off the couch and threw it at Azalea, hitting her square in the face. Azalea's gun went off with a loud bang, but Tish didn't have time to listen to that. She crossed the room in three paces and shoved Azalea as hard as she could into the bookcase. The gun went skittering out of her hands and Azalea sprawled on the floor looking up at Tish in shock.

Then, with a wordless scream, she launched herself off the floor and back at Tish. On panicked instinct Tish lashed out and punched her. Azalea staggered back just as the front door swung open. Nash reached through the open door, pulled Azalea off her feet and slammed her onto the front porch with a hard thud that made Azalea squeak like one of Coats' toys. With a knee on her back, Nash yanked her into handcuffs with the efficiency of long practice.

"Well," said Tobias, dusting off his hands as if a job had been well done, "that's what I call perfect timing."

Got your gun put away already, didn't you, Granddad?

Through the open door Tish could see the lights of Nash's squad car parked in the drive-way.

"I really am going to have to take some sort of class on punching," said Tish, panting a little, and examining her knuckles. "I keep having to do it and I really don't think I'm doing it right."

"No problem," said Tobias. "I know a guy."

CHAPTER 28

NASH

Tish sat on the back patio and waited for Nash to come be mad at her. At least tonight she'd had the forethought to bring wine out along with her blanket. Using the remote, she flipped on the candle chandelier. Out in front of the house, Detective Spring had arrived just as everything was winding down, which meant everyone had to start all over with their stories. Tish had gone first and then deemed it wise to get out of the way. Nash had been disturbingly professional through-out the entire situation. Which meant that he was probably really, really mad. She just wasn't sure which part he was going to be the most mad about.

She pulled the blanket tighter around herself and tried to think about what she was going to do if Nash really did want to break up. Cry and drink a lot seemed the most probable answers. Sarah had talked to him right before the sting operation. Tish hadn't had the courage to ask if he'd said anything personal. She took a sip of wine and went back to waiting. Just when she thought she'd actually have to go find him, Nash came around the corner of the house and stopped, staring at her. She waved.

That was dorky. But he's just standing there. What am I supposed to do?

"Do you have all the statements you need and everything?" she asked, when he didn't speak.

"Yes," he said without moving. "But Detective Spring is still annoyed."

"He should stop hanging out with us then," said Tish.

"It's an occupational hazard."

"Being annoyed or hanging out with us?" asked Tish.

"Both," he replied.

"Are you annoyed about Azalea?"

"No, you called me. You had back-up and you got it on tape. It's not ideal, but for you that was practically by the book."

Tish tried not to look as smug as she felt.

"Also, I can teach you how to punch things if you want," he added.

"You'd have to talk to me to do that," said Tish.

With a sigh he came over and stood next to the lounger and she leaned back in the cushions, tilting her head to look up at all six-foot-four of him. He opened his mouth and shut it again as if the words he'd been looking for weren't in there.

"I'm sorry," said Tish and he looked startled. "If I have ever made you feel like a plan *B*. You are definitely Plan *A* material and I would never want you to think I don't believe that."

His shoulders sagged.

"You don't," he said. "You never do. That was Nora. Our entire marriage felt like a Plan *B* that was forced on her because we got pregnant."

Tish grimaced. She hated that idea. Claire was a brilliant little bundle of radiance. She hated that Nora might resent Nash, let alone Claire.

"I spent a lot of time trying to make that up to her, but I could never make up for the fact that her life didn't turn out like she wanted."

"Like anyone's life ever turns out the way they expected," said Tish. "Tell her to join the club."

He shrugged. "I can't change her. I gave up trying a long time ago. But I hate the feeling of always compensating for something and I don't ever want to go back to doing that."

"Do I do that?" asked Tish, wishing she could hug him, but feeling pinned in by her own blanket and the fact that he was standing. "I don't think... You're not..." She struggled for the right words. "I don't ever want to do that to you."

"You don't do that. I'm saying that's what I'm afraid of. That's my baggage and I'm sorry I tried to blame you for it."

"Oh, good," said Tish, relaxing back into the cushions, as a wave of relief swept over her. "That makes me feel better. I don't want you to feel that. But I couldn't figure out what I had done to make you feel that in the first place, so then I couldn't figure out what I could change."

Nash gave a half-chuckle and dropped into the lounger next to her. He rubbed his hand through his hair tiredly before looking up at her.

"Yes, well, since I've had twenty-four hours to think about what my problems are and what I would like to change, I have realized that I don't want to change anything. The truth of the matter is that you have always done everything you told me you were going to do. Including this business. You've never dropped anything and moved on. Your *track record,* or whatever bullshit phrase I used, is that you are the person I turn to when I'm in trouble because I know that I can count on you. I'm just insecure because I've only ever been here on Orcas and I worry that this—that I—am not exciting enough for you. You could be off doing anything and sometimes, at the end of the day, I'm not sure why you would be here."

Tish laughed. She could see it was hurting his feelings, but she couldn't stop. She struggled out of the blanket and sat up.

"Nash… No, this is a first name conversation. Emmett, I am insecure because you're very… secure in who you are. And you understand all these things that I don't. Like, parenting, and adulting, and math. I saw your study book for the traffic collision course and it scared the bejeezus out of me. That's not the point, but it's late and I'm tired. My point is that while I appreciate that you and Granddad act like I can do anything, the truth is that I can't. I don't have a college degree and I don't have a consistent resume in anything but acting. And no matter what I told Sarah, I can't be an architect. I can only act like an architect."

"Did you want to be an architect?" Nash looked lost. She didn't blame him.

"No. They're under-qualified engineers who think they're creative geniuses. It's just that when you're a kid you hear *you can be anything!* And when you're an adult you get told *you can't do that* and sometimes the distance between those two is astoundingly short and shocking. I left acting and slammed my face into a lot of shut doors because of the choices I'd made and dealing with the loss of both my dream of acting and the death of *you can be anything* is really, really hard. Sometimes it feels like someone tossed me out of the boat and I'm just flailing around in an unfamiliar sea hoping that someone comes by to rescue me. But then I came here. And people here believe that I can actually do things and no one says *no*. They say, *take a sweat lodge and think on that,* which is weird, but they don't say *no*. I know I landed on this island on accident, but I am staying on purpose. I am making something real here. Something permanent and important, that helps people, and will be a significant place in people's lives. That's exciting for me. And you're exciting for me because I love you and I don't do that very easily and I…"

Her voice cracked and the tears spilled out of her eyes and Nash grabbed her off of her lounger, pulling her over to his chair and into his lap, hugging her tight.

"Sorry I'm an idiot," he said into her hair. "I love you."

"I love you too," she sniffed.

"Did you just wipe your nose on my shirt?"

"Maybe," said Tish, leaning back and wiping her nose on her sleeve. "Do you want me to wash it for you?"

"No," he said, with a chuckle. "Definitely not." Then he put his hands on both sides of her face and kissed her. Tish melted against him as the kiss deepened.

"Oh God, not again," said Tobias, opening the back door. "Quincy, you're not filming are you?"

Tish broke away from Nash as they both heard Quincy's faint reply from inside the house.

"You showed him the video?" asked Nash, looking pained.

"He said we looked cinematic," said Tish. "Also, that led to reviewing Quincy's other footage and that's how I figured out that Tate was Penelope's boyfriend. So it was for the best. Also we're up over a quarter of a million views, in case you were wondering."

"That frightens me," he said.

"Tish come in here and tell us which wine we can drink," said Tobias. "I don't want to mess up the wedding."

Tish sighed and rested her forehead against Nash's.

"We're going to end up sneaking around just as much as ever, aren't we?" asked Nash sounding amused. "Just to get some privacy."

"Maybe," said Tish. "Come on. I'd better make sure that Sarah isn't standing too much on her broken ankle and that Granddad gets wine."

"I'm still unclear about what happened to Sarah," complained Nash. "When I talked to her earlier, she just mumbled something about resisting arrest and blushed."

"Remember Greg?" asked Tish, picking up her blanket.

"I generally try not to," said Nash. "But yes."

"So he went to arrest someone at an event Sarah was working. And the jerk resisted arrest and knocked Sarah down a flight of stairs and broke her ankle. Anyway, now they're dating."

"The guy that got arrested is dating Sarah?"

"No! Greg and Sarah!"

"Oh. That makes more sense. That's nice. They share a similar view on work clothes."

Tish giggled. "They will make a spiffy looking couple."

"Yeah," said Nash, sliding his arms around her again, "but can they get a quarter of a million views for quoting Shakespeare."

"Not even close," said Tish, grinning.

"Seriously," barked Sarah, leaning out the door. "Less kissing.

More wine!"

"There's a bottle open on the counter!" Tish yelled back.

"Also," said Nash, clearing his throat, "I'm sorry about going grocery shopping. I was preparing to get in the car to come see you and Ray just climbs in and starts talking about his Costco list. I couldn't figure out how to get out of it."

"It's because you're not comfortable with lying," said Tish. "I understand and accept that about you."

He snorted. "Thanks. I think."

He leaned in for another kiss and Tish sank into him, feeling like the world had righted itself.

"We probably ought to go in," said Nash, not sounding very certain, but Tish sighed.

"Yeah, probably," she agreed.

Tish went into the kitchen, holding Nash's hand. Tobias was already pouring. Detective Spring seemed to have calmed down and was inspecting one of Quincy's drones on the kitchen counter. Quincy was excitedly pointing out features to him. Sarah was sitting with her foot up on the other chair.

"Well," said Sarah, looking up at them, "everything all good?"

"Yeah," said Tish, looking at Nash. "I think so."

CHAPTER 29

SUNDAY – POST EVENTS

"Tish!" Claire dropped off the motorcycle and sprinted toward Tish.

"Mind the helmet!" Tish yelled, holding out her arms, but flinching to one side.

Claire cannonballed into Tish, but managed to be surprisingly soft on the headbutt to Tish's midsection.

"There's my unicorn princess," said Tish, as Claire took off her helmet, her dark brown hair, the same color as her father's, tumbling out in waves. Nash followed more slowly, working on parking the bike and hauling the groceries out of the saddlebag.

"Nope," said Claire, her blue eyes sparkling. "Today I'm a warrior princess and I am smiting the unholy wights of Orcas! Dad got me a sword and everything!" She pulled a plastic sword that was strung across her back by a piece of yarn.

"Good gravy," said Tish, unconsciously echoing Tobias. "I didn't realize we had a wight problem."

"Did you know wights are just, like, early Celtic zombies?" asked Claire.

"I did not," said Tish.

"Hey Mr. Yearly," said Claire waving to Tobias on the porch.

"Hello Claire. Who are we slaying today?"

"Wights!"

"Oh, excellent. I've got some paper zombie shooting targets I think. We could string them up on the back porch for sword practice."

"Yay!" Claire shook her plastic sword in the air.

"When did you get shooting targets?" asked Tish.

"Ordered them off the internet. Figure it's been a while since I practiced and I really ought to if I'm going to keep up my permit. They were having a sale on zombies."

"I have a spot I use out back on my property," said Nash. "You can come over if you want to do some target practice."

"Trying to butter me up?" asked Tobias, glaring at Nash.

"Why's Dad trying to butter you up?" asked Claire.

"Because neither he or Tish told me they were walking out together," said Tobias and Tish froze.

Shit! Granddad!!

"What's *walking out*?" asked Claire.

"What the young people call dating."

"Really?" demanded Claire, turning to look at Tish and Nash, her expression an emoji of hope.

"Um," said Nash, and Tish found she was smiling awkwardly.

"Is Dad your boyfriend now?" demanded Claire, turning directly to Tish.

"Yes," Tish said firmly.

I am being direct and honest. This is not awkward. We are doing this.

"Sweet!" Claire added a fist pump for extra emphasis. "Oh, wait. You didn't tell me either. Does that mean I get to be buttered up?"

"I bought you a sword—what more do you want?" demanded Nash, sounding outraged, but Tish could tell from the smile on his face that he was pleased to have the band-aide ripped off.

"Well, the shield to go with it," said Claire. "And a real pocket knife. I'm going to be eleven soon. I should be able to cut things on my own."

"I've got a spare," said Tobias. "Come on in. I'll get it down for you."

"What? No, I don't think that's a good idea." said Nash.

"Oh, relax. Ten's plenty old enough," said Tobias. "It's only a Swiss Army Knife."

"Yay!" exclaimed Claire, shaking her sword in the air again.

"Mark my words," said Nash, as Claire and Tobias disappeared into the house, "there will be blood."

"2007," said Tish automatically. "Earned Daniel Day Lewis an Academy Award for Best Actor."

"What?"

"*There Will Be Blood*? It's a movie…" She petered to a stop.

"I love you," said Nash, "but I feel that possibly you and Tobias don't have the same focus on safety that I do."

"I got a pocket knife when I was nine," said Tish. "And I still have all my fingers and toes. It will be fine."

"I'm really not sure where she gets the need to be violent. I swear she just used to like rainbows and cupcakes and ponies and stuff."

"She still likes those things," said Tish, deciding not to mention the book that she and Claire had read a few months back about a dragon and her princess and the various amounts of sword wielding that had followed. "She just also wants to slay some wights, right some wrongs, and you know… have her own pocket knife."

Nash looked skeptical, but didn't say anything further. Tish tugged him into the kitchen. By the time burgers were on the grill Tobias was showing Claire how to whittle and Tish felt smug.

Nothing is going wrong today. Everything is perfect.

The wedding on the previous day had been just as beautiful as the first one and Sarah had liked every single Instagram post. Quincy had taken down the dumb story about Matt Jones. Although, Tobias had insisted she leave the one about him up. And Nash and Claire looked happy. Everything really was perfect.

Tish stirred the dressing over black rice salad, reading carefully off the recipe that Talia had sent over.

"Burgers will be done in a few," said Nash, going by with a plate of cheese slices, and dropping a kiss on her cheek. Tish watched him go out to the deck, struck again by the idea that Nora, his ex-wife, was an idiot. Blaming Nash for not getting the life she wanted seemed like a cop out. Tish had wanted to be a movie star, but life hadn't handed her that. That wasn't anyone's fault. That was just how it was. But if Nora couldn't be happy in the life she was currently living then maybe she should be looking at herself instead of trying to blame anyone else.

Maybe Nora needs to do a sweat lodge.

Tish chuckled to herself and decided that some thoughts probably didn't need to be shared. Life was never going to go according to plan, but that didn't make it bad.

This life is an adventure.

Tish carried the salad out to the dining room and surveyed the table. It looked like they had everything but ketchup. Ten-year-olds required ketchup for everything. She was about to return to the kitchen when her phone rang. She took it out and checked the caller ID, preparing to dismiss the call unless it was someone absolutely vital.

Tish paused, her finger raised, staring at her phone in disbelief.

CORA PERALA.

Butt dial—has to be.

There was just no way that her old agent would be intentionally calling her three years after they had parted company. Tish walked into the den and swiped the call button to green.

"Hello?" Tish tried not to sound too uncertain, but she really wasn't sure what to expect.

"Oh, my God, Tish, tell me that's you," demanded Cora.

"Hi Cora," said Tish. "Yes, it's me."

"No, tell me that's you in the video because I just swore on a stack of People Magazines that it was and that I could totally have you on a call on Monday."

"What video? Cora, what are you talking about?"

"Shakespeare at the tower!"

"Oh my God," said Tish. "You saw Quincy's drone footage on

Mt. Constitution."

"I have no idea what half those words mean, but it was the one where you and the totes adorbs free climber with the ass that won't quit were just Shakespearing it up on a castle someplace."

"Yes, that video. Yes, that's me. And my boyfriend."

"Should have known. You always did have good taste. Look Tish, I know it's been forever. And thank God, you haven't gotten fat or anything since I saw you last. You look fantastic. The windswept look is so hot right now. I don't even know where you are, but I said you were out of state. That's right, right? It looked out of state."

"Yeah, I'm in Washington."

"What, seriously? That didn't look like DC."

"The state of Washington."

"Oh, that makes more sense. Fish and rain and apples and shit. Got it. OK, but honey, here's the thing. Shit's about to get real. Because there's a guy. He's got a script."

There's always a guy with a script.

"It got optioned by 20th Century. It's a feature. It hasn't got a name attached to it yet, but they're casting and scouting locations right now! This thing is happening."

Tish felt the words wash over her, bringing with it the familiar sense of urgency and excitement. Everything in Hollywood was always *right now*. Something was always *happening*. Adding more exclamation points was always better.

"And," continued Cora, "somebody brought in your clip and everyone lost their mind. Fortunately, I know the camera guy doing the principal shooting. He worked with you one time… I think on that yogurt commercial? Anyway, he called me up and asked if that was you. Which it was sooo you! I just got off the phone with the director. They love you. They love your look. They love the location. They want to talk. Like, now, now, now. I told them I'd book a conference call for Monday."

234 I BETHANY MAINES

"Monday?" repeated Tish.

"Yeah. Tomorrow. I do not have to tell you how big this is. A feature! So? What do you think?"

"Um," said Tish, looking through the open door to the living room where Nash was petting Coats and talking to Tobias while Claire sharpened a stick from the yard into something that could kill zombies. "I mean... It couldn't hurt to talk to them, I guess."

LOVED IT?

Please consider leaving a rating on Amazon, Goodreads, or Bookbub. Reviews help authors gain advertising opportunities and new readers. Your positive reviews make a difference!

WANT MORE?

For a free e-book visit:
www.**bethanymaines**.com

WANT MORE ADVENTURES FROM BETHANY MAINES?

TRY THE DEVERAUX LEGACY SERIES

The Deveraux Family: wealthy, glamorous, powerful… and in a lot of trouble. Senator Eleanor Deveraux lost her children in a plane crash, but she has a second chance to get her family right with her four grandchildren – Evan, Jackson, Aiden and Dominique. But second chances are hard to seize when politics, mercenaries, and the dark legacy of the Deveraux family keep getting in the way.

TAKE A SNEAK PEEK AT BOOK 1

THE SECOND SHOT

SATURDAY
MAXWELL AMES

I have better uses for my mouth.

The words were etched in his brain.

Maxwell Ames looked across the room at Dominique Deveraux and felt himself physically flinch at a memory-driven whip of embarrassment.

An eighteen-year-old Dominique had arrived at college with an ice queen reputation and a pair of legs that had fueled half the hot dreams on campus. But it hadn't been the legs that had gotten to Max—it had been her lips. Max had taken one look at Dominique and decided he wanted, no, *needed* to know what those lips felt like on his body. And he'd declared, drunkenly, to an entire frat party that he would melt the ice queen. He hadn't doubted for a minute that he could do it. He was a senior. He was a nationally ranked college wrestler—his body showed his effort—and he rarely had to do more than lift a finger to get panties to hit his floor. Perhaps it had been the liquor that had made him stupid, but whatever the reason, he'd simply walked over and told her what he wanted her to do to him. He recognized his mistake the second he heard the words come out of his mouth. Her horrified expression only confirmed how badly he'd misjudged. Then she'd gone from shocked to furious, but instead of slapping him, she'd pulled herself up to her full height, looked him in the eye, and declared loud enough for the rest of the room to hear: *I have better uses for my mouth.* And then he'd stood there and let her pour the entire contents of her red solo cup down his front.

And now, six years later, his father had dragged Max into the

Galbraith Tennis and Social Club and directly into revisiting one of his top ten stupidest moments.

"Dad," said Max, turning to look at his father.

"She donates two-k a year," said his father, staring across the party hall at a woman in beige everything. "She's worth like eighty million. Would it kill her to scrounge a little more change out of the couch cushions for needy kids?"

"Dad," said Max again.

"Yeah, what?" asked Grant Ames, finally making eye contact.

"You didn't say this was a Deveraux party."

"Uh, yeah?" said Grant, looking away again—probably scanning the crowd for more targets. "Oh, that's right. You went to school with them, didn't you? Dominique and Aiden? They're probably around somewhere if you want to dig them up. Eleanor usually commands appearances from the family at these little shindigs."

Eleanor Deveraux was running for congress. Again. Or still. Whichever. These *little shindigs* were fundraising events masquerading as cocktail parties. Max didn't know why she bothered. Her nearest competitor was a bitter Republican that sounded crazy even to his constituents. But his father, always on the hustle, spared no thought about why the party existed—he simply enjoyed that it did. And of course, it hadn't occurred to Grant to mention to Max who was hosting.

After the frat party incident, Max hadn't even had the courage to apologize to Dominique. His only consolation was that during all their other encounters she had treated everyone in the room with an equal amount of cool disdain—he hadn't been singled out. Generally, she hadn't even acknowledged him, let alone what had happened.

"You said we wouldn't be here long," said Max, looking back at Dominique. Her golden blonde hair was longer than the last time he'd seen her, laying in soft waves against her pale skin. Those lips that had made him lose his judgement were painted a wine red that emphasized their size. Her conservative pencil skirt and long-sleeve, high-necked blouse should have taken her allure down a notch, but as far as he could see, she was even more gorgeous than she had been in college.

Max had been with plenty of beautiful women—hell, his last girlfriend had been a model-slash-actress. Dominique shouldn't have been able to make the impact she did. But here it was, six years later, and Dominique still hit him like a Mack truck to the libido even when the only skin he could see was her knees.

"We won't be long, I promise," said Grant, scoping the room, oblivious to the direction of Max's gaze. "I need to make the rounds. Say hi to a few people and then we'll be off for burgers."

It was a lie. Max didn't know why he'd thought his first visit to his father's in over a year might warrant special treatment—particularly, since his entire childhood held evidence to the contrary. He wondered if there was a point in adulthood when a parent's failings stopped mattering so much.

Dominique nodded along as the guy next to her talked. He was a lean, good looking twenty-something with black hair and a designer suit. Max watched in surprise as Dominique burst out laughing at whatever he'd said—Dominique had never been very demonstrative in public. Her laugh made the guy grin, but, still talking, he leaned over and snagged something off her plate. Dominique smacked at his hand, but the man leaned further away, dragging the morsel with him, and popped it into his mouth. She flicked at his ear, miming patently faked annoyance. In equally mock penance, her companion lowered his head and held out his plate and Dominique made a show of selecting something in recompense. The only person he could remember bringing out that sparkle of playfulness in her had been her brother, Aiden. It seemed that the ice queen had been melted after all.

Still chewing his stolen goods, Dominique's companion looked up and scanned the room, homing in on the location of the other Deveraux family members. Max followed the man's gaze to the matriarch, Dominque's stately and poised grandmother, Eleanor, holding court by the bar at the far end of the long, narrow room. Then he shifted to Dominique's red-headed investment manager cousin, Evan, amongst a bevy of Wall Street bros in the middle of the room. And last, Dominique's brother, the equally blonde Aiden, hovering by the buffet table in front of a wide expanse of floor-to-ceiling windows.

All of the Deveraux children had lived with their grandmother after a plane crash had left them orphans sometime during their early teens. Max remembered thinking how nice that had sounded when his father had missed every single one of his college meets and was late for graduation. He supposed it hadn't really been pleasant for the Deveraux cousins, but at least they'd had each other and Eleanor.

Max realized, too late, that the scan was continuing on to the new arrivals in the room, which, in this case, were Max and his father. Max found himself awkwardly making eye contact with the guy and knew that he'd been busted staring at Dominique. He broke eye contact and turned to follow his father.

Max pretended to be absorbed in his father's conversation with a white-collared, black-shirted Jesuit priest. After a few minutes of discussing the endowments and scholarship funds, Max's eyes glazed over and he looked around the room, desperate for anything to take his mind off his desire to blurt out a question about pedophiles. How did anyone take priests seriously anymore? He found himself fidgeting with one of the tiny decorative pumpkins placed on the bar-height tables and biting his tongue.

With Halloween and the election around the corner, the party was decorated in a patriotic harvest theme. The red leaves and orange gourds seemed attractive, but Max thought the hay bales by the buffet table seemed a bit too folksy for the Deveraux, not to mention the tennis club locale. He suspected that the entire reason for their existence was to support the stars-and-stripes-bandana-wearing scarecrow. After all, a politician couldn't fundraise without at least a nod to the flag.

He snuck another glance at Dominique and realized that her boyfriend was scanning again. Same pattern—Deverauxes first, then new arrivals, then the rest of the room. There was something professional in the appraising stare, and Max felt the weight of it resting thoughtfully on him. Max checked his watch and angled so he could watch Dominique and her guy. She chatted in an easy, unaffected way, but at a minute fifteen, her boyfriend made another scan. Then again a minute later. It was definitely a more than a casual glance. Max tried to get a better look at the guy. What was he? Boyfriend, bodyguard, security? The suit was expensive, but he was drinking water as he watched the crowd.

Dominique reached out and put her hand on his arm, tugging impatiently, demanding attention. The guy laughed and complied, turning toward her with an affectionate smile. He was definitely not the hired help. For some reason, that burned. In the intervening six years, Max had put Dominique out of his head. Mostly. Sort of. Max would never have admitted it out loud, ever, under any circumstances, including a court of law, but Dominique had always been one of his go-to fantasies. He was perfectly sure that she hadn't thought about him once in that time. So why did he feel jealous of this guy?

Max turned back to his father and tried to focus on the conversation. Dominique was none of his business. What did he care if she dated someone with an over-active sense of security? None. Of. His. Business.

Grant moved on and Max followed him dutifully, the same way he had when he was twelve. He was a prop to his father's socializing. He met a dozen people and forgot their names instantly. Finally, he turned away from a blocky woman in a Chanel jacket and found his father about to introduce him to Dominique and her date.

"Max, I don't know if you've met Jackson, but you went to school with Dominique. Max is staying with me for a few weeks while—Hey, Frank! Frank! Be right back. I've been trying to get five minutes with that guy all month." Grant buzzed off and left Max staring uncomfortably at Dominique and her date.

"So, Max," said Jackson, his expression derisive, "do you need Dominique to get you another drink? We could send the catering staff out for some beer and solo cups."

Max glanced at Dominique, who was visibly restraining a laugh.

"No," said Max, trying not to feel like an ass—any hope that she'd forgotten him or the incident slipping away. "I think once was enough." Did she really have to tell everyone?

Dominique actually did giggle this time and her boyfriend looked amused by her laughter, but his attention was pulled away.

"Nika, what is Aiden doing?" asked Jackson, looking past Max.

"Um," she squinted toward the door, "exactly what you told him not to do?"

Jackson sighed. "OK, I'll be right back." He ducked around Dominique, his jacket swinging open. For a second, Max clearly saw the strap on a shoulder holster and outline of a gun. Max looked back at Dominque, but she seemed not to notice. She was watching her brother attempting to sneak out of the room and biting into her bottom lip with a frown. She transferred her gaze back to Max and smiled, but it was the same old cold smile.

"I'm glad you can laugh about that uh... incident," he said, deciding to man up and do what he should have done six years ago. He glanced down at the floor and realized that she was only conservative from the ankle up. Her heels were stacked, strapped, and had a black satin bow at each ankle that begged to be untied. "I really apologize for that," he said, tearing his eyes off her feet.

She looked startled and suspicious.

"I was a total asshole," he added.

"Um." She frowned, then smiled—a real smile this time. "Well, apology accepted."

It was his turn to feel surprised. He hadn't expected her to simply believe that he was sorry. "And I wouldn't say total. I'd go ninety-eight percent."

"Ninety-eight percent?"

"Well, I'll give you a one percent discount for being young, dumb and in college."

"Yes," he agreed fervently.

"And another one percent for standing there for the entire cup of beer."

"I knew I'd earned it," he said. She glanced over his shoulder, still following the action across the room.

"Your boyfriend's a little intense," he said.

"My boyfriend? You mean Jacks?"

He wanted to comment on the intimate shortening of their names. Jacks seemed weird, but he liked Nika. On the other hand, it really was none of his damn business.

"Does he always carry a gun?" he asked instead.

"Oh, you know..." she said, trailing off and not answering the question. Max decided that meant the answer was yes. "Grandma has gotten some... Well, they're death threats, really, in the last few weeks. She's chairing that Senate Committee Hearing on Absolex. And nothing brings out the crazies like Big Pharma."

"I don't understand," he said. "I thought that was about government fraud?"

"Absolex falsified research and then sold their drug Zanilex to the VA as a solution to treat complex PTSD. Suicide rates sky-rocketed. Turns out that, in fact, it makes the symptoms of PTSD worse, particularly the paranoia and depression. Or at least that's what Grandma intends to prove. She's going to haul the CEO out on the carpet next week. But ever since the hearings started, she's been getting hate mail."

Max looked around the party. "Where is the Secret Service?"

"None of the threats have been active. It's all kind of vague. And she's not a party leader or anything. So, no Secret Service."

Max frowned. If he had been Eleanor, he would have been putting his foot down and demanding an investigation. He also wouldn't be hosting a party and looking as relaxed as she did.

"Besides," continued Dominique, "we have Jackson. Although, even he couldn't get her to cancel this stupid party. She claimed that we all just didn't want to go."

He raised an eyebrow and she looked guilty.

"That may be partially true. Anyway, Jacks said if she was going to insist on having the party, we should at least be smart about it. He gave us all rules and hired additional security. Of course, Aiden is not following the rules. I would accuse him of being willful, but it's more likely that he's just not taking the threats seriously."

Max nodded. His memory of Dominique's older brother was a sunny personality to whom nothing serious was allowed to adhere and who never seemed to get mad about anything.

"I expect Jacks will tell him about a secret stash of bourbon under the bar and rope him back in."

"Sounds like Jackson knows what he's doing then," said Max, turning to look at the two men who were now making their way back toward them. Aiden stopped to adjust the bandana on the scarecrow with a disapproving shake of his head.

"He does," agreed Dominique, looking up at him with a flash of a smile, "but Jackson isn't—"

Whatever she had been about to say was drowned out by the sound of a car engine and then a thunderous crash as a car exploded through the windows, slammed through the buffet table, plowed across the room, and buried its nose in the far wall.

FIND OUT WHAT HAPPENS NEXT IN...

THE SECOND SHOT

OR TRY THE SHARK SANTOYO SERIES

Fresh out of prison and fresh out of luck, twenty-something Shark wants back into The Organization. But when Geier, the mob boss with a cruel sense of humor, sends Shark to the suburbs to find out who's been skimming his take, Shark realizes he's going to need more than his gun and an attitude to succeed. With the clock ticking, Shark accepts the help of the mysterious teenage fixer, Peregrine Hays, and embarks on a scheme that could line his pockets, land him the girl and cement his reputation with the gang—if he makes it out alive.

"Anti-heroes, bad guys, uncles and the dynamic crime-fighting duo of Shark and Peri equal reading bliss, especially if you like some heart, brains and wit with your down-and-dirty grit. All I can add is READ IT."
—**Tome Tender Book Blog**

TAKE A SNEAK PEEK AT BOOK 1

SHARK'S INSTINCT

CHAPTER 1
SHARK: ROLLING THUNDER LANES

Shark Santoyo rubbed a hand over his prison buzz cut, and considered his options. They appeared to be death or accounting.

He wondered if he could make it to Mexico before the FBI

caught up with him. His jailhouse college degree had given him a basic understanding of American History, Psychology, Criminal Justice, and a hatred for the *Grapes of Wrath*, but higher-level accounting had not been part of the curriculum.

That was unfortunate, since his current mission in life was to find where Big Paulie had put Geier's money, and Big Paulie had chosen to rather inconveniently die of a heart attack mid-beating rather than reveal that information. Shark's only clue was the red leather ledger with the rambling, scribbled out, crisscrossing columns of numbers, and the gold-stamped *Fred Abernathy* on the cover. There had been efforts to find the wayward accountant, but so far he was in the wind.

A vacuum cleaner started up on the far side of the room. Shark both ignored and enjoyed the sound. He didn't know if the layer of filth covering every surface was due to Rolling Thunder Lanes being a closed suburban bowling alley or because it was the base of operations for wise guys, but he was starting to feel like the OCD germophobe in his cell block who had eventually tried to scrub his cell mate's face off with a potato brush. Fortunately, Shark was now at the top of this particular pyramid. He might be dead in a week if he couldn't find Geier's money, but at least he'd go out in a damn clean bowling alley. He'd even had them open the blinds on the front windows. Bright October sunlight streamed in, illuminating all the grime and blinding him as it bounced off the white pages of the ledger.

He put on his sunglasses and flipped another page. He had no idea what he was staring at. He sensed a YouTube video on accounting in his future. Later, once he was alone, and no one would know.

Someone slid into the booth across from him and he looked up, expecting one of the low-level scumbags that floated through here. He wasn't sure why these suburban dipshits seemed to think he could be pushed around, but he was getting tired of correcting their misunderstanding. But sitting across from him in the booth was a girl—thick brown hair pulled into a loose braid on the right side, purple hoodie, hazel eyes, no make-up. She looked somewhere between fifteen and twenty. He had a hard time judging, since every sixteen-year-old girl he'd known since he was ten had looked over twenty-one. He had no idea what to say to her.

"We're closed," he tried. "No bowling."

"Do I look like I'm here to fucking bowl?" His mysterious apparition had a potty mouth. It was an incongruous as it was cute—like an aggressive Corgi.

He looked around the empty bowling alley. He had no idea what bowlers looked like; he'd never actually been bowling. His supposed bodyguards were lounging against the bar, unaware of the five foot four inch security breach sitting across from him. He flipped the ledger closed.

"How did you even get in here?"

"Through the kitchen. If you look like a kid and stay out of people's way, they assume you belong to somebody."

"OK," he nodded, trying to figure out how he was going to block that in the future. "How about, *why* are you here?"

"I'm here because you just took over from Big Paulie, so now you run the Fives and Blue Street," she said.

Took over, that was a polite way of putting it.

"And what is any of that to you?"

"Blue Street." She pulled his unused fork over to her side of the table, then paused to make a disgusted face when the fork proved to be sticky. He sympathized. "Blue Street is in an ongoing turf war with the 38th Street crew"—she pulled the spoon into an L shape with the fork, bowl to tines—"which is where Lincoln High School is." She put a sugar packet in the corner of the adjoining silverware.

Shark heaved a sigh. This had been going somewhere. She had been interesting. "And you want me to call them off your high school?"

"No, I want you to apply your foot to Blue Street's ass and get them to do their fucking jobs."

Behind his sunglasses, Shark blinked.

"Look, I get it," the girl said. "You're new, and you're probably hearing a lot of chatter about how they can't push too hard because one dead kid in the schoolyard and the police will crack down, and then everyone gets rolled up like a window shade."

"The metaphors haven't been as good as that, but yes."

She flashed a smile. "They're not wrong. Dead kids equals bad. But everyone is stuck staring at the problem from here." She tapped the fork. "When you need to be looking at the problem from here." She laid the pepper shaker down parallel to the fork, but at the end of the spoon. There was a huffing sound as Zip and Marko jogged up. "Oh good," the girl said, showing zero fear. "Which one of them is the waiter?"

Shark looked at his bodyguards. Marko was Italianish, heavyset and forty-something, usually in jeans and a black leather jacket, and hadn't said one word about working for a younger man. Zip was a decade younger, equally well-padded, always dressed in a track suit, and had been pissy about the assignment, but so far he had followed Marko's lead on everything. "Either one," Shark said. "Seems like that's what they're good at."

"Great. I'll take a cherry Coke," she told Zip.

Zip looked at Shark.

"You heard her," said Shark.

Zip's expression said he wanted to argue. "I'll just…" He

glanced at Marko for support, who gave him nothing. "I'll just go do that then." He headed for the bar, while Marko unfolded his Sports section and took a seat a few tables over. It was a location that said *I know you can handle a kid, but I feel like I should look like I'm doing something.*

The girl watched them leave. "What are the odds that Coke comes back spit-free?"

"Not good," said Shark. He slid his Jack and Coke across the table to her and she took a sip.

"Oh." She made a face. "How do you drink that stuff?"

"It's an acquired taste."

"But why acquire it?"

"Because at some point," Shark said, "you like feeling bad."

She didn't say anything, but looked like she was thinking it over. She tried another sip and slid the drink back. "Not today."

"So tell me about the pepper."

"The pepper is everything above Jackson."

"That belongs to the Ukrainians," he pointed out.

"Yes." She smiled, and this time there were teeth. "I know. And up until now the Ukrainians have been staying out of it."

"What do you mean *up until now*?"

"38th Street's been getting restless. They want a bigger slice of the pie. They've been intending to take it out of Blue Street, but would it be such a huge surprise if they hit the Ukrainians' stash house on Jackson?"

"Not a surprise. But what would they make them do it?" She had a firm grasp of the politics of the territory—probably better than he did. He hoped it didn't show.

"They don't really have to do it. You can do it. It just has to *look* like they did it."

Shark did a quick mental calculation about the amount of money they could expect to find in a Ukrainian stash house at the end of the month. It seemed like a possible solution to Geier's money problem. Although, the last time a girl had come to him with a plan he'd ended up in prison, so maybe he should be hearing alarm bells, not seeing dollar signs.

He wasn't sure what to make of her. Most girls, most women, if they wanted something from him, they hedged, they angled, they hinted. Things were suggested, but never actually stated. Also, there was generally a lot more cleavage. He stalled, trying to get a feel for her. "And what if the Ukrainians decide to just roll through 38th Street and onto Blue Street? Then you're right back to where you started."

"My focus is on 38th Street's current personnel; I need them gone. But for what it's worth, the Ukrainians are set to have a civil war."

"There haven't been any indications of that. My intel says they're stable."

"Your *intel* doesn't sit next to Andriy's younger sister in Pre-Calc. They don't know that she's been sleeping with his second-in-command and that she's pregnant. The right words to the right people at the right time and the Ukrainians could be pretty damn unstable."

"Cherry Coke," offered Zip.

"Cherry Coke," said Shark. "That sounds good. Why don't you give me that one, and go get another for the kid?"

There was silence. Shark didn't have to look up to know Zip was sweating.

"You know," said Zip. "I didn't do the garnish right. I'll be right back."

Marko looked after him with a frown. "I'll help him," he said, folding his paper. Shark ignored them both, focusing on the girl.

Shark took off his sunglasses and set them on the table. Born with pale gray eyes, he knew most people found a hard stare from him creepy, an effect enhanced by the scar running through his right eyebrow. Leaning forward, he stared at the little shark who didn't like alcohol. She met his stare levelly. "Why come to me? Why not take this directly to the Blue Street crew?"

She shook her head. "Blue Street won't listen to me. Too many boobs, not enough dick. I did some recon and I think you're the first person on the food chain with more than two brain cells to rub together and enough power to make it happen."

"What's in it for you? Why do you care?"

"No one owns the school because all the crews have family there. That makes it an open territory for independent operators."

"Such as yourself?"

"Such as myself. But that arrangement doesn't mean we're unaffected by what goes on out here. And right now 38th Street is inconveniencing me. I need them, and specifically their leader Tall Jimmy, to go away. Preferably permanently, and without a lot of fuss or a long lead time."

"Two cherry Cokes," announced Marko, setting down the glasses with a flourish. This time there were cherries dangling from the rims.

Shark leaned back and put his sunglasses back on. "What are you bringing to the table?"

"Intel, a plan, and a few other items." She took a cherry off the glass and crunched it between her teeth, leaving the stem on the table.

"I'll think about it."

She slid a card across the table. "This is my number."

It was blank except for digits. How did she have better business cards than he did?

"I need to know by tomorrow."

"What happens tomorrow?"

She slid out of the booth. "I move on to plan B."

Shark watched her walk out the front door. She walked quickly, with firm feet. No hip wiggles, but no tripping or awkwardness either. She knew they were watching, but she didn't waver. Even some of the guys who had been around awhile couldn't walk from the table to the door without looking back. The girl had balls.

He tapped the card on the table. "Call Blue Street," he told Marko, when the door closed behind her. "Tell them I'm coming for a visit. Tell them to call in anyone in their crew who goes to the high school."

FIND OUT WHAT HAPPENS NEXT IN...

SHARK'S INSTINCT

ABOUT THE AUTHOR

Bethany Maines is the award-winning author of action adventure and fantasy tales that focus on women who know when to apply lipstick and when to apply a foot to someone's hind end. When she's not traveling to exotic lands, or kicking some serious butt with her black belt in karate, she can be found chasing after her daughter, or glued to the computer working on her next novel.

ALSO BY BETHANY MAINES

CARRIE MAE MYSTERIES

Bulletproof Mascara

Compact With The Devil

Supporting The Girls (Mini-Mystery)

Power Of Attorney (Mini-Mystery)

High-Caliber Concealer

Glossed Cause

The Second Shot

A PNWA 2019 Literary Contest Award Winner

GALACTIC DREAMS

When Stars Take Flight Vol. 1

The Seventh Swan Vol. 2

A Book Excellence Award Winner

SAN JUAN ISLANDS MURDER MYSTERIES

An Unseen Current

Against the Undertow

An Unfamiliar Sea

SHARK SANTOYO CRIME SERIES

Shark's Instinct

Shark's Bite

Shark's Hunt

Shark's Fin

Made in United States
Orlando, FL
20 December 2022

27368602R00143